Sacred Gift

BOOK II IN THE
SACRED JOURNEY SERIES

D1522782

KAREN HULENE BARTELL

Sacred Gift

BOOK II IN THE
SACRED JOURNEY SERIES

KAREN HULENE BARTELL

P
Pen-L Publishing
Fayetteville, Arkansas
Pen-L.com

OTHER BOOKS BY KAREN HULENE BARTELL, PHD

Sacred Choices: Book I in the Sacred Journey Series

Belize Navidad

Sovereignty of the Dragons

Fine Filipino Food

The Best of Korean Cuisine

The Best of Taiwanese Cuisine

The Best of Polish Cooking

American Business English

With love to Peter William Bartell.

With admiration for the dedicated volunteers, staff, and clergy who provide support and solace to help post-abortive women bridge the chasm between unspoken sorrow and forgiveness.

THE MISSION OF NUESTRA SEÑORA DE LA PURÍSIMA CONCEPCIÓN looks much as it did in the early 1700s when it served as the mission's center of religious activity. The solar illuminations highlight several celestial and religious events, including the Feast of the Assumption. The National Park Service, which manages the grounds of the mission, is open for tours 9:00 a.m. to 5:00 p.m. every day except Thanksgiving, Christmas, and New Year, although tour times can vary.

MORE INFORMATION AT:
www.NPS.gov/SAAN/learn/historyculture/conc_history1.htm

TABLE OF CONTENTS

OF CABBAGES AND KINGS

"…more things in heaven and earth . . . than are dreamt of…"

— *HAMLET*, WILLIAM SHAKESPEARE

After Judith tucked Angela Maria in for her afternoon nap, she watched her adopted baby.

Fascinated, the infant focused on the wall. Her eyes rapidly tracked the sunlight's muted play of light and shadow on the wall, as if watching a movie.

Judith noticed the baby's eyes open wide in wonder and then crinkle, as if thinking or laughing. Chuckling to herself, Judith shook her head. *What is she doing?*

Her eyes glued to the wall, the baby watched the streaming video that only she could see. She saw tall pyramids, nearby palms swaying, their leaves waving in the virtual breeze.

She listened intently to the audio, a voice that spoke only in her inner ear.

"Mesoamericans built step pyramids," said the baby's personal narrator, Toci. "More like the Mesopotamian ziggurats than Egyptian pyramids, the Mesoamericans built the largest pyramid in the world, the Great Pyramid of Cholula."

The wall her private movie theater, Angela listened and watched the moving images, intrigued.

ℰ

"I'm too big for a nap," Angela Maria complained. With a frown, she pursed her lips.

"You're growing up way too fast," said Judith, tucking her in. She sighed. "But you're still only two, and two-year-olds need naps."

Angela pouted. "Abby says I'm too old for naps."

"Abby?" Judith chuckled. "Who's Abby?"

"My best friend, Abigail, but she wants me to call her Abby."

"Really," said Judith, swallowing a smile. "Where did you meet Abby, at the playground?"

"No, she comes and visits me."

"Where?"

"Here, in my room. She's here now," said Angela, "by the closet."

Judith turned her head, humoring her. "By the dresser?"

"No, on the other side of the closet, by the window." Angela knitted her brow. "Don't you see her?"

Judith smiled as she nodded. "I see. You have an imaginary friend."

"What's imaginary?"

"A person who only exists in your mind."

"No, Abby's real." Angela's knitted brow turned into a serious frown. "She's my sister."

"Your sister?" Judith cocked an eyebrow as she leaned over to kiss her. "Tell Abby it's nap time. Sweet dreams, baby."

As Judith closed the door, she heard Angela whispering. "Mom said we have to take a nap."

She walked into Sam's office, chuckling. "Angela certainly has an active imagination."

"Why do you say that?" Sam looked up from his computer.

"She has an imaginary friend, Abby, that she says is her sister."

"Maybe she's lonely." He lifted his eyebrow. "She's an only child."

"True, maybe we should enroll her in classes or take her to play dates," said Judith. "Let her be around kids her own age."

"I don't like kindergarten," announced Angela.

"Why not?" Judith glanced at her daughter as she drove.

"The kids are mean." Angela's brows furrowed together.

"Mean? Why do you say that?"

"They make fun of me when I talk to Abby, Toci, and Nana."

Judith's ears perked at her daughter's words. *Toci's another aspect of Tonantzin.* "Who's Toci?"

"Toci's my grandma."

Stopped at the light, Judith asked, "Have you heard me speak of Toci?" The girl shook her head. "Then how do you know that's her name?"

"She told me. She tells me all sorts of things."

"At school?"

Angela shook her head. "No, at home."

"How?"

"She shows me movies on the wall and teaches me about them."

Judith smiled at the girl's imagination. "Who's Nana?"

"You know, Nana, your mother."

Judith gasped and covered her mouth with her fingers. "Angela, my mother passed away when I was a little girl, not much older than you." She took a deep breath. "You can't see her."

Angela shrugged. "But I do."

"My mother's dead." The light turned green, and Judith pulled into traffic.

Angela looked at her mother. "But I see her."

At Angela's First Communion, Sister Pastora handed her a small, tissue paper wrapped box.

"What is it?" Angela asked, dark eyes dancing.

"Open it and see," said Pastora.

Angela inhaled the wrapping paper's distinctive odor. Bright-eyed, she smiled, as if proud she had guessed a riddle. "That's Nana's scent."

"What?" Pastora squinted as she looked from Angela to Judith, trying to understand.

Judith scratched her ear as she shrugged. "Angela has imaginary playmates."

"Nana's not a playmate," said Angela. She looked from Judith to Pastora. "Nana's your mother."

Pastora went pale. Her eyes flashed wide open as she studied the girl.

"Our mother's dead."

Angela shrugged. "I know, but I see her." She smelled the tissue wrapped gift again. "And I can smell her cologne."

"Go on, open your gift," said Judith, tactfully shifting her seven-year-old daughter's focus.

The girl undid the wrappings. Then she put the yellowed box to her nose, inhaled, and turned to Pastora. "This was your mother's, wasn't it?"

Pastora glanced at Judith, her eyes wide. Wordless, she nodded.

Angela lifted off the box's cover. Inside, nestled on cotton, lay an antique blue rosary.

"Nana's." Angela reverently picked it up, stared at it, and then held it to her heart.

Two days before her eighteenth birthday, Angela went shopping with Judith. They entered the mall through the anchor store's perfume department. Chandeliers hung overhead. Mirrored walls reflected row upon row of glass bottles lining the shelves. Displayed behind glass-encased counters, the yellow, pale-orange, and icy-blue perfumes called out to shoppers through their fragrance and packaging.

Angela lifted her head and inhaled. "Nana's scent."

"What?" Judith turned toward her daughter.

Still sniffing the air, Angela said, "I smell Nana's fragrance." She looked into Judith's eyes.

Judith studied the girl's shoulder-length dark hair, high cheekbones, and creamy complexion. She gazed into her dark eyes. *Who is this young woman? This college girl can't be the baby I adopted.*

"Don't you?"

Judith shook her head, realizing she'd been daydreaming. "Don't I what?"

"Don't you smell Nana's fragrance?"

Before she could answer, a woman eagerly approached with a bottle of perfume and fragrant, grosgrain ribbon samples.

"Would you like to try this?" She held the bottle like a can of pepper spray, poised to shoot.

"No, thanks." Judith turned up her nose as she walked away, her automatic response to aggressive sales tactics.

"I would," said Angela.

"Hold out your wrist," directed the heavily made-up saleswoman.

Angela smiled but made no attempt to move. "I'd prefer a sample ribbon."

The woman handed her one, and Angela waved it in front of her nostrils, inhaling.

"We're running a special on it today. Do you like it?"

"Mom, smell this. Do you recognize the scent?" Angela held it up to Judith's nose.

Judith wrinkled her nostrils. "It smells like vanilla."

"Good nose," said the woman. "It's Vanilla Missions, been around for years, but now it's making a comeback. Do you like it?"

Angela turned to Judith. "It's Nana's scent." She turned back to the saleswoman. "I'll take a bottle."

When they finished shopping, Angela and Judith waited for Pastora in the mall's bistro. Hand-lettered chalkboards displayed the menu. Faux gas lamps set a cozy, cheerful mood, and the high-backed booths provided privacy.

"This shopping's worn me out." Taking a deep breath, Judith leaned back.

"That's what iced tea's for." Angela sipped her tea and smiled. "It revives you."

"Not when you're my age." Judith chuckled as she appraised her daughter in her new blouse. "At least you won't be starting college threadbare. With all the bags and boxes in the trunk, I could barely close it."

"Thanks, Mom." She grabbed her hand. "It's been great shopping with you."

"You don't turn eighteen every day." Judith smiled and then sighed. "Eighteen . . . are you sure you want to start your freshman year during summer school?"

"We've been through this." Angela stifled a sigh as she sat back, letting go her mother's hand. "It's the only way I can graduate in three years. I want to get through with school and on with my life."

Judith shook her head. "I can't understand how a daughter of mine is so opposed to education."

"I'm not opposed to education. I'm just against marking time in classrooms."

"What alternatives are there?"

Angela took a deep breath and looked hard at her mother, debating.

"Remember when I was little, I told you how Toci tutored me?"

"You had an active imagination." Judith grinned. "I'll give you that, but I was hoping you'd pursue an academic career."

6

"I'm not you, Mom. I have different goals." Angela took a deep breath and counted to five. She consciously put on a smile. "Let's not spoil a good day with an old argument."

"I'll drink to that." Judith held up her iced tea.

As Angela clinked her frosted glass against Judith's, she saw her aunt approach.

"Pastora, come sit next to me." She slid over and patted the leather seat beside her.

Pastora sat down and sniffed the air as she hugged her.

"What's that scent?"

Angela grinned. "Can you guess?"

"It's familiar." Pastora sniffed the air again and squinted, staring into space, thinking. "It reminds me of something . . . someone . . ."

"Give up?"

With a sigh, Pastora folded her hands and put them on the table. "I can't place it."

"It's your mother's scent, Vanilla—"

"Vanilla Missions," said Pastora, her clouded eyes sparkling at the recollection. "Yes, now that you mention it, I do remember." She leaned toward Angela and breathed deeply. "I'd forgotten. How did you know?"

"I recognize it." Angela bit her lip, debating whether to say more, sensing where it would lead. *I'll be eighteen.* With a self-affirming nod, she gave herself permission to speak her mind. "It's Nana's scent."

"Nana? Not this again." Heaving a sigh, Pastora faced the girl. "I thought you'd outgrown all your childish notions about ghosts."

Judith grimaced. "Pastora, do you want some iced tea? I know I need a refill." She waved the waitress over.

Pastora shook her head as she addressed Angela. "I've said it before, and I'll say it again. There's no such thing as a ghost."

"What about the Holy Ghost?" asked Angela, trying to suppress a mischievous smile.

"You know what I mean. I'm talking about spirits." Pastora raised her eyebrows. "Father Schmidt wrote that the cult of spirits is nothing but a substitute religion."

"Then what about angels?" asked Angela. "Aren't they spirits? As Christians, aren't we encouraged to believe in them?"

"Angels and the Holy Spirit, yes, but not other spirits," said Pastora. "The *Bible* doesn't mention ghosts."

"Yes, it does." Angela cocked her eyebrow.

"Where?"

"In the Old Testament."

Tilting back her head, Pastora's eyes narrowed as she watched her niece. "Where in the Old Testament?"

"In First Samuel," said Angela, interpreting it as a challenge. She sat up straight. "Saul talked the Witch of Endor into conjuring up Samuel's spirit."

"You're taking it out of context." Pastora shook her head. "Believing in spirits is simply not in keeping with God's wisdom—"

"What can I get for you ladies?" asked the waitress, handing Pastora an open menu.

"More iced tea to start with," said Judith. "Pastora, what are you having to drink?"

Pastora grunted as she turned her attention from Angela to the menu before her.

"Water, please, with a lemon slice."

"And while my sister's deciding what to order, I'll have the Reuben sandwich." Judith turned to her daughter and winked. "What are you having?"

Angela grinned at her mother for changing the topic. "Let me see." She opened her menu and purposely deliberated, giving her aunt ample time to decide. "I'll have . . . the Greek salad and . . . vinaigrette dressing on the side."

Her pencil poised, the waitress turned toward Pastora. "And what'll it be for you, Ma'am?"

"I'll have a BLT sandwich, please." Pastora folded her menu and handed it back to the waitress with a warm smile. Then she turned toward Angela and Judith. "Now, where were we?"

"We were just saying how it doesn't seem possible Angela's going to be eighteen," said Judith. "Where did the time go?"

SACRED GIFT

*"The intuitive mind is a sacred gift and the
rational mind is a faithful servant. We have created a society
that honors the servant and has forgotten the gift."*
— ALBERT EINSTEIN

Driving home on I-35, Angela glanced at her mother.

"Thanks for steering the conversation during lunch."

"You know how any talk of spirits or spirituality gets my sister's goat . . . ghost." Judith chuckled.

"Why is that?"

Judith shrugged. "Maybe it's because I used to lecture on religious studies at the university. She told me I turned the sacred into the secular, but I don't recall her having any problem with spirits." She stopped and thought, staring into space. "If I recall correctly, Pastora used to tell me ghost stories as a child, good ones, scary ones that raised the hairs on the back of my neck."

"I wonder what changed."

"Who knows? Time, circumstances change people. It could be any one of a thousand reasons."

"And you," Angela looked at her mother, "how do you feel about me seeing spirits?"

"You don't, anymore, do you?" Judith eyed her daughter's profile. "I mean, you had an imaginary friend as a child, and you used to talk about Toci and Nana occasionally, but you haven't brought that up in years, not until today. What triggered it?"

"Nana's scent." Angela pulled the aromatic ribbon from her pocket, held it to her nostrils, and inhaled. She glanced sideways at her mother. "I do, though."

"Do what?"

"See spirits." Angela took her eyes from the road long enough to watch her mother's reaction.

Judith's nostrils widened as she took a deep breath, remembering her own encounters.

"Somehow, you don't seem surprised." When Judith didn't respond, Angela asked, "Have you ever seen a spirit?"

Judith rubbed her eyebrow and nodded. "A long time ago. It's been nearly nineteen years since it happened, but, yes, I have."

"Really?" Angela blinked as she turned toward her mother.

"Eyes on the road, please. I want to get back to Austin in one piece."

"Okay." Angela dutifully focused on the road ahead. "But tell me about it."

Judith snorted, recalling. "Ceren, Pastora, and I were at the Basilica of Our Lady of Guadalupe in Mexico City. I had climbed to the top, near Saint Michael's chapel. Somehow, I felt drawn to two winged angel statues standing guard in front of it."

"Angel statues," said Angela, eyes on the road. "One of them was the Archangel Michael, wasn't it?"

Judith turned sharply. "Why do you ask?"

"My birth mother told me how she was drawn to Michael's statue."

Nodding, Judith's mouth twisted into a half smile. "You could definitely say Ceren was drawn there."

"But this is your story." Angela stole a glance. "What did you see?"

Judith looked off into the distance, focusing on the past.

"At first, it wasn't what I saw, but what I heard." She glanced at Angela. "Giggling."

"Giggling?"

Judith chuckled. "A child's laughter. At first, I thought the girl was making fun of me. Then it became a game of peek-a-boo. From the corner of my eye, I'd glimpse her peeking out from behind the statue. Then, as I turned, she'd dart back behind it."

"Did you ever see her?"

"Yes," Judith nodded, "several times, but she was as elusive as fog."

"What did she look like?"

"She was a dark-haired little girl, wearing an ankle-length, dazzling white, Mexican wedding dress. It was a vintage, crocheted dress, with a scalloped hem."

Angela's forehead furrowed. "Somehow, that sounds familiar."

"It should." Judith snorted. "That describes the dress you wore for your First Communion, my cut down wedding dress."

"Oh, this is just a story." Angela scoffed. "I thought you were telling me a true experience."

"I was."

Angela shook her head, as if trying to clear it. "Okay, I'm confused."

"When I married Sam, I found a dress that reminded me of the giggling girl's."

"Giggling girl?"

"That's what I called her." Judith grinned. "You were always fascinated with that dress as a child. Then, when you made your First Communion, you begged me to let you wear it."

"I vaguely recall that."

"That day, you were the spitting image of the giggling girl."

Angela took a deep breath. "I remind you of her?"

"You did then . . . and now." Judith looked at the young woman beside her, trying to superimpose the images. She tilted her head, debating. "You're nearly eighteen. Maybe it's time you knew."

"Knew what?" Angela blinked.

"When your birth mother was pregnant with you, an image visited her in a dream. Ceren recognized the face she had seen in so many paintings of Our Lady of Guadalupe. That image told Ceren she was the child she carried, *you.*"

"Our Lady of Guadalupe . . . how—"

Judith shook her head. "It was a dream. All I know is the giggling girl was also the image in my dream that transformed into a young woman . . . who called herself the Aztec goddess Tonantzin. In that dream, she said, 'I am your daughter, the child your friend carries.'"

"' . . . your daughter, the child your friend carries,'" Angela repeated slowly. "So you and Ceren both knew, even then, that she'd give me up for adoption and you'd raise me?"

Judith pressed her lips together into a thin, white line. "It wasn't quite that straightforward, but that's the gist of it." Beginning to wish she hadn't brought it up. Judith sighed. "These are just dreams I'm retelling and nothing more."

"Maybe, maybe not." Angela cocked her head, scrutinizing her. "Did your dream tell you anything else?"

Judith inhaled sharply. *Is this the right moment to tell her? How will she feel about it?*

"In the dream, Tonantzin also said, 'I am the child you discarded. I am the young mother you could have been.'"

"Discarded . . ." Angela caught her breath as she studied her mother's face. "So you—"

"Had an abortion," said Judith, finishing her sentence. With a sigh, she peered at Angela, her shoulders slumping as that familiar wave of remorse washed over her. *What's done is done. I can't change the past.*

"So I'm your atonement child?" whispered Angela.

Judith nodded and swallowed. "I can't bring back the child I aborted, but I can give you all the—"

"You can't, but I can."

"You can what?" Judith winced as her head suddenly began to pound. She pressed her fingers into the niche between her eyes to dull the pain. Squinting, she scrutinized Angela's face. "I must have misunderstood. You said—"

"You can't bring back your daughter, but I can," she shrugged, "in a manner of speaking."

Judith opened her mouth to speak, but no words came out.

"Remember my 'imaginary' friend? Remember how cute you thought it was when I talked to her, called her Abby, and told you she was my sister?"

A grunt passing for an answer, Judith nodded.

Angela met Judith's eyes. "She wasn't imaginary. She's real. She's the soul of the daughter you aborted."

Judith gasped. "What are you saying?"

"I can see your daughter." Angela spoke while she kept her eyes on the road. "I can speak with her."

"Here? Now?"

Shaking her head, Angela smiled as she maneuvered through the traffic. "Let's wait till we get home."

A half hour later, they pulled into the garage.

"Is she here now?" asked Judith, pushing open the car door.

Angela looked internally and, grimacing, shook her head. "Uhn-uh." She opened the trunk, and they gathered the shopping bags and boxes.

Unable to meet Angela's eyes, Judith focused on juggling the boxes. "What does she look like?"

"Her looks have changed over the years." Angela held open the kitchen door for her mother. "It's as if she's grown along with me." She studied Judith. "Does that make sense?"

The older woman shrugged. "Why not? In my dream, the giggling girl transformed before me in moments. Why couldn't she take on the appearance of a child gradually growing into adulthood?" She forced herself to meet Angela's eyes. "You said she was about your size when you were a child?"

"Yes, she seemed to match my growth." Angela used her hands to indicate the heights. "She was a toddler when I was that age, then a child, then an adolescent with me, but, during high school, she seemed to age quickly. She became more like an older sister.

Then, as she became so much older in appearance, she seemed like an aunt. Now she has gray hair. I think . . ." Angela drew in her breath, "maybe this image reflects Abby's true age, what she actually looks like."

Judith set the shopping bags on the granite-topped island and hung her purse on the nearest kitchen chair. "She would have been fifty-eight." She peered up into Angela's face, but the girl wasn't watching her. "Would that be about right?"

Angela was staring across the kitchen's island toward the open space living area. In a hushed voice, she said, "She's here."

"Where?"

Pointing, Angela said, "By the fireplace."

Judith suddenly felt weak-kneed and slumped onto the chair. She groaned as her head began throbbing again, and this time her heart was hammering along with it. She pressed her fingers against her sternum, trying to slow its beat. Squinting, she scrutinized Angela's face.

"What does she look like?"

"The first thing you notice about her is her smile." Angela spoke in a whisper. "She's happy, so very happy. Her smile practically glows."

Equally fascinated and frightened, Judith wanted to hear more. She struggled to catch her breath.

"What else?"

"She has chubby cheeks and dark eyes. Her hair had been dark brown when I first met her, but now it's salt-and-pepper, mostly salt." Angela turned toward her mother with a half-smile. "She liked that description. She's laughing."

"Ask her . . ." Judith stopped, unsure where to begin. Swallowing hard, she spoke in a whisper. "Ask her if she can forgive me."

"She says all was forgiven years ago, decades ago. There's only love." Her eyes glistening, Angela turned toward her mother. "Can't you feel it? Her love for you is overwhelming. It fills the room."

Judith swallowed the painful lump in her throat as she brushed away her tears.

Angela's smile fled at the sight. "Don't cry, Mom."

"I can't help it." Judith began shivering. "This is too much, too much."

Angela leaned over and put her arm around Judith's shoulders. "Abby understands. She's leaving in a moment, but . . ." standing up, Angela looked toward the living room, "she has a question, something she's wondered about." She looked back at her mother. "Had you chosen a name for her?"

Judith brought a shaky hand to her forehead. "I never allowed myself that luxury. If I had, it . . . it would have been harder to . . ." Her voice trailed off as she gazed blankly toward the living room.

"Abby said she always sensed something about the name 'Helen.'"

Gulping air, Judith suddenly felt she was suffocating.

"That was my mother's middle name." Her breathing constricted, she undid the top button of her blouse with her trembling hand. "I'd always thought I'd have another child, and, if it were a girl, I'd name her after my mother."

"After Nana." Angela paused, as if listening, and then chuckled. "She wants us to call her Helen." Her smile faded. "And she realizes how hard this is for you." Angela lifted her hand in a wave. "So she's making this short. She's gone."

Judith rose unsteadily to her feet. "I . . . I feel a little lightheaded. I'm going to lie down for a while."

The smile vanished from Angela's lips. "Do you need any help?"

"No, I'll be all right." She took an uncertain step and lost her balance, grabbing onto the island for support.

"Mom!"

Angela reached for her, but Judith waved her off.

"I'm fine. Just have to lie down for a while."

Judith tried to take shallow breaths, but, as she walked through the living room, she started to hyperventilate. *Breathe slowly, slowly.* She started trembling as she passed the fireplace. Whether from fright or the suddenly icy temperature, she was unsure, but by the time she reached her bedroom, she was shaking uncontrollably.

Judith climbed on top of the bed and pulled a comforter around her. As she stared up at the ceiling, she recalled the last day the spirit had lived. She remembered waking up from the anesthesia the day she'd had the abortion, fifty-eight years before.

Eyes still closed, she had heard a voice ask, "Why is that girl crying?"

She had peeked through half-open eyes and recognized one of the girls from the clinic's waiting room.

"Some of them do that," an attendant had said, shrugging. "Cry."

"Is she all right?"

"She'll be fine."

Judith remembered lying there, hurting inside and inside. Both her womb and soul had ached.

Too weak to sit up, she had lain on her hospital gurney, looking at the other recovering women. Two rows of gurneys had lined the walls. The long, rectangular recovery room had simulated a hospital ward, except for its fast pace.

As each postabortion patient recovered, her gurney had been wheeled away, and another had taken its place, methodically, like clockwork. Watching the cycle of death as her anesthetic wore off, Judith had almost felt detached—until the pain began.

The cramps had been stronger than during her heaviest period. Originating in her abdomen as a feeling of pressure as the anesthetic faded, the cramps had become a steady ache that developed into increasingly painful spasms and uterine contractions. Then the pain had radiated to her pelvic region, sacroiliac, and lower back.

Pulling up her legs to relieve the pressure had put her into a fetal position. As she gently rocked herself to relieve the pain, she had squeezed back the tears stinging her eyes.

My baby should be in a fetal position, not me.

With a sinking heart, Judith recalled feeling the flow of blood between her legs. Not menstrual blood, it had been her baby's.

Helen's blood. My aborted baby was a girl, and she has a name. Helen.

FAMILY RESEMBLANCE

*"Like branches of a tree, we grow in different directions,
yet our roots remain as one."*

— ANONYMOUS

The phone rang. Angela caught it on the first ring before it could wake Judith.

"Angie?"

She smiled. Only one person called her 'Angie'—her birth mother.

"Hi, Ceren. Great to hear from you. What's up?"

"I'm in Austin for a conference and wondered if you and Judith would like to meet me for dinner?"

"I know I would." She winced. "But I'm not sure Mom will feel up to it."

"Why, nothing's wrong, is it?" Ceren's concern came through the phone.

"No, she's just had a long day. She took me shopping, and . . ." Angela caught herself before mentioning Helen, "it wore her out. She's lying down."

"Go easy on her." Ceren chuckled. "She's no spring chicken. How old is Judith now, seventy-nine, eighty?"

"Eighty-four."

She whistled. "Wow, I'd forgotten."

"She hides her age, but Mom's definitely slowing down." Angela scratched the back of her head. "I'm concerned about her. Sometimes . . ."

"What?"

Angela sighed. "Sometimes I want to say things, express my-self, share things with her, but," she sighed again, "I'm afraid I'll say too much . . . or that I've said too much. Then I worry about her health."

"Geez, Angie, what did you say to her?"

"Can we talk about it at dinner?"

The first thing Angela noticed was the salad bar. It ran nearly the length of the restaurant. Lettuce framed each rectangular dish set in crushed ice, creating a frosty green base. Protected by a glass sneeze shield, the salad bar was topped with immense, red, flowering plants. A built-in wine rack covered two walls, displaying hundreds of labels. The other two walls were painted in dark colors, their expanse broken by dozens of gilt framed oil paintings.

Then Angela spotted Ceren, waving from one of the linen covered tables. She smiled at her birth mother, still dark-haired and vibrant at forty-four. *Hope I look like her at her age.*

Angela kissed her cheek, admiring her youthful complexion, and then sat across from her.

"Good to see you."

"You, too. It's been what, five, six months? Too long." Her eyes hungrily took in the girl's appearance. "You're letting your hair grow." She leaned back, scrutinizing her daughter. "And is it my imagination, or is your hair darker?"

Starting with a smirk that grew into a grin, Angela pushed her dark, shoulder-length hair behind her ears.

"You don't miss a thing, do you?" She nodded. "Just put a temporary rinse on it."

"Goth girl or steam punk?" asked Ceren, her eyes twinkling. "What look are you going for?"

"It's only a temporary color." Angela shrugged. "Just wanted to see how I'd look with black hair."

"Of course you did. You're eighteen. It's only natural you'd want to try out a few personas."

Uncomfortable with Ceren's summary, Angela changed the subject. "So what conference brings you to Austin?"

"The Mid-America Art History Society's. There was a special showing at the Blanton. Then there were sessions on various topics." Ceren's eyes lit up. "But the one I liked most was about sixteenth century concepts of art."

"Right up your alley." Angela grinned at her mother's enthusiasm.

"Guess I do get excited about art." Ceren chuckled. "Did any of my love for it rub off on you?"

Angela took a deep breath. As she studied the vase of fresh rose buds and baby's-breath on their table, she picked her words carefully.

"You've certainly dragged me to enough art shows to find out. I enjoy looking at art, but," pursing her lips, she shook her head, "it's not something I'll pursue."

Ceren sighed. "I'd hoped you might follow in my footsteps, study art history, teach it, but you're your own person." She raised her eyebrow. "Always have been."

The waiter approached the table with two menus.

"Good evening. Let me know when you're ready to order." He started to hand Ceren a menu, but she held up her hand.

"Thanks, but I'll just have the salad buffet."

"And you, miss?" He turned toward Angela.

"Same for me, please." She smiled at Ceren. "Judith and I had lunch with Pastora today. I'm still full from that."

He gestured toward the salad bar. "Help yourselves when you're ready."

Their chairs made no sound as they pushed back from the table. Angela started toward the salad bar with Ceren following.

"What's that scent?" Ceren breathed in the wafting fragrance. "Are you wearing a new cologne?"

"Got it today. Vanilla Missions. Like it?"

"Definitely has vanilla in it." Sniffing, Ceren added, "Clean, yet lingering."

"Actually, that's what started the whole issue today."

Ceren picked up two plates, handing one to Angela. "What issue?"

Angela lowered her voice. "This is Nana's scent."

"Nana." Ceren squinted. "Who's that?"

"That's Mom's mother, but I always called her Nana." Angela reached for the seafood salad, but a little boy dashed in front of her, snatching at the tongs. She sidestepped him, helping herself to the cucumber orange tossed salad instead.

"I thought Judith's mother had passed away when she was a little girl." As Ceren reached for the tongs to pick up the gazpacho salad, the little boy grabbed at them but missed.

Angela raised her eyebrow at him as a warning. "She had."

"Okay, I'm confused."

Angela glanced at the little boy, obviously eavesdropping. "Let me tell you about it when we get back to the table."

By the time they had cleaned their plates, Angela had relayed the story, and they returned to the salad bar for seconds.

Again Ceren picked up two plates, handing one to Angela. "So you mean to tell me you can see spirits?"

Angela hunched her shoulders and grinned. "Yup."

"Why didn't you ever tell me?"

"I did. I told everyone about my invisible friends." Rolling her eyes, Angela took a deep breath. "At first, everyone thought it was cute, but in school all it brought me was heartache. Teachers called it childish. Kids thought I was weird. In self-defense, I started keeping it to myself." She helped herself to the seafood salad as the little boy looked on.

"And you said I don't miss a thing. Hah!" Thinking aloud, Ceren studied her daughter. "So this is your 'super power.'"

"What?"

"I always wondered." Ceren chose from the smorgasbord of salads, adding samples to her plate.

"Wondered what?"

Ceren shrugged. "With your background, I wondered if you'd have some sensitivity, some special gift."

"What do you mean, 'with my background?'"

"Now that you're nearly eighteen—"

"You're not talking about the dreams you and my mother had of me, are you?"

Ceren turned sharply. "You know about those dreams?"

Angela nodded. "I just learned this afternoon." She gave a wry chuckle. "But those dreams didn't have any significance, did they? I mean, it wasn't as if they gave you any specific message."

Silent, Ceren chewed her lip.

Angela studied her birth mother. "Did they?"

Ceren reached for her hand. "There's something I've never told you." Her chest heaving, she took a deep breath.

Hanging on every word, the little boy moved in closer. Angela watched him through the corner of her eye.

"Let's wait until we get back to the table." When they sat down, she leaned forward. "What was it?"

"I'd always meant to tell you sooner, but . . ." With a deep breath, she took Angela's hand across the table. "I've beat around the bush long enough." She sighed. "Angie, when I was pregnant with you . . . I nearly aborted you."

"You what?" Angela lurched, in the process letting go Ceren's hand.

Ceren shut her eyes and nodded. "It's true. I almost aborted you."

Angela felt the color drain from her cheeks. "It's been hard enough to come to terms with you giving me up for adoption. Now you tell me you almost killed me?" Rolling her eyes, she shook her head. "This has been quite a day. First, Mom tells me there's some connection to Our Lady of Guadalupe or some ancient, Aztec goddess. Next, you tell me I nearly never was." She glared at her birth mother. "What else?"

"Your father—"

Angela threw up her hands. "Oh, so now you're going to tell me about my birth father, too? All these years, I've begged you to tell me about him, but you'd never open up. You'd only say," she mimicked, "'when you're older.'"

"Well, you are older." Frowning, Ceren's eyes burned into her. "Do you want to hear about him or not?"

Angela suddenly resented the woman she had trusted all her life—the birth mother who had given her up for adoption, yet who had always been a part of her life. It was too much to learn she had nearly killed her, as well. Yet the topic of her mother's near abortion morbidly fascinated her. Now that it had been broached, she wanted to know more, not have the subject introduced only to be switched.

"I want to hear why you wanted to abort me."

"The stories are interconnected. To hear one, you need to hear the other." Eyes narrowing, Ceren gave her a sharp look. "Deal with it." As soon as the words left her mouth, her expression softened, and she grimaced. "I've had to."

Angela scrutinized her. *Ceren's been close to me all my life. I've loved her like an aunt, like I love Pastora, but this . . .* She shook her head slowly. *This is proof she not only rejected me after I was born, she never wanted me in the first place.* Despite the sting, the older woman's tone and expression subdued her. Angela sighed.

"Okay, tell it your way."

"Jarek—"

"Jarek." Opening her eyes wide, Angela rolled his name over her tongue. "So that was his name."

Ceren scratched her ear. "How do I keep this neutral?" She took a deep breath. "Let me just preface it with this. Judith never called him Jarek, only Jerk."

Shaping her lips into an O-shape, Angela gave a quick exhalation. Ceren nodded. "You get the idea."

"If he was so bad, why did you marry him?"

"Jarek could be very persuasive. He had electrifying blue eyes that sent chills down my spine." Ceren's eyes took on a faraway glaze. "When we first married, he was my prince charming. He made me feel I was living in a fairy tale."

"Sounds romantic." Angela hunched her shoulders and smiled. "So he swept you off your feet?"

"You could say that. We had a two-hour engagement."

"Wait a minute." Angela held up her hand. "Don't you mean two weeks or two months?"

"I meant two hours." Ceren cocked an eye at her daughter.

"Then you must have known him a long time before he proposed?" Ceren shook her head. "Not really, two weeks."

"Two weeks?"

"If nothing else, your father was impulsive."

"I'd say." Despite the tone of the conversation, Angela had to grin. "These tidbits are tantalizing. They make me want to hear more. Where were you married, in Austin?"

Ceren shook her head. "Carlsbad, New Mexico."

"What were you doing there?" Angela squinted.

"We'd attended a Southwest Art seminar at Sul Ross State University in Alpine," said Ceren. "On the way back, we stopped for dinner at a steakhouse. We'd been argu—" She looked at her daughter, and her expression softened. "We'd had a disagreement. Very long story short, your father proposed."

"And you accepted, just like that?"

"Not just like that, but almost." She gave a wry grin. "It was a two-hour drive to Carlsbad, so I had two hours to mull it over and back out. Even with a frantic, last-minute search for the county clerk's office, we had our marriage license in hand, had said 'I do' in front of the county judge, and were out the door before the courthouse closed at five for the weekend."

"How did you feel about marrying so suddenly?"

Ceren's eyes flashed momentarily. "It all happened so fast, none of it seemed real. When I say it was a fairy tale, I'm not exaggerating. I kept waiting to wake up from the dream."

Angela couldn't resist asking. "Was it his kiss that woke you?"

Nodding, Ceren smiled at the memory. "It was our first kiss as husband and wife. We were standing beneath an ancient live oak on the courthouse grounds that hot August afternoon while we planned our next step." She laughed to herself. "As he put his arms around me, I got a bad case of the giggles."

"What was so funny?" Ceren's mirth contagious, Angela could not help smiling.

"That's pretty much what he wanted to know. As soon as he pressed his lips against mine, I got the silliest notion. An image of Snow White popped into my head. All I could think about was the prince waking her with a kiss."

"Why was that?"

Ceren shrugged. "The proposal, our marriage had all happened so fast, none of it seemed real until he kissed me and brought it to life." She took a deep breath, collecting her thoughts. "It's as if his kiss grounded me, making the whole idea take root, have any substance." She looked at her daughter. "As I held him, as I felt his arms around me, it occurred to me he was the only thing tangible in what otherwise seemed like a fairy tale." Then the corners of Ceren's mouth drooped.

Responding to her expression, Angela said, "I take it there was an awakening."

"Oh, yeah." Ceren took a deep breath as she slowly nodded. "It happened the night I discovered your father was married to another woman."

"You mean he'd been married before? You were his second wife?"

"Oh, I was his second wife all right."

"So you found out about his ex?"

Pursing her lips, Ceren shook her head. "No, I mean he was already married to his first wife when he married me."

"He was a bigamist?" Blinking, Angela raised her eyebrows.

"Why do you think I waited until you were eighteen to tell you these things?"

25

Angela grunted. "My family history sounds more like a social services assessment."

Ceren reached for her hand. "Angie, maybe this will help you understand why I decided to give you up for adoption. I didn't want to bring you into that dysfunctional scenario."

Angela tried to crack a smile. "This heart-to-heart talk isn't giving me the warm fuzzies I'd thought it would, but I'm a glutton for punishment. Go on. I want to hear what happened."

Ceren gave her hand a friendly squeeze and let it go. "I began asking myself hard questions. What if our marriage isn't legal? What if he has no intention of being a husband to me, a father to you?"

"So you were pregnant with me when you found out?"

Ceren nodded. "I wondered how I'd earn a living, both while I was pregnant . . . and after I'd had you. I wondered how I could manage as a single parent. Would it be fair to you?" She turned toward Angela, her eyes red. "All my plans, my dreams of raising a family with him, were nothing but fantasies built on lies."

"Weren't you were lecturing at the time?" Angela peered at her. "Wouldn't the university have had maternity leave or some kind of social safety net?"

Biting her lip, Ceren shook her head. "His first wife told me she'd have my contract terminated. She said I'd never work again in that university or any other. She threatened to ruin my career, my reputation, my livelihood, my life. I was desperate."

Her lip upturned in disgust, Angela muttered, "Dear ol' Dad." She grimaced. "What did you do?"

"That night, after his wife hung up on me—"

"Wait a minute." Angela held up her hand. "You're telling me you found out all this from a phone call?"

"Yup, from his wife," Ceren nodded, "while I was alone in Mexico, pregnant with you."

Angela rolled her eyes. "Fairy tale, huh? What a prince of a guy."

"My husband's wife called me a whore, informed me I wasn't married, and that I was about to be dismissed for 'spreading rumors.'" Ceren's chest heaved. "I was so frustrated, I threw the nearest thing I could find against the dresser. It was a book called *Raising Baby with Smiles*, and it shattered the mirror. Looking at the silver splinters scattered across the floor was like seeing the shards of my broken dreams."

"Wow."

"You'd asked earlier if there were an awakening."

"Yeah."

"That night ended my fairy tale romance with your father."

Angela met her mother's eyes. "That book, *Raising Baby with Smiles*, did throwing it have anything to do with your feelings toward me?"

Sitting at her full height, Ceren straightened her back. She started to speak, swallowed, and tried again.

"I remembered . . . someone's advice about the pregnancy. She'd told me to lose it. Get rid of it. Not to ruin my career, my life, because of some stupid mistake. She'd told me to take care of it."

"Take care of it?" Angela studied her mother. "'It' being me and 'take care of' meaning 'abort,' right?"

Ceren nodded. "I reasoned, without a baby, there'd be nothing holding me back from dissolving the . . . the 'relationship' with your father." She turned toward her daughter. "I can't even call it a common-law marriage. It wasn't anything. It doesn't have a name. Though I'd married your father in good faith, the marriage was a sham. I was desperate, and yes," her eyes settled on Angela. "That was the first time I considered aborting you."

"There were other times?" Angela rubbed her forehead. "I'm beginning to feel like the red-headed bastard at the family reunion."

Ceren twisted her mouth into a wry smile. "Seeing you here as a vibrant young woman, I can't imagine how I ever considered such a thing." She lifted her hands helplessly. "But then, in the first weeks of pregnancy, you were a concept. You didn't seem real. It was like gambling with Las Vegas chips. Cardboard, not cash. At the time, you don't realize how much is at stake, how much you could lose."

"You said there were other times." Ceren nodded. "When?"

"There was the night I almost swallowed the abortifacients."

"And that didn't kill me?" Raising her eyebrows, Angela gave an exasperated sigh.

"*Almost* swallowed the abortifacients, I said." Ceren grimaced. "The operative word is *almost*, but I certainly intended to take them."

"What stopped you?"

"I reread the bottle's label one last time. At first, I thought my tired eyes were playing tricks. The label read 'effective up to ninth week of pregnancy.'" Ceren shook her head. "I couldn't believe it, but when I checked the calendar and calculated the time, it had been eleven weeks, plus who knew how many days between my last period and conception."

"Maybe it wasn't forgetfulness." Her breathing shallow, Angela found it disturbing to hear of her birth mother's intent to kill her. Easier to acquit than accept, she grasped at straws. "Maybe deep down you didn't want to abort me."

Ceren winced. Angela saw the pain reflected in her eyes.

"I wish I could say that, but . . ." she looked down at her hands and then into her daughter's eyes, "I have to be honest. Postponing the decision wasn't intentional. First there was the amniocentesis to prove paternity and the two-day wait for the results. Then the jer . . . your father appeared on the doorstep . . . and disappeared. Somehow two weeks flew by."

Angela digested that. "So what did you do?"

"I took a bus to Mexico City. Abortions there were legal and free."

Angela raised her eyebrows and took a deep breath. "What changed your mind?"

Ceren opened her mouth to speak, sighed, and started again. "I don't know where to begin. So much happened that day, *Día de Muertos Chiquitos*—"

"*Dia de* . . . what?"

SACRED GIFT

"It's the Day of the Little Dead, the day Mexico celebrates the souls of the children who've died. I remember surges of people wearing skull-painted faces passing me on the sidewalk, watching me with their blank, black eyes. As absurd as it sounds, I had the unreasonable feeling that the grinning skull faces knew I was on my way to the abortion clinic and were jeering at me."

"If you felt ashamed," Angela shrugged, "it's understandable to think others could sense your guilt."

Ceren gave a short, somber nod. "It was the half-decorated faces that caught my eye—grins that began on natural features and crossed the face to become painted-skull smiles. I stared at the half-skull makeup, the faces caught between life and death, relating."

"Even though it was a holiday, the abortion clinic was open?"

"It was a cultural, not a civic holiday." Ceren grimaced. "Death doesn't take a holiday."

"So what changed your mind?"

"I had to wait several hours for an appointment, so I went to the Basilica of Our Lady of Guadalupe. There I saw—"

"The Archangel Michael, right?"

Ceren turned sharply. "Have I told you this story?"

"You told me you were drawn to Michael's statue."

Ceren nodded as she inhaled. "That's right. When you were a little girl, I told you how he's been my special guardian."

"And mine, you said."

Her expression hardened. "Let me tell you just how special. I'd stopped for water at the vendor's stand one level below Saint Michael's Chapel. The woman in line ahead of me started a conversation. She told me she went there every *Día de los Angelitos* to remember her little angel. While she was talking, she kept fingering a necklace of tiny skulls on her chest. 'The *Basílica de Guadalupe* is a sacred space,' she told me."

"Sacred space," Angela repeated in a whisper.

"At first, I dismissed the macabre necklace as costume jewelry for the holiday. But then the sun reflected off her metal belt and arm band, catching my eye. Fashioned like a snake, the flexible belt coiled around the woman. The belt's two ends looked like a snake's head swallowing its tail, clasping her waist. A golden armband, also in a serpentine shape, wrapped itself around her withered bicep."

A chill passed over Angela, and she shook it off. "To hear you describe it, it sounds creepy, although . . ."

Ceren nodded knowingly. "It was."

"She seems vaguely familiar. It almost sounds as if you're describing Toci."

"Toci? Who's that?"

"For lack of a better word, she was my tutor, my 'grandmother.' She taught me all through my early childhood." Angela smiled, remembering fondly. "I called her Toci."

"Toci? Interesting. That was one of Tonantzin's names." She scrutinized her daughter. "What do you mean 'taught' you?"

"Call it what you will—daydreams, spirits—but until I was seven, Toci would act like a narrator to videos that only I could see and hear."

Ceren studied her. "How do you know she wasn't just your imagination?"

"Because she taught me so much." Angela raised her eyebrow. "You can't imagine knowledge."

"Justin once said, 'Dreams can seem real, and memories can be tangible.'"

Nodding, Angela gave her a wry smile. "So what happened with the old woman at the Basilica?"

"I nicknamed her the 'Snake Lady.'" When Angela chuckled, Ceren smiled and continued. "The woman—"

"Snake Lady," said Angela.

". . . told me the womb is a sacred space."

"I thought she said the Basílica was a sacred space." Angela squinted, trying to absorb it.

"Both, she said both are sacred spaces."

"And she's the one who convinced you not to abort me?"

Lifting her head, Ceren nodded.

"Then I owe her a lot."

Ceren nodded as she stared out into space. "There was more." She turned toward her daughter with a grimace that passed for a smile. "But that's another story for another time. As I recall, this conversation started when we were talking about you. Like I said, with your background, I always wondered whether you'd have a special sensitivity. Tell me about your gift, Angie."

Angela shifted her gaze from her birth mother to the little boy eavesdropping behind her.

"There's someone here who seems very curious about you."

Ceren followed her line of sight and turned in her chair. "Where?"

"Right behind you."

Ceren looked again and, turning back, frowned at Angela. "What are you talking about?"

"Do you know a little boy who's eleven?"

Ceren's frown momentarily became a scowl. "I'm not following..."

"Have you ever had an abortion or a miscarriage?"

Ceren's eyes flew open. Her jaw slack, she spun around in her chair to search behind her. When she saw nothing, she turned back, ashen. In a whisper, she asked, "What do you see?"

"I see a boy, who tells me he's eleven." Angela turned her focus toward her birth mother. "Did you have an abortion or a miscarriage eleven years ago?"

Ceren nodded. Staring at the table, she said, "Maybe you remember I was pregnant at your First Communion."

"I recall seeing you that day." She looked off, remembering. "In fact, that was the last day I ever saw Toci, but I never knew you were pregnant."

Ceren took a deep breath and nodded. "I miscarried later that day." She lifted her moist eyes. "Do you see my baby?" Angela nodded. "What does he look like?"

Angela assessed the boy as she described him.

"He has dark, wavy hair. The back of your chair is level with his chest. I'd say he's about five feet tall. He looks like you—has your creamy complexion and big, dark eyes." She laughed.

Ceren half turned in her chair to look behind her, her eyes shifting left and right. When she saw nothing out of the ordinary, she turned back.

"What's so funny?"

"He says I look like you. He can see the family resemblance."

Ceren's eyes lit up. "What else does he have to say?"

Angela's smile drooped as she listened. "He has a message for you, something he's been trying to tell you."

In a soft voice, Ceren asked, "What is it?"

"He says not to blame yourself or his father."

"Justin," she whispered. When a small sob escaped Ceren's lips, Angela moved closer and took her hand.

"What's wrong?"

"Nothing . . . everything." Ceren squeezed Angela's hand. "I wasn't going to mention it. I've hidden it for so long, but this convention isn't the only reason I came to Austin." She swallowed. "I needed time away from Justin to think about us."

"Are you saying what I think you are?" Angela squinted as she scrutinized her birth mother. "Mom says she knew you and Justin were meant for each other the moment you met."

Ceren gave her a wry smile. "That was true in the beginning, but after the miscarriage our relationship became," she sighed, "strained."

"How so?" Angela watched the boy come around to the front of their mother's chair and gently touch her shoulder. He stood between them, his back to Angela, partially blocking her view.

Ceren shivered. "I guess we silently blamed each other for the baby's death." She looked up. "At first, we avoided bringing up the subject, and then . . ."

Angela watched her look into space, not realizing she was staring into her son's eyes.

"Then?"

"We tiptoed around the topic. After a while, the miscarriage became such a sore subject that the only time we'd bring it up would be during an argument." Lifting an eyebrow, Ceren sighed. "Lately, that's been often. Bickering's become the norm."

The boy rested his hand on Ceren's knee and peered into her eyes, as if trying to communicate. In the process, he brushed the napkin from her lap, and it fell to the floor.

"We've never discussed what really happened, how the baby's death affected us," said Ceren. "As we pushed it deeper, it festered. The miscarriage became a wedge that's driven us further and further apart."

Ceren leaned down to retrieve the napkin. She shivered as her torso passed through the boy, and he did an abrupt about-face. When he saw Angela trying to peer around him, he seemed surprised to learn he was standing in her view. His eyes opening wide, he quickly stepped aside.

"I was only trying to get her attention." The boy's words infiltrated Angela's mind. "I didn't realize I was standing between you two."

"Any more than you realized you were coming between your mother and your father?"

He shook his head.

"What?" Ceren gave Angela a sharp look. "Are you talking to him?"

Angela nodded.

"What's he saying?"

"He said he never meant to interfere." Angela looked from the boy to Ceren. "All he's ever wanted is for you to acknowledge him and—"

"Acknowledge him? How could I?" Frowning, Ceren scoffed. "He's dead."

"But he lives on in your memory." Angela shook her head and paused, listening. "No, he says I got that wrong." She started again. "He says your regrets have drawn him here, bound him to you."

"What?" Ceren pressed her fingers to her temples. "None of this is making sense."

Concentrating, Angela focused on the thoughts he sent. "He's wanted your attention, so he could give you that message. He doesn't want you or his father to blame yourselves. He wants you to release him, to forgive each other and let him go, let his spirit rest."

Ceren's eyes opened wide. Raising her eyebrows, she silently questioned Angela.

"Yes, that's true." She nodded. "He says I got it right that time."

"Got what right?" Ceren eyed her daughter skeptically.

"I don't actually hear his words." Angela struggled to explain how she could communicate. "It's a better description to say I telepathically 'hear' his thoughts in my mind, but I don't always get the translation quite right. Sometimes, I miss the subtleties." She snickered. "Okay, he says I usually miss the subtleties."

Ceren's scowl softened into astonishment. "He's teasing you?"

Angela shrugged. "Guess you could call it that."

"It's hard to believe you can see spirits." Ceren gave a wry smile. "In fact, I didn't believe you at all." Her eyes homing in on Angela's, she slowly shook her head side to side. "Not until you started bantering with him."

"Now you believe me?" Angela watched her birth mother's reaction closely.

Ceren scratched her ear. "Let's just say," she grimaced, "the less stilted this encounter, the more plausible it seems . . ."

"But you're withholding judgment?"

"The verdict's still out."

Angela exchanged a crooked grin with the boy and then turned to Ceren.

"He thinks this is funny. It's the first time I've heard him laugh."

"He's happy?" Ceren looked relieved.

Angela pressed her lips together. *How much do I let on?*

"I wouldn't say he's happy." Angela took a deep breath. "Like I said, this was the first time he's laughed."

"Then how does he feel?" She looked hard at her daughter. "Or is 'feel' the right word?"

"Feel, feelings." Angela gave a mirthless chuckle. "Now that I'm 'coming out of the closet' about being sensitive to spirits," she sighed, "I have to be sensitive to your feelings, too."

Her chest heaving, Ceren squinted. "If you've got something to say, say it."

"He . . ." She peered at her mother. "Does he have a name?"

"If the baby had been a boy, we were thinking of naming him Esteban," said Ceren, "after Justin's grandfather."

"Esteban." Angela rolled the name over her tongue and then smiled at her birth mother. "He likes it."

The boy leaned over and kissed Ceren on her cheek. She put her hand where his lips had touched her.

"What was that?"

"What did it feel like?" asked Angela.

Ceren's eyes fell on the fresh flowers on the table. Her hand still caressing her cheek, she stared at the white roses and delicate gypsophila.

"It felt like a baby's breath. Was it?" she asked in a whisper.

Angela nodded. "He kissed you."

Ceren's eyes glistened. Blinking back the tears, she swallowed and nodded.

"Is he . . . at peace?"

"Not really." Angela paused, choosing her words carefully. "I won't say Esteban's spirit is earthbound, but it's stretched between heaven and earth. He says your feelings for him interfere with his ability to move into the spiritual realm. He—"

"But I love him."

"He knows that." Angela grimaced. "Esteban says it's precisely because you've loved him so much that you can't let go. You haven't been able to move on, so—"

"Neither can he. What you're trying to tell me is I'm holding him back."

"Exactly." Angela nodded. "You haven't learned to live without him, so Esteban's spirit has become attached to those feelings. The umbilical cord stretches from this world into the next."

Ceren was thoughtful for a few minutes. Then she took a deep breath.

"This is a night for stories. Would you and Esteban like to hear how his father and I met?"

LIKE A HEART NEEDS A BEAT

"You know you're in love when you can't fall asleep because reality is finally better than your dreams."

— ANONYMOUS

Father O'Riley and Pastora waved from the back seat of Sam's car.

"We'll meet you at the restaurant in Puebla," Judith called before closing the car door, giving her a sly smile and a wave.

Ceren nodded and waved as she climbed into the passenger seat beside Justin.

As they drove off, Justin turned toward her, wearing a sheepish grin.

"We've been set up."

Ceren nodded, chuckling at the last-minute seating arrangement.

"They weren't very subtle, were they?"

He shook his head. "Hope you don't mind riding back with me." He glanced at her, taking in her chocolate-brown eyes and creamy complexion contrasted against her coffee-brown hair.

She felt his eyes on her and turned toward him. Looking into his dark-brown eyes, she swallowed hard, squirmed, and fibbed.

"Not at all."

She crossed her fingers, still tingling from his touch earlier, when his arm had brushed against hers. Static electricity had made the hairs of her arms stand on end, reminding her of her episode with St. Elmo's Fire. Just thinking of it made the hairs on the back of her neck stand on end, but she hugged the door, keeping as much distance between them as the front seat allowed.

This is so soon, too soon. I'm not ready, am I?

"I'm glad," he said, his eyes on the road. "This will give us a chance to get to talk, get to know each other."

She nodded but could think of nothing to say. After a pause, she began, "The baptism—"

Speaking simultaneously, he said, "Didn't the baptism—"

They laughed. "Okay, you go first." She rubbed her forehead and tried again.

"The baptism was beautiful—the flowers, the music."

He nodded and glanced at her. "What happened back there?"

She started to answer but then thought twice. "What do you mean?"

"When you gasped during the baby's baptism, you looked like you'd seen a ghost." Wearing a quizzical frown, he took his eyes from the road momentarily to watch her. "Did you see something?"

She took a deep breath, debating. *Should I confide in him? Though practically a stranger, he's certainly someone I'd like to know better.* She scratched her head. *But what would he think?*

"Yes?" Wearing a wry smile, he glanced at her again. Ceren noticed he had a dimple. "Hey, I can't keep taking my eyes off the road. Something happened. Something disturbed you back there. What was it?"

She cautiously peered up at him through her eye lashes.

"You don't know me that well, and . . ." she turned away, gave a nervous laugh, and finished in a whisper, "you'll probably think I'm having a relapse into my postpartum anxiety disorder." She glanced back in time to see him raise his eyebrows, though he kept his eyes focused on the road. "See? I saw that. I knew it. You already think I'm crazy." She shook her head. "Nothing, I saw nothing except Angela Maria laughing." Chest heaving, she folded her arms across her chest.

Chastened, his eyes turning down at the sides, he grimaced before he glanced at her.

"I'm sorry. It was an involuntary reaction. You prepared me to expect something odd. I promise I'll keep a poker face—no expression, no sign of disapproval . . . or approval." He smiled, his dimple reappearing.

She inhaled deeply through her nostrils. Then, biting her lip, she scrutinized him.

"Do I pass muster?" he asked, his dimple deepening, his eyes twinkling as he glanced again at her.

She chuckled. "Only if you keep your eyes on the traffic."

"Duly noted."

Partly serious, partly joking, Ceren said, "And, days from now, when Sam asks you why we never 'clicked' after his and Judith's set-up, you can repeat the story I'm about to tell you." Inwardly, she groaned. *Hope I'm not making a mistake.* "On *Dia de los Muertos*, I . . . I went to the Basilica, where an old woman talked to me about Tepeyac being sacred space and the womb being sacred space. She had a profound effect on me."

She glanced at him sideways, watching his reaction.

Expressionless, he nodded.

"The woman was swearing a snake belt and a snake armband. I thought they were simply that: accessories." She looked at him sharply, watching for any sign of criticism or sarcasm. When she saw none, she continued. "Even when I saw her necklace of tiny skulls, I thought it was costume jewelry for celebrating the Day of the Dead."

He glanced sideways at her. "Okay, so where's the weird part?"

She took a deep breath before plunging in. "You asked if I saw something today. I did. I saw the old woman."

"Where, in the congregation?"

She shook her head. "No, she was on the altar during the baptism."

Inhaling, he ran his fingers through his thick, dark hair but said nothing.

"I know it sounds far-fetched," she said. "There's more, and this is the weird part. The snake belt and armband weren't accessories. They were . . . alive."

"Snakes?" He did a double take.

"That's what was making Angela laugh during her baptism."

Ceren watched him blink and chew his lip as he took in her words, seeming to process his thoughts. She raised her eyes in a silent prayer. *Please don't let him think I'm crazy.*

Finally, after what seemed an interminable pause, she asked with a nervous laugh, "Was that weird enough for you?"

"Pretty much." Giving her a sidelong smile, he chuckled. "But I've heard weirder." He drove along, silent, seeming lost in thought, and then asked, "Do you have any family here in Mexico?"

"No, I was an only child, and both my parents have passed away."

"So you're an orphan."

She snorted. "That's what Pastora said."

"I was an only child, too, sandwiched in-between aborted siblings."

She gasped, not believing her ears. Her body tensed at the mention of abortion, yet she warmed to him, to the fact that he was no stranger to abortion: a common bond.

"You were a middle child, really, but brought up as an only child." She looked at him, trying to fathom his thoughts. "Was it lonely?"

"Very." His expression darkened. Then he shrugged. "I always felt I was missing something that I couldn't quite put my finger on. Even as a child, I sensed . . . missing parts. Though I loved my parents, I never felt I was part of a family." He glanced at her. "You know what I mean?"

She nodded. "You were an extension of them—annexed, but unnecessary—a third wheel." She took a deep breath. "I was an only child, too, but I always felt like the proverbial 'other woman,' part of a triangle instead of a family."

"What do you mean?" He squinted as he looked at her.

"I felt like an interloper. My parents had each other, and my only niche was as 'the other woman,' always outside looking in, never even a part of conversations."

"You and I shared different yet similar childhoods."

"I always wanted a big family to make up for that." Then looking down at her bare ring finger, she shook her head and sighed.

"What?"

"I've made such a mess of things." She grimaced.

His hand lightly touched her shoulder. "You made the most you could out of a sad situation. You made Judith and Sam parents, something they weren't able to do themselves, and you gave Angela a loving home." He shook his head. "That doesn't sound so bad to me."

She turned up a corner of her mouth in a wry, half smile. "But I miss her. Angela was a part of me for nine months, a part of me that's gone forever."

"That's not true. You're in her life. You have an open adoption. It's just that you're her auntie instead of—"

"Her mother," she filled in, biting her lip to keep it from trembling.

Reaching over, Justin squeezed her shoulder. Ceren's eyes opened wide and then instantly narrowed. Reassessing his motives, she shifted her weight, leaning away from him, toward the safety of the passenger door. She was grateful for the distance of the car's console and emergency brake separating them.

It's too soon, way too soon, for these maneuvers.

Stiffening, Justin seemed to take the hint. He looked at the time and drew back to the driver's side.

"They'll think we got lost." He smiled slowly and chuckled.

Ceren returned his smile, simpatico with him once more now that he was chastely behind the wheel. She sighed. *What a difference twelve inches makes.*

"Look, there's Popocatépetl," Ceren said. "It's such a clear day. No smog. No haze. The early morning fog's lifted. Its column of smoke looks—"

"Like a smoking gun," Justin said, "circumstantial evidence of premeditated eruption with the intent to explode."

Shaking her head, she laughed. "Lawyers and their jargon."

"Volcanoes have always fascinated me." He winked. "I love their raw power."

"If you like volcanoes, you'd love the view from Cholula. You get the best views from Our Lady of the Remedies."

"Really?" He turned to look at her. "Why?"

"It's located on the peak of the world's largest pyramid."

He peered through the windshield and then cocked his head toward her.

"What do you say we visit it?"

She hesitated, considering the idea.

"After all, you promised Sam you'd show me the local sights." He grinned, showing his dimple.

WARP AND WOOF

"I may not be your first love, first kiss, first sight, or first date—I
just want to be your last everything."

— Anonymous

Three weeks later, they parked at the base of the pyramid and began climbing the steep road.

"What a gorgeous day," Ceren said, breathing deeply. "The air's so clear, you'll get a great view."

"I already am," he said, staring at her. She turned her head, following the sound of his voice, and he looked away quickly. "Of the volcano."

Ceren studied him, her eyes narrowing. Then she dismissed her suspicion with a shrug.

"Just wait till we get to the top. Popocatépetl seems near enough to reach out and touch." The uneven pavement took her by surprise. Trying to regain her balance as she slipped, she extended her arm.

"Got you." Justin caught her hand as his eyes drilled into hers.

"Thanks." Extricating her hand, she met his gaze. "Guess I'd better watch where I'm going."

"The path is easier if you have something to hold on to." He grinned and, palm up, held out his hand.

She hesitated, then, swallowing a smile, shyly took his hand.

They passed a woman on the roadside, weaving with a hand-held loom. Ceren slowed her step to watch as the weaver pulled and pushed the wooden shuttle boards, compressing the strands of yarn into scarves and shawls.

"I love how the strands combine into these colorful patterns."

"Something like life, isn't it?" he asked.

Ceren nodded slowly. "Tying up loose ends, making a tightly knit fabric from loose threads, yes, it is."

"The woof and warp of life."

"I've heard those terms, but I don't know what they mean," she said.

"They're Middle English terms for weaving." Crouching, he pointed to the threads of the weave. "See? The horizontal threads are the woof, while the vertical threads are the warp."

"In other words, the fabric of life," she said, nodding. "I like that. How do you know such obscure words?"

"I took a class in Chaucer and ended up with a second minor in Middle English."

When he stood up, Ceren realized how tall he was. Craning her neck, she peered up into his eyes.

"Doesn't sound like a pre-law prerequisite to me."

He chuckled. "I said second minor, with English my declared minor. I just like Middle English. What can I say?" With an endearing smile, he cocked his head to the side and shrugged.

"There's more to you than meets the eye, Justin Garcia." She looked at him in a new light, taking in the nuances of his smile, the tiny crinkles around his eyes. When her eyes held his a beat too long, she cleared her throat and looked away.

"So," asked Justin, as he handed the weaver a coin. "Which one do you like?"

Ceren fingered through the selection, finally choosing a red, white, and rose colored plaid.

"This one."

"Why, what's different about it from the others?"

"See how she's woven two colors, red and white, into all these rosy shades? She's made the whole more than the sum of its parts." Fingering the material, feeling its texture, Ceren looped it around her neck. Then she rested her eyes on him. "Thank you."

He shrugged. "Glad you like it."

"It's a perfect souvenir of this day, this place, something created right here."

They continued up the steep road as it narrowed into a pedestrian path. When the incline became nearly vertical, the path turned into a stairway.

"There's that smoking gun again," Ceren said, pointing at Popocatépetl in the distance. Justin laughed. Then Ceren saw something glinting in the fading sunlight. A stone. She tried to pick it up, but it stuck hard in the ground. "Like the pyramid, the stone's widest third is buried out of sight."

"Let me pry that out for you." Justin used his pocket knife to dig it from the ground. As he held it in the palm of his hand, it reflected the light in a kaleidoscope of blues and greens.

"It's a moonstone," she said as he offered it to her. She turned it this way and that, letting the light play on its iridescence.

"Did you know that moonstones were once thought to be solid moonbeams?"

"No, but they're my favorite gemstone."

"Really? Look, here's another." Justin retrieved a second stone from the same location. He rolled it in his hand until he saw its brilliance in the matrix.

Ceren held her stone next to his, fitting their rough edges together. "It looks like they had been one stone originally. See where they fit together?"

They looked from the fitted stones to each other.

"What a coincidence finding both parts," he said.

Ceren shook her head. "Not by chance. I believe everything happens for a reason."

"I also believe there's a purpose, a pattern to life." He touched her scarf and smiled. "Just like two colors make a pattern."

She matched her rock half to his. "Like two halves make a whole."

She looked into his eyes, watching how their corners tipped up in a subtle, private smile. *He understands.* Ceren inhaled deeply.

His eyes never leaving hers, he leaned over and brushed her lips with his. As their lips connected, she briefly held his before slightly leaning away. *It's so soon, too soon.* She paused, her lips millimeters from his.

Questions flooded her mind, but her mouth could not form words. His breath tickled her moist lips. Teetering a millimeter closer, then farther, she stood poised between returning his kiss and backing away. She inhaled his breath, wanting to take the initiative, wanting to return his kiss, wishing she could answer his silent, but articulated, question. Half of her said jump; the other half said pull back.

Scuffling feet and muffled voices warned them a group was approaching just moments before they rounded the corner and came into view. Ceren pulled away, but too late. Her quick movement drew a giggle from one of the women as they passed. Justin grinned sheepishly and waved. Ceren felt her cheeks burning. She moved into Justin's warmth, instinctively seeking shelter.

As she buried her face in his shoulder, he put his arms around her, screening her from the barrage of sly grins.

After the group left, Ceren tipped her face to look up at him but stayed in his arms.

"Thank you." Cheeks flushing, she smoothed the wisps of windblown tendrils escaping from her tightly pulled back hair.

"For what?"

She took a deep, cleansing breath before answering and then shrugged.

"I don't know, for shielding me from their stares and giggles." Her voice hardened as she recalled Jarek. "Some people seem to enjoy humiliating others publicly."

Feeling his grip tighten, she looked up, watching his dark eyes glisten as they homed in on hers.

"If you truly care for someone, their ache becomes yours. You don't hurt someone if you feel, if you share their pain."

She stared at him as his words sank in, comparing him to her annulled husband, a bigamist, who had married her without mentioning he was already wed. How opposite they were.

Justin broke the gaze first, letting one arm slide behind her waist.

"C'mon, let's visit Our Lady of the Remedies and then get a cup of coffee."

Ceren looped her arm behind his back. *This feels so natural, so right. For the first time since I gave up Angela for adoption, I actually feel happy.* As they climbed the remaining steps, she glanced up at his face and smiled shyly.

SUPPOSALS

"Love demands infinitely less than friendship."

— GEORGE JEAN NATHAN

Months later over lunch, Justin pushed a small, velvet box toward Ceren. She tilted up her eyes to peer at him through her lashes. Wordless, she questioned him with her lively eyes.

He laughed. "I know that look. Open it, and find out for yourself."

The lid opened to reveal a moonstone ring set in a band of silver, and she gasped.

"It's beautiful!" Lifting the ring, she turned it left and right, letting the stone's iridescence reflect in the light. "It has such fire. Look at the greens and blues." Then she stopped to watch his expression. "Is this . . . ?"

He nodded. "That's the stone you found on the pyramid last May."

She sighed and then held it out to view it again. "And you had it cut and set. It's gorgeous—thank you!"

She leaned across the table and squeezed his hand. Then, as she began to place the ring on her right hand, Justin took it from her. Wearing a nervous smile, he placed it on her left hand.

Tensing, she drew back her hand. "What . . . what are you doing?"

His eyebrows rose as he opened his mouth to speak. As his eyes sought hers, he paused. Chuckling self-consciously, he started again.

"Normally, words come easily for me, but not today. Originally, this ring started out as a pendent, nothing more than a souvenir to remind us of our first date."

48

Tilting back her head, she drew in her breath and then whispered, "What made you decide on a ring instead?"

She watched his Adam's apple bob as he swallowed.

"I wanted to ask you . . . a question, but it's so soon after your annulment that I was afraid you'd say you weren't ready."

Her eyelids flew open, but before she could say anything, Justin pushed on.

"Let's . . . let's just call this a friendship ring, admit we're best friends, and see where it leads." His dark eyes peered at her intently.

Silently, she held up her left hand, splaying her fingers so she could better see the ring's sparkle. Then she took his left hand in hers.

"Yes," she said solemnly.

His eyes flashed momentarily and then narrowed as his forehead puckered into a quizzical frown.

"You wanted to know what I was asking you. What are you answering 'yes' to?"

She looked at him, looked at the ring, and then, taking a deep breath, stared him in the eye.

"If this is a rehearsal, I'm practicing saying 'yes.'"

His eyes lit up. "Yes?" He pulled her left hand toward him and kissed her fingertips. Then he turned her hand over and kissed her palm.

"So 'yes' to being friends, and 'yes' to—"

"Let's just see where it leads," she said, smiling.

"A friendship ring?" asked Judith, her voice high-pitched and dubious over the phone. "What is this, high school?"

"What do you mean?"

"You're not 'going steady,'" said Judith, "so is this a wedding proposal or what?"

"He's testing the waters—"

"Tell him to defecate or abdicate."

Muffling a sigh, Ceren rolled her eyes. "We both want to move slowly."

"You both?" asked Judith.

"Well, it's so soon. I mean, I don't want to rush into any-thing prematurely."

"So you might want to call it a soft wedding proposal—or, instead of a proposal, maybe call it a supposal." Judith's snort served as a laugh.

With a delayed chuckle, Ceren realized she was joking.

"Okay, have it your way. Justin 'supposed' to me."

"How do you feel about that?"

"I feel terrific." Ceren took a deep breath. "Actually, I'm terrified."

"Terrific or terrified?"

"Both." She laughed. "Oh, it's good to talk with you, Judith. I miss you and your sense of humor. Now, catch me up on what you're doing. How are you and Sam enjoying married life? How does it feel being back in the States? How's retirement?" She paused a beat. "And Angela Maria, how's she doing?"

"I'm loving it all: marriage, Texas, retirement, family life," Judith said.

"Not a hint of sarcasm," Ceren said with an incredulous gasp. "You actually sound sincere."

"Why shouldn't I?"

"I recall when cynicism was your default mode—and it wasn't so long ago."

Judith laughed. "It's all due to marriage." Then her tone became playful. "I recommend it, and as soon as possible."

Ceren could almost see the mischievous glint in her eyes.

"You couldn't resist adding that, could you?"

"I'm serious. Speaking from experience, I heartily recommend that you marry Justin—"

"So," Ceren said, changing the subject, but in a louder voice than she had intended, "how's Angela Maria?"

"She's doing great." Judith's voice nearly chirped. "She's growing like a weed. Said her first word yesterday—mama. Sam said she was just babbling, but I heard it as clearly as I hear you: mama."

Ceren inhaled sharply. Though she had meant to shift the focus off marriage, she was not prepared for Judith's burst of enthusiasm. The maternal pride in Judith's voice shrieked as abrasively as a jet engine's whine. Clenching her fists, digging her nails into her palms, Ceren forced herself to answer in civil, even tones.

"That's wonderful. Good, I'm glad to hear it." She paused, her jealousy hard to swallow. "Well, I'd better run. I've got to prepare for my classes."

"Do you have to go so soon? I was hoping to hear more about you and Justin." The smile came through Judith's banter.

"Have you forgotten what it's like to be a working girl?" Ceren struggled to keep it light.

"Not really." Judith chortled and then gasped. "That reminds me. I stopped by the university yesterday to box the rest of my books, and guess—"

Ceren's heart began thumping so loudly it drowned out Judith's words, but she could deduce. Hyperventilating, she closed her eyes, and, with a forced calm, answered, "You saw the jerk, right?"

"Yes, he was packing. The word in the faculty lounge is his contract was terminated before the ink dried on his divorce." Judith snickered. "Couldn't happen to a nicer guy."

"Yeah, well, gotta' run." She forced herself to breathe deeply, slowly. "Give my love to Angela—and Sam," she added quickly before hanging up.

The resentment was overwhelming. No matter that she was grateful to Judith and Sam for helping her through a difficult time, she envied them, begrudged them having Angela.

And I miss Angela Maria, ache for her.

And now this. *Why did she have to mention Jarek? Why? Why now?*

The anger toward him only fueled her resentment at having given up her baby. Ceren closed her eyes. Shutting out her surroundings, she tried to imagine what life would be like with Angela. She tried to visualize feeding her or putting her to bed. Unable to envision caring for Angela in her own lifestyle, she struggled to imagine caring for Angela in Judith's. After several fruitless minutes, she opened her eyes.

It's useless.

She scrutinized herself in the mirror. Wrinkling her nose at her reflection, she pinched the rolls of fat at her waist and spoke to her image.

"All I have left of Angela is the baby bulge, not the baby." Her eyes began to brim. "I made my choice."

A wry voice echoed in her head. *I made my bed.*

"That's right, and I may have to lie in it," she snorted, angrily wiping away the tears, "but I don't have to wallow in it." She grabbed her lesson plans, stuffed them into her briefcase, and, heading to her office, slammed out the door.

As she crossed through the Zocalo, Ceren heard someone calling her. She looked left and right but saw no one she knew.

"Hello, hellooo!"

She looked again and saw Pastora coming up the walk. When Ceren waved and began walking toward her, Pastora's face lit up, and she picked up her pace.

"Haven't seen you in a while," Pastora said, hand to her chest as she caught her breath. "How are you doing?"

Ceren shrugged. "Okay." Forcing a smile, she struggled to keep up her end of the pleasantries. "How are you?"

Pastora took in Ceren's posture, and her smile fell away. "What's wrong?"

"Nothing," Ceren said. "Why?"

"Your tone, for one thing," Pastora said. "Your body language for another."

"I'm fine."

Pastora shook her head. "I've known you for over a year, Ceren. I can tell when you're pretending. Where are you headed?"

"My office. I have to finish my lesson plans."

Pastora's expression was questioning, but she did not probe. Instead, she said, "I'll walk you there."

"Suit yourself." Shrugging, Ceren turned, and they fell into step together.

"How's Justin?"

"He's fine."

Pastora nodded. "You're fine; he's fine." She paused. "How's Faith . . . I mean Judith? Have you spoken to my sister lately?"

Ceren felt the blood drain from her face.

"Ah, so Faith's the trouble," said Pastora. "What did she do?"

Ceren sighed. *It's hard, if not impossible, to hide anything from Pastora.*

"It's nothing she did. It's . . . it's what she has. She has Angela. She has Sam. She has a family, while I . . ." She swallowed.

"While you have what—memories, regrets?"

"Try jealousy, resentment," said Ceren, chewing her lip. "I don't feel very gracious at the moment."

"Are you sorry she adopted Angela?" Pastora watched her closely.

She breathed deeply before answering. "No, it was the right thing, at least at the time, but . . ."

"But what?"

"I just . . . I resent the fact that I won't be there for Angela's first tooth, first step, the scent of her baby lotion, the softness of her hair . . . or her voice calling me mama."

"You miss Angela."

Dropping her head, she nodded. "I'm her mother, and I didn't even get to name her! Sometimes, I wish . . ." Ceren angrily brushed away a tear.

"You wish what?" Pastora's expression hardened as the creases around her eyes deepened.

"Sometimes I wish she'd never been born." The tears began welling up. "Sometimes I wish I'd had that abortion."

"Don't say that, Ceren!" Pastora's eyes flew open. "You don't mean that."

"Oh, yes, I do." The tears beginning to flow, she added, "If Angela had never been born, no one would have her."

"Think how happy you've made Faith and Sam." Pastora placed her hand on Ceren's arm.

"That's just it." Ceren pulled away, her eyes narrowing. "I don't want them to be happy while I'm so miserable."

"So if you can't have Angela, you don't want anyone else to have her, either. Is that it?" Pastora's eyes blazed. "How selfish you are."

Pastora's words hit her like a slap in the face. Ceren moved her lips to reply, but no words escaped.

"How can you be so self-centered?" Pastora paused, breathing deeply, and then started again in a kinder tone. "You've been through, are still going through, a lot."

Ceren nodded, head still bowed, sniffling.

"Have you ever heard of Raphael's Vineyard?"

Ceren shook her head as she wiped away a tear. "What is it?"

"It's an organization that helps postabortive women," said Pastora. "You need to speak with people who've been through this, people who understand."

Ceren shrugged. "But I didn't have an abortion."

"No, but you can identify with it. You've lost a baby. It's easy to forget that recovery's not accomplished in one selfless act or in six months, or in sixty years. It's a process."

Ceren hung on her words, remembering the last time she had seen Angela. *She was such a wide-eyed, intelligent baby—always watching, always touching, exploring with her tiny fingers. You could almost see the wheels turning in her little brain.* Ceren felt a corner of her mouth tugging, tipping up. A snort passed for a chuckle.

"What?" asked Pastora, watching her subtle smile unfurl.

54

Ceren raised her eyebrow. "I was just thinking." She sighed. Refocusing from the past to Pastora, she asked, "Do you have any information about it?"

Ceren clicked the emailed link. Of the twenty symptoms of postabortion trauma listed, she related to seven. Her chuckle was a groan. *Pastora was right. Again.*

She clicked another link and found several types of Raphael's Vineyard retreats: daily, weekend, seven week support groups, and one-to-one companioning.

Only one problem, they were all located in the States. She shrugged, about to dismiss it, when she had an idea. *What about my frequent flyer points? Texas is only a short flight away.*

The decision took all of five minutes. She signed online for the soonest and shortest retreat, Saturday's, and booked a flight to San Antonio to stay the weekend.

GIFT OF GOD

"Sometimes the only way the good Lord can get into some hearts is to break them."

— FULTON J. SHEEN

The retreat met in a converted house on the church grounds, located alongside a railroad track. Train after train rushed past the old house, the metallic whine high-pitched as the trains approached, the roar lower in tone and decibel level as they sped past. The sound reminded her of a scene from an *I Love Lucy* rerun, but she found it hard to smile.

Trying to be discreet, she watched the other participants. Two appeared to be retreatants and two staff members.

Who comes to these retreats? Dumb idea. I don't belong here. I'm not one of them. I didn't have an abortion.

"Help yourselves to coffee and cookies," said Martha, introducing herself as one of the volunteer staff. "We'll get started in a few minutes."

Ceren passed judgment: *Friendly, yet not smothering.* Beginning to breathe, she poured a cup of coffee and chose from an array of homemade breakfast breads and cookies.

"We're expecting two more to join us," said Maria, who introduced herself as a counselor. The door opened, and a middle-aged man walked in. "Joe, thanks for coming." Addressing the group, she continued. "Because we're expecting a couple, we've asked Joe to attend, so the man doesn't feel uncomfortable being the only male in our group."

Ceren smiled inwardly, relating to feeling awkward, but their concern for the attendees helped put her at ease.

Five minutes later, Martha returned from the kitchen.

"It seems our couple has car trouble, so they won't be able to join us, after all."

"In that case, let's get started," said Maria. Turning to Joe, she added, "You're welcome to stay if you like."

"Thanks, but as long as there'll be no men in today's group, I'll bow out." With a smile and a wave, he was gone.

Ceren stole glances at the other two retreatants. *Do they feel as anxious as I do?*

Maria opened with a short prayer. Then in a composed voice she began.

"Abortion has many consequences, many costs, that aren't recognized by society. You might not link certain behaviors as responses to abortion, but ask yourself if you've ever experienced any of these. Do you deal with chronic grief or remorse? Do you feel alienated, on the outside looking in? Do you have anger issues, addictions? Do you get panic attacks, flashbacks, or nightmares? Do you have a problem with anniversaries or other reminders of your abortion? Do you have trust or commitment issues?"

Ceren was careful to control her facial expressions, but inwardly she nodded at nearly every example. *I'm in the right place, after all.* With that realization, a sense of well-being began seeping into her pores. She breathed deeply.

"We're here to listen," continued Maria, "to empathize and help guide you along the healing process. Just remember, you're not alone."

Martha nodded, adding, "The basic fact of abortion is the loss of a child." Ceren flinched. "That child was your daughter or son, but also someone else's grandchild and someone else's neighbor, sibling, or cousin. Whether or not this loss is acknowledged, the grief is real." She looked at each of the attendees. "Not everyone here has had an abortion. For me, it's the grief of a grandparent."

Pausing, she glanced at Maria, as if seeking moral support, and then took a deep breath. "I insisted that my teenaged daughter have an abortion. In fact, I drove her to the clinic. That was twenty years ago, and I still have no grandchildren. My daughter's sterile." She gave a brittle smile and shrugged. "Who knows whether that's the cause, but my heartache is real."

Maria said, "My first husband and I had just gotten married and were a semester away from graduation when we aborted our baby. We weren't ready, or so we told each other. We'd have others, we said. Eight months later, on what could easily have been that baby's birthday, we divorced. In one way or another, we've all experienced the loss of a child—and its consequences. As you see, no one's here to point fingers or throw the first stone.

"Each of you will have ten minutes to tell your story. During that time, no one else may speak or interrupt. This is your time to express what's in your heart." She surveyed the three attendees. "Who'd like to go first?" A girl, who had introduced herself as having been in the navy, raised her hand.

"I'm postabortive, but really we're all postabortive. It's something like postwar." Her snort served as her cynical laugh. "Think about it. Everyone knows someone who's had an abortion." She looked from face to face. "Those of us here know the pain it causes first hand, but there's also a ripple effect. No one's exempt. In the early sixties, it was the Cold War. Beginning in the late sixties, it was the Cold Heart."

Her jaw worked, and she swallowed before continuing.

"Jim and I had lived together a year, and we'd made arrangements to get married the following June. He'd found a job with a software company in Austin and moved in with his uncle. I'd visit him on the weekends, and it was during one of those visits that I got pregnant.

"Though I'd kept track of my cycle with the rhythm method, I had a feeling I was pregnant. I just felt hungry and moody, so I bought a home pregnancy kit. Sure enough, a little blue ring told us that, on schedule or not, married or not, we were about to become parents. Jim didn't give me the hip-hip-hooray and pat on the back I'd expected. Instead, he said I'd have to get rid of it—and now. 'Why?' I asked.

'Simple,' he said. 'We have no money.'

"I told him that as long as we had each other it was enough, that we'd make it somehow. I just couldn't have an abortion.

"That's when he threatened to leave me. I was terrified of losing him. I had no one else, so I made the appointment. Somehow, my mind wouldn't let me think of it as killing a baby. Instead, it seemed like I was just being rational, realistic. After all, so many girls I knew had had abortions. The only thing that worried me was losing my fiancé.

"That day of the abortion finally came. That's what I call it: *that day*. Jim dropped me off at the clinic. He said he'd pick me up afterwards, to call him when I was finished. As I walked into the waiting room, I looked at the grim faces.

"A few of the girls were alone. Some had a boyfriend, husband, or friend with them. A few even had their mothers, but all of them looked anxious. An assistant called me into a 'counseling' room and explained how they were going to perform a simple procedure. They were just going to remove the lining of my uterus. She never used the word baby or fetus. She said I might experience a little discomfort, a little cramping. What a joke. There was a lot of cramping.

"She had me put on a bile-green hospital gown and paper flip-flops. Then she positioned me on the table, with my feet in the stirrups. When she called in the doctor, he looked young enough to be in med school. I don't know what his point was, but he showed me a series of tapered metal rods that he'd use to widen the cervix.

"For whatever reason, I started fixating on the rods." She glanced at us, her expression distasteful. "I was trained in the Medical Service Corps, so I know a little about the dangers of reusing the same equipment without proper sterilization. 'Have they been sterilized,' I asked the doctor. I half sat up, so I could view the room better. I didn't see an autoclave. When he didn't answer, I repeated, 'Did you use an autoclave?' The doctor leaned over me. His face inches from mine. I could feel his breath on my face. My eyes blinked as he enunciated his 'P' with a puff sound. 'This equipment is cleaner than you are!'

"I died. I crawled into some tiny hole and died at that moment. His words made me feel so dirty, so contemptible, that I lay back down and didn't say another word.

"I remember looking up at the ceiling as they gave me a local anesthetic and began to dilate my cervix. The pelvic cramps were excruciating, but what screams in my mind is the sound of the vacuum, literally sucking the life out of me.

"After it was over, an attendant asked if I was all right. Too stunned to answer, I just looked at her. She led me to an improvised recovery room filled with cots instead of beds. There must have been thirty or forty cots. Each one contained a girl at a different stage of recovery. Some were being helped up, while others just lay there, dazed. Others, like me, were just coming out of the anesthetic. Except for a few sniffles and muffled sobs, the room was silent, dead silent.

"The last stop at the clinic was a lecture on contraceptives. Before the talk began, I called my fiancé to pick me up, but there was no answer. I tried his home number. I tried his cell. I waited for over an hour, calling and calling, but he never came. Finally, I took a cab home, wincing with each bump the cab hit in the road.

"The next morning, he showed up at the apartment, stinking of stale cigarettes, beer, and cut-rate cologne. I packed without saying a word and left. I felt alone. I was all alone. I couldn't tell anyone, not even my parents. That was the beginning of my loneliness, my isolation." She sniffed contemptuously. "It's a little souvenir of the abortion that still haunts me.

"A couple years later, I finally worked up the courage to tell my mother over the phone. Just before saying goodbye, I said, 'By the way, I had an abortion,' and hung up. She actually dealt with it better than I thought. She gave me the Christening gown I'd worn at my baptism. I'm saving it for . . . when my husband and I conceive a child, although, after ten years, we're still waiting." Her words hung in the air as she slumped in her chair."

"Thank you for sharing your story with us," said Maria. "We hope you'll be able to put that Christening gown to good use soon." She smiled warmly and then surveyed the other two attendees. "Who'd like to go next?"

"I will," said a soft-spoken girl. "Last Christmas vacation, I had a strong craving for milk. All I wanted to do was sleep and drink milk. It got so I was walking around with a gallon jug of milk, drinking from it randomly throughout the day. How weird is that? I mentioned it to a friend, but she shrugged it off, saying that everything was fine. Then I started getting nauseous. At first, I thought it was the flu, but instead of getting better, it got worse.

"I have news for you. Morning sickness isn't just for breakfast, anymore. Whoever named it morning sickness had no idea that it can come at any time, or that it can last all day long. I used up my sick leave because I felt so sick all the time. During Christmas vacation, I couldn't go to any parties because I'd throw up at everything I smelled. Even the thought of food made me vomit, and it would last for hours. I finally admitted that I might be pregnant and bought a pregnancy test.

"Sure enough, two of the three tests in the kit were positive. I called the clinic and scheduled an abortion the next day, New Year's Eve. My pregnancy symptoms were nausea and super-tender breasts. At the clinic, they performed an ultrasound. Then they told me about a DIY medical abortion that I could do in the privacy of my own home. I was so glad I wouldn't have to spend any more time at the hospital than necessary. I jumped at it."

She half-smiled, wistfully.

"Funny thing, though, I asked to keep the ultrasound picture. I don't know why." She shrugged. "In fact, I even spent a little time talking to the baby. I'm not sure why I did that, either. I even recall a moment when I felt happy to be pregnant, although that moment was short lived when I reminded myself that the fetus growing inside of me soon wouldn't."

She nodded at the first girl, who had told her story. "Like with you, the attendant took me into another room to explain the process. Only I had to take the first pill then and there. That would prevent the fetus from growing, she told me. Within the next two days, I'd have to take the pain medicine and then thirty minutes later insert another set of pills into my vagina to begin terminating the pregnancy. Her directions were clear, nothing complicated.

"Late New Year's day, I decided to start the abortion process. That way, I'd have a chance to sleep through some of the pain. After I inserted the abortion pills, I went to bed, with the pain medication beside me and a towel underneath me.

"An hour later, the pain woke me up. I moaned, I was in so much pain. I was sick to my stomach. I took pain killers and tried to go back to sleep. I dozed a few minutes and woke up again in excruciating pain. I thought for sure there would be a lot of blood, but there wasn't a drop on the feminine pad. I looked through my medical cabinet to see if I had any pain killers stronger than the Motrin they'd given me." She rolled her eyes. "No such luck.

"The worst cramp sent me running to the bathroom. I checked and saw one drop of blood drip into the toilet. I gently wiped and felt something. I held my breath. On the tissue was a miniature baby, perfectly formed, a little over an inch long. I must have broken the sack.

"He looked so calm, so undisturbed, he seemed to be sleeping. I'm sure he was a boy. Fragile and salmon pink, his skin was almost transparent. I touched his little body for a while, not exactly caressing him, but sort of. It was partly awe and partly curiosity. I saw his white ribcage through his salmon colored skin. The ribs looked as delicate and white as fish bones. The black dots were his eyes. I noticed his tiny tongue showing through two, thin, pink lines that were his little lips. I could even make out his nostrils, two dark specks. I touched his hands. Each finger smaller than a sharpened pencil point, his mini fingers rested on his chest. His tiny toes curled against the toilet paper. He looked like a baby—just in miniature.

"What's weird, I couldn't flush him down the toilet. I had just aborted him, killed him, but flushing him—that would be too cruel. I felt sorry for my baby, for the life that I had just ended. I took him in my hand, feeling his spine against my skin, and I gently placed him on a clean piece of tissue paper.

"I felt pressure against my bladder, so I pushed, and the sack passed, its color the same salmon-pink as my baby's skin. The pain was intense momentarily but then left as soon as it passed. I put the little baby aside while I wiped away the blood and washed my hands. Then I picked him up again, wanting to touch him, hold him, even though he was dead, even though I had just killed him.

"As I walked back to my bedroom, I covered his little body with my other hand so I wouldn't accidentally drop him. Finding an old contact lens case, I put him in one side, covered him with saline solution, and closed it. This child, yes, child, deserved a burial. I can't forget that little man. I cry for him every time I think about how innocent he looked after what I'd done to him."

She sat there silently until Maria said, "Thank you for your poignant story." When the girl did not move, she asked, "Is there anything else you'd like to add?" The girl shook her head and abruptly sat back in her seat, seeming to retreat back into her thoughts.

Maria smiled warmly and said, "Looks like you're next."

Ceren began by synopsizing her story. She mentioned the bogus, bigamist marriage—as well as the annulment, friendship ring, and reluctance to commit. Then she looked to Maria for affirmation.

"But I didn't have an abortion, so I'm not even sure if this is the problem, or if this is where I'm supposed to be. I nearly aborted—in fact, came within minutes of doing that. Instead, I gave up my baby for adoption. It's an open adoption and to my friend, but last week when she told me about my baby speaking her first word—mama—to her, I couldn't help but feel I've made a terrible mistake.

"Initially, when I made the decision, I was relieved, knowing that my friends would give my baby a safe and loving home. That relief's been followed by doubt and grieving. Now that choice is coloring my whole future."

With a bittersweet pang, she thought of Justin. She took a deep breath.

"When I was pregnant, I had to decide whether to carry the baby to term or abort. Once I decided to carry the baby to term, I had to consider, should—could—I raise my baby myself, financially, emotionally, physically? As a single parent, would I have the time and energy to both support us and nurture her? Raising her with the birth father was out of the question, and I have no family to help. Foster care wasn't a consideration, so the only other option was placing her for adoption.

"At the time, I thought I was doing the right thing. Now, I'm not so sure. There's been . . . let's just say that decision has caused me some emotional distress. I miss her. I had this child inside me, next to my heart every moment of every day and every night for nine months. Suddenly, she was gone. There was nothing. There is nothing, a void. It isn't natural. I miss her, yearn for her. I wish I could hear her call me mama. I wish I could smell her hair when I bathe her or look into her eyes and debate whether she has my mother's eyes or if she looks like her birth father.

"I didn't abort my baby. She's not dead, but, in many ways, I am. I ended my life when I gave her up for adoption, and I feel so lost."

Ceren sat back in her chair, looked at Maria, and said, "Thank you."

"Thank you for bringing up the distinction between abortion and adoption, as well as the similarities." Maria smiled wistfully. "Do you have anything more you'd like to say?"

Ceren took a deep breath, pursed her lips, and shook her head.

"In the past, I've had naive notions about both adoption and abortion," said Maria, speaking to them all, but with her eyes focused on Ceren. "Being especially inexperienced regarding adoption, I've had to ask a lot of questions. My main question was why do women who find themselves unexpectedly pregnant chose abortion over adoption. Particularly, why do they choose abortion when so many of them profess to believe it's wrong? Here's one of the answers I received recently at a conference."

Listening, leaning toward Maria, Ceren found herself sitting on the edge of her seat.

"Pregnancy, especially unplanned pregnancy, includes a loss of self." Gesturing as she spoke, Maria said, "Carrying to term and giving birth to the baby involves losing yourself, but saving the baby. Abortion can delay a loss of self, but loses the baby. In many ways, adoption is the most difficult choice of all since you feel both the loss of self in carrying the baby to term, as well as the loss of the baby."

"It's a lose-lose scenario," Ceren mumbled under her breath.

"I'm told it can feel that way," said Maria with a wry smile. "On the other hand, and at the same conference, mind you, I heard it put this way. Abortion's the decision not to be pregnant, while adoption's the decision not to parent. The author of these definitions was vehemently opposed to the previous counseling. In fact, she called the assertions biased and stereotyped. She said women have no moral duty to 'lose themselves' or 'give till it hurts.'

"A third speaker at the convention compared and contrasted abortion to adoption. She said one's over before it begins, while the other leaves the mother with empty arms and full, aching breasts." Maria looked at the other two attendees. "However, after my abortion, my breasts lactated, and my heart ached. There's grief in both. Abortion and adoption are not a dichotomy, with one at one end of the emotional spectrum and the second at the other end. They share many similarities." She turned toward Ceren. The smile came through her voice. "Hope this helps you decide whether you're 'supposed' to be here. I'm glad you are." Then she nodded to Martha.

Rising, the older woman said, "We've shared some of our faith journeys with each other. Now, let's begin another journey of healing. For this, we'll need the grace of baptism. Please stand as we renew the promises we made in baptism."

At the end of their renewal, Martha lit a candle. One by one, each woman lit her candle from Martha's.

"Remember, you are each a child of God." Then, calling on Jesus, the Light of the World, she led them in prayer.

After they blew out their candles, they shared a quiet moment. Ceren breathed deeply, assessing the retreat. *I feel a little calmer inside. For the first time in . . . since I gave birth to Angela, I don't feel the need to rush or make up time . . . or make up for my failings.*

"Next, we're going to do a little writing exercise." Martha handed out folders as she spoke. "You're going to write about your stumbling blocks since the abortion—or adoption. There are a few questions to answer, as well. Be honest. This is for you. There's no need to share unless you feel the need."

The attendees began writing. Except for the scribbling of pens on paper, the room was quiet.

Ceren began recalling details and answering questions quickly, until she came to the last question. What was the worst effect of this experience? She wrote, *the worst part of this adoption is my inability to forgive myself.*

When the pens were laid down, Martha continued. "This exercise was the start of an inward journey to help recall the details of your abortion—or adoption—more clearly," she said, glancing at Ceren. "Turn the page, and you'll find a series of questions to help spur your memory further. Take a moment to read these over now, and then read them again in a few days. Write down any emotions or memories you recall, and share them with someone who supports your healing journey. Finally, bring these memories to the Lord in prayer. Through this, truth and kindness will meet. If we share our truth with God, He'll meet us with kindness."

Ceren looked up from their assignment. After the others finished, Maria began speaking.

"We have one more exercise before we break for lunch. Are you familiar with the story of the woman at the well, the woman who had five husbands and was living with a sixth?"

Ceren nodded.

"This is a dialogue version of Chapter Four from the Gospel of John. You'll see that the Samaritan woman's words are italicized. Martha and I will read the other roles, but the three of you will read the woman's dialogue."

As they read through the skit, one line resonated with Ceren. *Sir, give me this water, so that I may never be thirsty or have to keep coming here to draw water.*

At the end, Martha gave them each a cup of water. Then she placed a punch bowl of water in front of them.

Maria said, "The water in this bowl represents the living water of Jesus. One by one, pour your cup of water into the bowl saying, 'Lord Jesus, I give You my whole life. Please give me Your living water.'" She looked from face to face. "All He wants is that you bring Him the truth of your life. Ceren, you start. Offer Him the 'water' of your life. Add your cup of water, signifying your life, your sins, and your regrets."

Ceren nodded. Mingling her water with that in the bowl, she spoke quietly.

"Lord Jesus, I give you my whole life. Please give me Your living water."

When each had poured in her water, Maria asked, "Can any of you remove your drops of water from the bowl?"

They shook their heads, smiling at the absurdity of the idea.

"In the same way that your cup of water mixed with the water in this bowl, your life combined with the Lord's. You are a child of God."

Ceren breathed deeply, internalizing the words.

The quiet girl, who had buried her aborted embryo, whispered, "When you asked if we could remove our drops of water from the bowl, I had an image. Instead of water, I saw drops of blood from our aborted babies mingled with the blood of Jesus."

Maria nodded. "What a beautiful image to end the morning's session."

After lunch, Martha said, "Turn to the next page of your workbooks. On the left, you'll see a list of actions. On the right, you'll see two columns: the before and the after. Take a few minutes to write how your life has changed the most since your abortion or adoption."

Ceren studied the long list, but only two jumped out at her: trust and marriage.

No wonder I want to 'take it slow' with Justin. I'm afraid to trust, to commit. I'm afraid any relationship will end, either by him abandoning me, deceiving me, or by my deserting him, my baby, or anyone else.

When all three had laid down their pens and looked up, Martha said, "Turn to the next page. This is a list of symptoms that women experience after an abortion. Look through these and circle the ones that apply to you."

Again, Ceren studied the long list, but only two jumped out at her: deeply buried anger and pregnancy anxiety.

What if I can't get pregnant? What if God punishes me for deserting my child?

"Would anyone like to talk about their symptoms?" asked Maria.

The woman who had been in the Medical Service Corps said, "Social alienation. Abortion is a taboo subject. Too embarrassed to speak about it to anyone, I grieved in silence and isolation. Finally, finally, I can talk about what happened."

Ceren nodded, empathizing.

The other woman said, "Maternal instincts. My body was preparing to give birth. The hormones were preparing me to become a mother. When I aborted my baby, I ended his life, but it took months for my body to stop manufacturing the hormones. Because I stopped the birth, I violated my maternal instincts. Because I couldn't tell anyone, I suppressed those instincts. I've wanted a baby so badly, but I . . . I've had relational problems ever since the abortion. Even eight years later, I have no boyfriend, no prospects of ever becoming a mother."

Ceren nodded, identifying with her situation. Different, but the same.

"Anyone else?" asked Maria, looking at Ceren.

Ceren looked down at the floor.

Martha said, "All right, let's turn to the next page. This is a list of questions to help identify postabortion stress. Look through these and circle the ones that apply to you."

Only two questions caught Ceren's attention. Do you have trust issues? Inwardly, she nodded. The other question was, Have you lost your faith? The words reminded her of Judith after she had had her abortion and changed her name. *I wonder if this retreat would help her.*

"Grieving is blocked until you acknowledge your losses," said Maria. "As long as you repress your losses from the abortion or adoption, you can't heal. Turn to the next page and circle the losses you've experienced."

Ceren circled child and self-respect.

"For me, it was dreams," said Maria. "After my abortion, I didn't dream. I only had nightmares, recalling my abortion."

"I circled dreams, too," said the quiet retreatant, "but I meant dreams as in aspirations. I lost all hope, any thought of goals."

"Recovery from abortion—and adoption—is an ongoing process," said Maria. "Each time you identify and understand a loss or a stress disorder, you become freer. You can bring that to God in prayer for healing, but, in the meantime, use it as a sacrifice of atonement."

Martha said, "We've all heard of the five processes of grief: denial, anger, bargaining, depression, and acceptance. These also apply to postabortion and postadoption reactions."

"The difference in these situations," said Maria, "is that relief is often felt before grief. It's the relief following the end of the crisis that led up to the abortion or adoption. That reprieve can last a short time, or it can last decades before grief surfaces."

"Another difference," said Martha, "is that, when the final stage of grief, acceptance, finally does come, it isn't something you can give yourself. It's something only God can give you: forgiveness."

"Through God, you receive the forgiveness of the child, and, finally, you can forgive yourself," said Maria.

The naval medic gasped. Though she did not say anything, Ceren could see the release in her. Her shoulders went limp, and she slumped back in her chair.

"Unresolved grief has side effects. Coping with it can affect other areas of your life. On the next page, you'll see some symptoms of blocked grief, unhealthy grief, and normal grief," said Martha. "Read these over and circle the ones that apply to you."

Ceren circled one of the forty symptoms: anger.

"Who'd like to share?" asked Maria.

The quiet retreatant raised her hand. "I circled perfectionism and workaholism."

Wearing a gentle smile, Maria nodded.

"Look on the next page. It shows the ways we cope by defending ourselves. Grief can lead us to overcompensate for something that can't be undone. There's no undoing abortion. All the volunteer work or overtime at the workplace can't make up for the lost baby. Anyone else?"

"Anger," said Ceren. "I can't get past the anger issue."

"Anger at others only hides our feelings," said Maria.

"And anger at ourselves," said Martha, "like the acceptance of grief, isn't something we can overcome by ourselves. Only God can help that. Only forgiveness relieves it—from God, from our children, and from ourselves. We can't do enough penance or prayer to make up—"

"For what we've done," said Ceren, finishing for her, her chin to her chest.

"No," said Martha, her eyes drilling into Ceren's. "We can't do enough penance or prayer to make up for what God's already forgiven."

"Our defense mechanisms helped us survive," said Maria, "but the past is behind us. There's nothing to fear from it anymore. Face it, and bring it to God in prayer."

TROPHIES AND SWINGS

"Sometimes not getting what you want is a brilliant stroke of luck."

— LORII MYERS

"Judith, I had to call you," said Ceren. "Have you ever heard of Raphael's Vineyard Ministry?"

"I've seen signs in front of churches, but I don't really know anything about it."

"It's a way to heal from the wounds of abortion and adoption."

Judith was silent.

"Are you there?" asked Ceren.

"Yeah, yeah, I'm just curious why you're bringing this up."

Ceren heard the reservation in Judith's voice, but instead of it dampening her enthusiasm, she chuckled good naturedly.

"Funny you should ask. I just finished a retreat in San Antonio, and I'm so excited about it that I wanted to share it with you."

"Where are you?"

"On the way to my hotel by the airport."

"Hotel? Why didn't you tell us you were coming to Texas? Cancel your reservation and stay here. We're south of Austin, only a forty-minute drive from you. Besides, we'd love to see you."

Along the interstate, Ceren started having second thoughts. The closer she got, the less certain she was of her last-minute decision.

I need to talk to someone about the retreat, and I'd like it to be Judith. More than anyone, she'd understand. Plus, I think she'd benefit from it, maybe as much as I did.

The thought of seeing Angela again, holding her once more, was sweet. A deep breath became a sigh. *But will I be able to handle the jealousy, resentment, and anger issues?*

She parked in front of their house, turned off the ignition, and debated. *Can I do this? Can I leave Angela again?* She finally got out of the car but left her suitcase in the trunk, just in case. As she waited for them to answer the doorbell, she muttered under her breath.

"Am I ready to put my new lessons into practice?" Closing her eyes, she said a quick prayer.

"Ceren, come in!" Judith opened the door, gave her a hug, and pulled her inside.

Standing just behind her was Sam, holding the baby.

"Hello, stranger, where's your bag?"

"Oh, I . . . I left it in the car." She could not take her eyes off Angela.

Watching her, Judith said, "Sam, would you get Ceren's bags?"

"Sure," he said, handing the baby to her while speaking to Ceren. "Got your keys?"

"Yeah." She broke her gaze long enough to fish in her purse for the car keys. "Here you go. Thanks, Sam."

"Good to see you," he said, giving her a passing hug.

"You, too," she said, distracted, her eyes solely focused on the baby.

Judith and Sam exchanged a glance before he went outside. Judith drew in her breath.

"Would you like to hold her?"

For a moment, Ceren's focus shifted to Judith. "Would I!" She reached out hungrily.

Judith hesitated for a microsecond before holding out the baby for Ceren.

"Oh, she's grown!" Ceren weighed her in her arms, astonished that Angela had gotten so heavy. Her surprise turned into a chuckle, which turned into tears. She held the baby against her heart, sobbing, until she regained control. Sniffling, she handed Angela back to Judith. "I'm sorry . . . it just . . . I wasn't—"

"It's all right," said Judith, just as Sam brought in the bag. "This reunion has to be emotional for you. How couldn't it be? Let's sit down."

Ceren nodded numbly, wiped her eyes, and sat on the sofa.

"Would you hold her?" asked Judith, gently placing the baby in her arms. "I think we could all use some iced tea." When Sam stood by, watching, she added, "Sam, could you help me in the kitchen?"

"Huh?" Turning toward the sound of her voice, seeing her expression, he said, "Oh, sure."

Eyes brimming over, Ceren looked up at Judith. Her whisper barely audible, she mouthed the words more than spoke.

"Thank you."

For a half hour, Ceren gently rocked the baby against her breast. Heart to heart with Angela, she rekindled the bond she recalled so clearly from the first nine months. She breathed in Angela's breath, smelled her baby shampoo scented hair. She fondled the tiny toes and gently traced the outline of her cupid lips with her finger.

Finally, Ceren took a deep breath. *If I ever wondered, I know now.*

A moment later, Judith and Sam walked in with iced tea. Eye lashes still damp, Ceren smiled at them.

"It's all right." She chuckled self-consciously as she shook her head. "I'm not going to try anything foolish."

Biting her lip, Judith placed a glass of iced tea in front of her.

"Thank you for giving me this unexpected gift," said Ceren.

Judith gave her a questioning look.

"For giving me this awareness," said Ceren. "Because of your generosity, I now know I did the right thing." She handed the baby back to Judith. "It's still not easy, but it's all right for me to let go." She took a deep breath.

Judith started slowly. "I'm guessing your retreat had something to do with your insights."

Ceren nodded. "Oh, yeah, it had a lot to do with it!" Looking at her surroundings for the first time, Ceren noticed a string of golf trophies on the mantel. Smiling, she said, "If I were a golf ball, the retreat was like setting me on the tee, but it was your 'golf swing' that propelled me."

SERENADING CEREN

"May songbirds serenade you every step along the way."

— IRISH BLESSING

Back in Mexico, Ceren told Pastora about her weekend.

"It's a shame you had to go to the States to attend that retreat." Wearing a determined frown, Pastora said, "We need to do something like that for the women here, in our community."

"What do you have in mind?"

Poring over the literature Ceren had brought back, she said, "Let's email them and see if we can arrange for a training session."

Ceren opened her eyes wide at the idea. "Wouldn't it be great if we could start a ministry team right here?"

"So, after the retreat ended," Ceren said, "I went to Judith and Sam's."

Justin watched her closely. "How'd it go with Angela?"

She flashed him a grateful smile. *He understands.* Then she took a deep breath before answering.

"Initially, it was tough. Seeing her, touching her, holding her broke my heart." She bit her bottom lip to keep it from trembling. "But then, you know what? The longer I held her, the more I realized it was the right thing. I had done the right thing for her." She lifted her left eyebrow. "Don't get me wrong. Leaving her again was the second hardest thing I've ever had to do, but I have a feeling it will get easier."

She reached for his hand. "Justin, I . . ." She looked down, embarrassed now that she had started this conversation.

"What?" He squeezed her hand. "Tell me."

"It wasn't only the retreat and reunion with Angela. Something else happened that helped me understand." She paused. "A sign, actually three signs."

He cocked his head. "I'm listening."

"While waiting for my flight, I saw a pond through the airport's window. Probably for drainage initially, it had developed into a small wetland. A row of turtles sat on a log, sunbathing. When a plane taking off disturbed them, they jumped into the water, one after the other, all in a line." She motioned with her hand. "Plop, plop, plop, plop, plop."

He gave a questioning smile and shrugged his shoulders.

"I'm getting to it. Next, a mother duck swam out from behind some cattails, seven little ducklings lined up behind her, all swimming in a row."

"Okay, these turtles and ducks, are they anything like the birds and the bees?"

"Not exactly." She chuckled in spite of herself. "Then, I turned around and saw a family walk into the gate area. They were dressed alike, looking like the von Trapp family from the *Sound of Music*. Eleven kids, they ranged from teenagers to toddlers to a baby in the mother's arms. They all seemed so self-contained in their family, so complete within themselves. Seeing them triggered something." She paused. "I realized that I'm not so afraid of . . . moving ahead . . . with marriage . . . starting a family with you."

Apparently unprepared for her declaration, he half choked, half chuckled. Taking a deep breath, he said, "You've certainly done some soul searching since we last talked."

"Call it a change of heart."

"We're so glad you could come to Puebla for our clinical training," said Pastora.

"I gained so much from my retreat in Texas," Ceren said, "but not everyone has the option to fly to the States. We thought it would help the local women if we could start a ministry team right here. We really appreciate you training us."

"Consider me more a mentor than a trainer," said Jan, wearing a warm, lopsided smile. "Like you, I experienced healing at a retreat after my abortion and was moved to help others through the program. Since then, I've started my own retreat center and helped set up two other sites. I wouldn't call what I do training as much as steering you in the right directions."

"I'm sure we can benefit from your experience," said Pastora.

"From where I'm standing," said Jan, surveying the half-dozen eager faces watching her, "you have a willing crew of volunteers. They're your most important asset. A facility is the next most important—and yours is perfect."

"We've practically memorized all the information you've emailed us, and the word's spread," said Ceren. "Three women have come forward already, asking when they can join a retreat."

"When are you holding your first one?" asked Jan.

"Saturday," said Ceren.

"Don't worry. I'll be here to guide you through it."

With a deep sigh, Ceren undid her ponytail and flopped on her bed after returning from the training. She kicked off her shoes and adjusted the pillow, too exhausted to shower or change. Unable to keep her eyes open, she began nodding off.

Ping, ping, ping. The sound at her window barely registered.

Bap, bap, thwap. She vaguely heard something bounce off her window, but began drifting off again.

Clunk, clunk, CRACK. Her eyes flew open. Scrambling out of bed, her brain still numb, she looked at the cracked window. "What the . . . ?" She pulled back the curtains and raised the window, ready to yell at whatever hooligans were disturbing her sleep and throwing stones at her window.

It took her eyes a few moments to distinguish the shadows in the dusk. Then she saw Justin, standing below her window, wearing a sombrero and holding something in his teeth.

When he saw her, he chivalrously swept off his ornate hat with one hand and took a long-stemmed rose from his teeth with the other. Apparently a signal, a four-piece mariachi band stepped out of the shadows and began playing "Besame Mucho."

Her hand automatically swept back her hair. Anger forgotten, her next thought was to tidy herself.

Justin missed his cue, and the band had to play the intro again. This time, he chimed in, serenading Ceren at the top of his lungs. His eyes focused only on her, he could not see the exchanged looks of the musicians behind him.

Ceren began smiling wider and wider. Touched by his romantic spirit, she found herself falling deeper in love with this passionate but tone-deaf man.

Lights came on from all sides of the courtyard. Windows flew open. When Justin finished, everyone applauded, whether for his musicianship or courageous lack thereof.

Ceren swallowed hard, touched that he would make such a romantic gesture. Her hand at her heart, she lifted her fingers to her lips and blew him a kiss, much to the crowd's delight. As the applause increased, Justin bowed with a dramatic sweep of his sombrero and faded back into the shadows. A moment later, Ceren's cell rang.

"Couldn't resist it," he said.

"Resist what?"

"Serenading Ceren."

She chuckled and then sighed. "I find you irresistible myself. That was an experience to treasure. Thank you!"

"In case you haven't noticed, I'm rather smitten with you." A smile came through his voice. "Have you eaten dinner yet?"

Adrenalin replacing her exhaustion, she smiled. "Nope, why?"

"I know a little café with candlelight and mandolin music."

"Be right down—just give me a minute to change."

"Don't change too much. I love you the way you are, you know."

"You silver-tongued devil, you." Shaking her head, she chuckled. "You sure know the way to a girl's heart."

"It's about time!"

Ten minutes later, she took the elevator. Freshly showered and hair still damp, she felt refreshed, renewed. *Or is it the thought of seeing Justin?*

From the moment she stepped into the lobby, his eyes held hers. Although the oversized sombrero was gone, he held out his arms for her, the long-stemmed rose in his hand.

She almost skipped into his embrace. She felt so happy with the world, so glad to be loved, so in love with him.

He lifted her off the ground and swung her in a circle. Ending with a kiss, he slipped his arm around her waist, and, turning, they walked out into the balmy evening.

BEJEWELED SERPENTS AND RINGS

"Patience is not an absence of action; rather it is 'timing.'"

— BISHOP FULTON SHEEN

"Let's visit Our Lady of Guadalupe's Basilica on her Feast Day," Ceren said. "It's such a special place for me that I'd like to celebrate it there."

Early on December twelfth, they stopped to purchase flowers at a neighborhood market before entering Tepeyac.

"Look at the flowers! Just look at 'em!" Her sweeping gesture included the floral stalls that ran the length of the street.

"Castilian roses outnumber everything else, two-to-one," said Justin.

"You and your analytical mind," she said, checking out each potted plant. "Oh, this is the one. The flaming red catches my eye." She reached for a poinsettia. "Its leaves look like they're on fire."

Feeling his gaze, Ceren turned toward him, watching him a beat too long. Justin's eyes blazed.

"What?"

He broke his gaze and half-smiled. Then touching the poinsettia leaves, he pretended to flinch.

"Ouch! It's a veritable burning bush."

"You goof." Chuckling, Ceren shook her head. "You can always make me laugh."

Justin tucked the plant in the crook of his left arm and reached for Ceren's hand with his right hand.

Strolling toward the basilica, they passed a man carrying a huge statue of Our Lady of Guadalupe on his back while he crept along on his knees. They joined the crowds of people bearing flags and banners of Our Lady of Guadalupe. Most clutched flowers protectively and wore their rosaries like necklaces.

Slowly, they followed the mass of people inching their way toward the tilma. Just before the crowd funneled into one lane, Justin reached up and set the poinsettia on the ledge overlooking the altar. The plant's red leaves joined hundreds of other potted plants, floral arrangements, and loose, long-stemmed roses.

"Have you ever been here before?" she asked.

He shook his head. "Heard about it, but this is the first time I've ever seen it."

Grabbing his arm, she pulled him into the fourth line, the farthest from the painting.

"Wouldn't it be better to be up front, closer?"

"No," she whispered. "You get the best view from the back. Trust me."

"I do," he said pointedly, looking into her eyes, giving her hand a tender squeeze.

Butterflies tickled her tummy. *Why did he use those words?* She looked at him, trying to read his thoughts, but the insistent crowd urged them forward onto the moving sidewalk.

As if the area bound them in a sacred pact of silence, it was not until the ride ended that anyone spoke.

"It lasted moments," Justin whispered, "but it seemed timeless."

She nodded knowingly. "There's something eternal in her presence."

They looked at each other, nodded, and then silently turned in unison, each reaching for the other's hand. As they passed through the gift shop on their way out, Justin suddenly stopped.

"You should have a souvenir of today."

His eyes flashed. She noticed a glimmer of a smile but dismissed it as nothing more than a friendly gesture.

"Maybe I'll do some Christmas shopping of my own," she said, starting toward the display cases.

"You stay over here," he said, wearing an unmistakably mischievous smile. "No peeking." With a cautioning, upraised eyebrow, he disappeared into the crowd.

Ceren passed the time window-shopping through an aficionado's eyes, comparing the creative art she saw on the walls to the kitsch.

Suddenly, Justin appeared in front of her, materializing out of the crowd.

"That was quick." Her eyes searched his hands for packages, then his pockets for bulges, but she saw nothing.

"Didn't find anything?"

He raised and lowered his eyebrows, à la Groucho Marx. "I wouldn't say that. I found you, didn't I?" He stepped closer, leaning in to her as if he were going to kiss her, and then pulled back, seeming to change his mind. "C'mon, let's get a cup of coffee."

Reaching for his hand was second nature. What surprised her was his stopping in his tracks and turning their friendship ring so the stone faced her palm.

"It digs into my hand," he said in answer to her questioning gaze. "We'll have to do something about that."

Tilting her head, she squinted, appraising him. "That's too leading a comment to let pass. What's up your sleeve?"

"Up my sleeve?" he repeated rhetorically, his wide eyes a parody of innocence. Then he made a show of checking his sleeve. "Why, nothing's up my sleeve." He left his words hanging.

"Hmmm." She scrutinized him through narrowed eyes, but, with a grin, took his hand.

As they crossed the side courtyard, something caught Ceren's eye. *Was that the old woman?* She paused, staring into the crowd.

"What is it? Do you see someone you know?"

"Thought I did." As they began walking forward, she looked behind her toward the throngs of people, but this time no one stood out. She shrugged. "Guess it was my imagination."

They bought coffee and found seats near the back of the tented shops.

"Oh, I forgot sugar," she said, standing up.

"I got it. Here," he said, pushing a sugar packet toward her.

"Thanks." She picked it up, then pausing before opening it, weighed it in her hand. *That's odd.* "What's this?"

"Open it and see." A quasi-smile played at his lips, while his eyes twinkled.

She looked at him quizzically, carefully tore the paper packet, and then peeked inside. Instead of snowy, white sugar crystals, she saw ice. She gasped as she gently tipped the packet's contents into her hand. An engagement ring!

Opening her eyes wide, she stared wordlessly, looking first at Justin and then, becoming introspective, focusing past him. She took a long, deep breath, aware of the step she was taking. *Contemplating this moment was one thing, but now that it's here.*

A thousand thoughts sped through her mind: the mistake of her first marriage to Jarek; the distrust she had for her own judgment; the grief, the loss of Angela Maria; the fear of making another bad choice, another mistake.

"Don't just sit there." He chuckled. "Say something. Better yet, put it on." When she sat motionless, he added, "Here, let me put it on for you." Then he paused, his expression drooping. "That is, if you want me to."

His disappointed tone broke into her trance. Blinking, she refocused, looking at him as if for the first time. She took in his open, expressive face, hesitant smile, and wounded eyes. Then she knew. *This is the man I love, the man I want to spend my life with.* She threw her arms around his neck. "Yes, oh, yes!"

With a quick peck on her lips, his comically twitching eyebrows suggesting more kisses later, he removed their moonstone friendship ring and slid the engagement ring on her fourth finger.

Her chest heaving, she sighed as she held up her hand, letting the light play through the marquise diamond cuts. A miniature disco ball, the ring refracted the sunshine into flakes of light that showered the scene like glitter in a snow globe. Ceren peered at and then through the shimmering flurries, her focus changing as the old woman came into view.

The woman wore what appeared to be an undulating, jewel-studded serpent around her neck. *A necklace? A snake?* Each flexible segment seemed a lithe row of diamonds, the bejeweled head clasping its tail. As their eyes met, the serpent lady's wizened face screwed into a jovial grin, and she gave a nod of approval.

"What are you looking at?" Justin asked.

Ceren blinked as if coming out of hypnosis. She looked at Justin and then back toward the old woman, gesturing with her eyes, inviting him to follow her gaze. "See that?"

"What?"

"That's the old woman I saw . . . that is, I thought . . ." The smiling face was gone. Questioning her vision, Ceren shook her head, shaking off her reverie. "The ring," she said, forcing herself to return to the present. Then, gazing into his expectant eyes, seeing his open trust and the love in his eyes, her fears of the future evaporated. She remembered why she had fallen in love with him. "It's gorgeous. I love it." She kissed him, meaning it. "I love you so much more."

"And I hope you realize how much I love you." His eyes, soft but resolute, confirmed it.

"But you didn't buy this in the gift shop," Ceren said. She playfully tilted her head to the side as she splayed her fingers, showing off her new ring.

With a chuckle, Justin produced a small package from his jacket's inner pocket.

"I wanted to hear your answer before giving you this."

"First an engagement ring, now what?" Ceren opened her eyes wide in expectation as she undid the gift's protective bubble wrap. It was a Christmas tree ornament. She read the inscription, "Our First Christmas."

"I didn't want to presume," he said as he watched her reaction. She did the math as she looked into his unwavering eyes.

"Christmas is thirteen days away. Are you thinking . . . do you mean you want to get married before Christmas?"

"Why wait?"

"Well . . . what . . . ?" Her mind spinning faster than her lips could move, she sputtered as she began listing the reasons. "What about a church and hall availability? Then, of course, guest lists to write, invitations to send, response time." Counting on her fingers, she added, "Florist, baker, caterer, musicians—"

"Is a big wedding that important to you?"

"I missed out on that with—" Her voice drifted off, recalling, yet reluctant to invite Jarek's memory into their moment. "I thought that lack of preparation might have contributed to . . . to the failure."

Justin took her in his arms. "What you had before was a sham, a lie, anything but a marriage. I don't believe a wedding cake makes you married any more than a birthday cake makes you a year older. It's the exchanged vows that make it a marriage, not the reception afterward."

"I do believe by not being married in church," she hesitated, not wanting to mention his name, but not seeing a way to avoid it, "Jarek and I set ourselves up for failure. At the very least, with a church wedding, I'd have known his divorce wasn't final."

He nodded his head. "A church wedding, a Mass, yes, I agree, that's necessary, but the rest of it?" He shrugged in answer to his question. "The rest is window dressing, in my opinion."

Sighing, she lifted an eyebrow. "I'd always imagined a big wedding, but . . ."

"Are the trimmings that important to you?" He gazed intently into her eyes. "If they are, say so. I'll do whatever you want, but neither of us has any real family to invite."

"That's true."

"We could have a celebration anytime, or renew our vows in a big wedding next month or even on our first anniversary. I just don't want to live apart from you any longer. I don't want to waste any more time. Exchanging vows doesn't need an audience. Let's get married in a private ceremony, and as soon as possible. I want to say goodnight and not have to leave." He held her at arms' length, watching her. "What do you say?"

"I don't want to be apart, either. I've been lonely since I moved to Mexico. Ever since . . . since Angela . . . I've felt a terrible void that I thought nothing, no one, could fill—until I met you. You've filled my heart. I only feel complete when I'm with you." Squeezing him in a bear hug, she kissed him. "Yes, let's get married, and the sooner, the better." Then, as a thought occurred, she pulled back, watching his response. "But don't we need to announce wedding banns weeks in advance?"

On the drive back to Puebla, Ceren called Sister Pastora with the news.

"Congratulations!" said Pastora, "That's wonderful news! When are you planning this blessed event?"

"As soon as possible," Ceren said, sharing a smile with Justin, who glanced at her from behind the wheel.

"You're not—"

"Oh, no," Ceren said quickly, feeling the heat rise in her cheeks, "no, nothing like that. We just don't want to wait any more. We want to live together as man and wife."

Sister Pastora's sigh of relief was perceptible, even over the phone. "Well, then, what good news, indeed!"

"Thanks," said Ceren, meaning it, and then pausing.

Pastora filled the void. "Is there anything I can do to help?"

"Actually," Ceren stole a look at Justin, trying to catch his eye. "We have a favor to ask. Do you know a way we could speed up the process?"

"What do you mean?"

"Do we have to wait for wedding banns or attend any pre-marriage counseling?"

"Wedding banns and pre-Cana counseling are there for good reasons, to help you be sure." Pastora paused, emphasizing her words. "To be certain that you're making the right move."

"I am sure," said Ceren, her unwavering conviction clearly audible.

Overhearing her, Justin flashed her a warm smile and reached for her hand.

"Let me see what I can do," Pastora said. "Have you found a church or asked a priest to marry you?"

"Not yet. You're the first to know."

"Let me speak to Father O'Riley. He may be able to help."

"That's a great idea. It would be wonderful if he could marry us."

"I've also heard of weekend retreats, where, instead of weeks of pre-Cana classes, engaged couples can spend a full day of counseling and learning sessions."

"That just might work." She swallowed hard to keep the tremor out of her voice. Turning toward the window, she brushed away the tears of relief. For the first time, Ceren felt getting married by Christmas was doable.

Hearing her strangled words, Justin took his eyes from the road long enough to look at her. He gave her knee an encouraging squeeze, and Ceren turned toward him, trying to smile through her tearing eyes.

"Don't worry," said Pastora, her soothing tone coming through the phone. "If it's a Christmas wedding you want, a Christmas wedding it will be."

MARIACHIS AND RAINBOWS

"Happiness is only real when shared."

— Jon Krakauer

"You're a real friend," said Ceren, giving Pastora an affectionate hug. "You made it happen. A Christmas Eve wedding, and here in my favorite church, the Chapel of the Rosario."

She looked around the chapel, seeing the familiar, gilded altar, onyx pillars, paintings, and Talavera tile. Tiers of red poinsettias cascaded over the altar, creating a carpet of red and green leaves over the white stone steps.

"The colors of Christmas," said Pastora, following her eyes.

"The colors of Mexico," said Ceren. Her cheeks ached from smiling so widely, but she could not stop.

"Happy?" asked Justin, coming up from behind, accompanied by Father O'Riley.

"Happier than I've ever been." Looking from him to Father O'Riley to Pastora, she said, "How couldn't I be, being here with the people I love, on the best day of my life?"

"If only Judith and Sam could have been here for the wedding," said Father O'Riley wistfully. "I miss them."

"And Angela Maria," added Ceren, biting her lip to keep her mouth from quivering. She looked down at the floor and mumbled. "That would have made it perfect."

Justin and Pastora exchanged looks.

"It's their first Christmas together as man and wife—and as a family," said Justin softly.

"Not to mention their first Christmas in their new house," added Pastora. Brightening, she patted the camera in her hand. "Now don't worry about them not seeing your beautiful wedding. I'm going to take lots of pictures with that camera they gave you."

"You're right." Her smile returning, Ceren hugged Pastora and Father O'Riley and kissed Justin on the cheek.

Glancing at the flowers on the altar, Pastora said, "You have the flowers, but where's the other half of the equation?"

"The what?" asked Ceren, squinting, cocking her head to the side.

"The music, what are you planning?"

"Oh, that's a closely guarded secret," Ceren said, looking at Justin expectantly. "What surprise do you have in store for us?"

"We've skipped the baker and caterer at our *boda menuda*, petite wedding," he said, "but there's one thing I didn't want you to miss out on."

He smiled deviously and motioned toward the door with a wave. Immediately, a procession of musicians began playing their trumpets and guitars as they filed into the chapel. Wearing silver-trimmed bolero jackets with jabots, mariachi pants, and mariachi sombreros, they commanded everyone's attention.

"A mariachi band," said Ceren with a delighted shriek. She drew him into a hug, crushing him against her powder-blue, silk suit. "This is perfect!" Then, whispering in his ear, she asked, "You're not singing this time, are you?"

He threw his head back and laughed. Ceren joined in, while Pastora and Father O'Riley looked on, wearing perplexed smiles.

Turning toward them, Ceren winked. "Justin serenaded me a few weeks ago. He was wonderful, but let's just say he shouldn't quit his day job." She gave Justin a warm smile. "Flowers and song, how appropriate for this day."

"And traditional," said Pastora, capturing it on film for Judith and Sam.

HIGHER EDUCATION

"Education is the movement from darkness to light."

— ALLAN BLOOM

Angela Maria waved goodbye to Judith from the cul-de-sac outside her dorm at the University of Texas in San Antonio. As the car became smaller and smaller in the distance, she could still see Judith's arm waving out the window until she turned left at the light.

With that last vestige of familiarity gone, she was alone. *Ohmigosh! This is it.* As she looked around, she swallowed. Near the dorms, she saw vignettes of other students moving in, their friends and families helping them. Everyone carried suitcases, boxes, or plastic laundry baskets filled with books, backpacks, and shoes. The scene was too graphic a reminder of her own situation.

Now what? A walk. Shoulders hunched, hands in her pockets, she started walking, hoping it would calm her, make the campus her own. With each footstep, she anticipated feeling a deeper sense of proprietorship.

As she strolled the walkways, she compared the buildings' architectural styles. An eclectic combination of new glass facades and old brick structures, she spotted a few windowless, concrete relics from the seventies thrown into the mix.

It's like every bad college movie I've ever seen. Students were everywhere, wearing all styles and guises. Shiny haired girls in buttoned-up blouses, pearls, and A-line skirts preened, while preppy, business majors in ties and vests appraised them through narrowed eyes. Jocks prevailed, wearing sports jerseys, even playing Frisbee in the quad. Girls modeling headbands and sixties hippie garb strutted along, their gypsy skirts flouncing with every step. Others cowered like embarrassed, overgrown children, their parents in tow, sporting ill-fitted jeans and loud T-shirts. Then there were the sullen goth girls and steampunkers, wearing their textured, black hair, thick eyeliner, and black nails like badges of honor.

Angela took a deep breath. Rolling her eyes, she muttered, "Home sweet home."

Overwhelmed instead of relaxed from her walk, she backtracked to the student residence for solace. Halfway up the stairs to her dorm, she heard punk rock. The closer she got, the louder the music. Then she noticed her door was wide open, and the rock was blasting from her room.

Covering her ears with her fingers, she tentatively poked her head inside the door. No one was there. The walls were covered with what appeared to be headstone rubbings. She stepped in and saw stacked boxes, clothes strewn on the bed, and an iPhone hooked up to a pair of speakers. As she turned down the volume, she took a deep breath, collecting her thoughts. *Apparently, my roommate's arrived. This is going to be one long summer.*

"Hey," said a goth girl, carrying an armload of black, charcoal, and purple clothes. She tossed them over the clothes already heaped on the bed.

Angela stared at her roommate. She wore laced-up boots over fishnet stockings with a black bustier over a short, black dress. Spiked black hair with a burgundy streak, dark black eyeliner, black lipstick, and black nail polish finished the look.

At a loss for words, she mumbled, "Hey."

"I see you found my speakers."

With a nervous grunt, Angela said, "Just turned them down a notch."

"No worries. Wanted to hear my fav sounds while I was out of the room. Music soothes the soul and all that."

"So I guess we're roommates."

"Yeah," said the girl, her head back, her eyes narrowed as she studied Angela. "I'm Develyn."

"Evelyn?"

"Develyn, short for Debra Evelyn, but everyone calls me Develyn." Her black lips parted in a smirk. "What's yours?"

Mimicking the girl's vocal style, she said, "I'm Angela, short for Angela Maria, but everyone calls me Angela."

"Ha!" The girl pushed her shoulder familiarly, knocking her back a step. "I like that. You're the angel, and I'm the devil."

THEN WHAT?

"Those who die go no further from us than God,
and God is very near."

— ANONYMOUS

Judith sat at the kitchen island, sipping her morning coffee. As if they had a mind of their own, her eyes returned to the fireplace time and time again. *Without Angela to see her, is Helen here now?* Judith snorted. *If a tree falls in a forest and no one's around to hear it, does it make a sound? If I'm not sensitive to spirits, does it mean they don't exist?*

Over the hum of the refrigerator, she heard the air conditioner kick in. Both acted as muted counterpoints to the rhythmic ticking of the clock. She sighed. *How quiet it is without Angela.*

The phone rang. *Angela?* Judith hurried to answer it.

"Judith, how are you?" Ceren's voice lilted as she asked the question.

She struggled to keep the disappointment out of her voice. "It's good to hear from you. Angela mentioned what a great time she had with you at dinner last week."

"Wish you could've made it."

Judith glanced at the fireplace. "Me, too, but Angela wore me out shopping that day."

"Actually," Ceren hesitated. "Angela's the reason I'm calling." She took a long breath.

"What's up?"

"Have you noticed . . ." she grunted uncomfortably, "has she said anything . . . unusual . . . recently?"

"Like what?" Judith was reluctant to offer any information until she was clear about Ceren's motive.

She sighed. "At dinner, Angela mentioned that she could see—"

"Spirits?" Judith chuckled with relief. "I didn't want be the first to broach that subject, but yes, she did. Did she mention it to you?"

"She mentioned seeing Nana and—"

"Helen?" finished Judith.

"Helen? Who's Helen?" asked Ceren.

Afraid she had divulged too much, Judith backpedaled. "Nothing. Who did she mention seeing?"

"Who's this Helen?" asked Ceren.

"You said Angela mentioned seeing Nana and . . . who?"

"Do you recall I had a miscarriage eleven years ago?"

"Of course. It devastated you."

"It did more that," Ceren muttered under her breath.

"What was that?"

"It's been a sore point between Justin and me ever since." Ceren grunted uncomfortably. "Angela said she saw the spirit of my baby . . . well, the spirit of my boy."

Judith glanced at the fireplace. "No. Other than mentioning she enjoyed her time with you, she didn't say a word about it. What happened?"

Ceren took a deep breath and brought Judith up-to-date.

"Have you discussed this with Justin?"

"Not yet. I wanted to talk with you first."

Judith cocked her head. "Why do you say that?"

"I'm . . . not sure how I feel about this."

"We always suspected Angela would have some special gift." Judith shrugged. "This may be it."

"But is this something new? Has Angela ever talked about this ability before?"

"As a child, she had an imaginary playmate," said Judith. "And remember at her First Communion, when Pastora gave her our mother's rosary beads, how she knew it was from—"

"Nana," finished Ceren. "Yes, now that you mention it, I do recall, but since those early years has she ever said anything or let on in any way that she could communicate with the afterlife?"

"No," Judith shook her head, "not until last week."

"Now you've got my curiosity piqued." Ceren snickered. "*You* mentioned Nana, and Angela mentioned her. What happened?"

Judith shared the story of meeting Helen.

"Wow." Ceren grunted under her breath. "How do you feel about it?"

Judith glanced toward the fireplace, and a chill came over her.

"I can't help but wonder if Helen's still here," Judith caught her breath, "or if there's any real substance to Angela's stories."

"That's partly why I wanted to talk with you before discussing it with Justin."

Judith nodded. "Without Angela's presence, I have no way of knowing whether or not Helen's here . . . or even if she *could* be here." She shuddered. "This whole revelation is unnerving, or maybe this is just a reaction to being alone. Without Sam and Angela here, this big, old house creaks and groans as much as my joints."

"You must miss her." Ceren's concern came through the phone.

"For the first time, I'm beginning to understand the separation anxiety you must have felt when you gave her up."

"The ache's dulled over time, but don't underestimate the anguish. It's real."

"After losing Sam, it's twice as hard for me with Angela leaving the nest."

"Circle of life," said Ceren.

From her tone, Judith could almost visualize Ceren's shrug.

"Circle of life and death, actually birth and death. Since Angela brought up the concept of seeing Helen's spirit, it's raised a lot of questions."

"Like what?"

"Like, will I see her when I die? Will I be judged?"

"Don't be so morbid, Judith."

"I'm not being morbid . . . just mortal." She sighed. "Things that hadn't bothered me earlier in my life are haunting me now."

"The abortion still bothers you?"

"Oh, yeah." Judith nodded. "First and foremost. Front and center."

"Then why don't you go to a Raphael's Vineyard Postabortion Retreat? It did wonders for me, and I've seen it help so many others."

"You've mentioned this to me before." Judith tried to stifle a sigh.

"But this time it's different. I think you're more open to accepting it than you were in the past. Judith, it'd be good for you. Trust me, it'd give you closure, peace of mind. Do it."

When Judith hung up, she dialed Pastora.

"Faith, what a pleasant surprise."

Judith smiled to herself. "Nobody but you calls me Faith."

"Habit," said Pastora in a bubbly voice. "What can you expect of a Sister but habit?"

Judith chuckled. "Do you still work with Raphael's Vineyard?"

"No, at ninety-two I've turned over the reins to younger women. Why?" Pastora's voice rose expectantly.

"I've been doing some soul-searching lately, and maybe it's time."

"Faith, you're thinking of joining a retreat, aren't you." Pastora's sigh was audible over the phone. "I prayed this day would come. What prompted it?"

Judith paused, struggling with an internal debate. *Should I mention Helen or Angela's role in the decision?* She shrugged. "It's just something Angela said, something that's long overdue."

EARPLUGS AND COMMUNICATION

"We are all butterflies. Earth is our chrysalis."

— LEEANN TAYLOR

Monday morning, Develyn got home at two thirty. Angela rolled over and covered her ears with her pillow, trying to ignore the noise as Develyn undressed in the dark.

Tuesday morning, Develyn came in at three thirty. Angela pulled earplugs from her drawer and rolled over.

Wednesday and Thursday mornings, Develyn came in at four thirty. Angela barely heard her.

Friday morning, Develyn came in at five thirty, sat on Angela's bed, and shook her until she woke up.

"You awake?"

Angela pulled the plug from her left ear.

"I am now. What do you want?"

"If we're going to be roommates, you and I have to get to know each other. Tonight, seven, wear black."

Homework assignments done for the weekend, Angela was waiting for her roommate Friday night at seven sharp. Dressed in black jeans and a T-shirt with an animal rights logo on it, she checked her watch for the third time and heaved a sigh.

At ten after, Develyn strode in, took one look at Angela, rolled her eyes, and said, "What is this? Cheerleader tryouts?"

"What?" Exasperated, Angela held out her hands as she shrugged. "You said black. I'm wearing black. Hello!"

Develyn laughed. "I love it when you get huffy. It's sooo . . . not you. Here," she said, pulling a skinny, black dress from her closet and throwing it on Angela's bed. "Try this on."

Angela looked at it. The dress had five sets of brass buttons on the front, creating a trim, nautical look with a flash of lace at the bodice.

"And why?"

"Because tonight is girls' night out. I wanna' get to know my roomie. You're on the preppie side," she scrutinized her, "but redeemable."

"Redeemable?" Angela smirked and took a deep breath. "Gee, thanks."

Missing the sarcasm, Develyn said, "No worries . . . oh, let me do your makeup. You won't recognize yourself!"

After Angela changed into the dress, Develyn applied white base to her face, followed by black eyeliner, black mascara, black lipstick, and black blusher. As a parting thought, she brought out a bottle of magenta hair spray and colorized a section of her hair.

"This is temporary color, right?"

"Sure."

By seven thirty, Develyn had done Angela's makeup and redone her long hair.

"It's brown, not black," she groaned, sizing up her hair, "but in the dark maybe no one will notice."

"Except for the red streak." Angela looked at her mascaraed reflection in the mirror and raised her eyebrows. "I look like one of the Black-Eyed children."

"That's the point." Develyn smiled for the first time Angela could remember. "How 'bout your hair? Like the look?"

"As long as the red washes out."

"Magenta," Develyn corrected, making a face. She shrugged. "It should."

"Not reassuring."

By eight, they had parked and made their way to the river front. As they descended one of the open staircases from street level to the River Walk, Angela caught her breath. Millions of twinkling lights reflected off the water, doubling the fairy land impact. Muffled sounds of gondolier tour guides slowly swept by as they guided their craft along the river. Gently jostling people—looking, not looking, talking, laughing—passed by.

"Now we enter the paseo," said Develyn.

"Paseo?"

"You know, the slow stroll along the River Walk, where the girls try on and show off their latest personas, and the guys strut their stuff." She winked.

Angela laughed at the image. It was the first time she had been there in the evening. Though she had visited the River Walk many times with her mother and Pastora, it had always been during the day. At twilight, her favorite time, just as the lights had begun glimmering, they had always left to get home before dark. Never had she seen this facet of the River Walk. Her eyes opening wide in anticipation, she looked out over the milieu of lights and life. *It's another world.*

"Fifteen miles of river front restaurants, bars, cafes, and shops to explore on foot." Develyn's black-painted lips parted in a grin. "And if you like history, you can even walk to museums, the King William District, and nearly three-hundred-year-old Spanish missions along this River Walk."

"You like history?" Angela cocked her head.

"Yeah, it's my major." The black lips smirked, and the right eyebrow arched. "But tonight, I'm looking for something else."

She touched a finger to her tongue and pretended to groom her eyebrow. "I'm on the prowl."

Her jaw slack, Angela took a deep breath, wondering if coming with Develyn was such a good idea. *She's my ride.*

"Don't look so scared," she said, chuckling. "I'm just messing with you."

Angela returned a nervous giggle.

"C'mon, let's grab a coke."

They bought to-go containers from the food court and brought them outside onto the River Walk. Sipping as they walked, they passed beneath the first bridge.

"Just a minute." Develyn took a flask from her purse. "Ever try rum and coke?"

"I don't think so—"

Develyn lifted her container's top and poured.

"That's enough." Angela pulled her cup away. "Just want to taste it, not bathe in it."

Develyn snorted and poured generously into her own cup.

"Hey, remember you're driving."

Develyn laughed and put away the flask. "You wanted to taste it. Do it!" She watched Angela's response. "What do you think?"

Angela took a sip it, rolled it around her tongue, and shrugged. "It's okay."

"Just introducing you to the finer things in life." She laughed, her white teeth contrasting against her black lips.

"Hey, Dev," said an interested male as he passed.

Develyn rolled her eyes and responded with a dejected, "Hey." She turned to Angela. "Quick, say something funny."

"What?"

Develyn broke out in a peal of laughter. Angela watched the boy slink away, his hands in his pockets, his shoulders hunched.

"What was that all about?"

"Nothing." She shrugged. "Keep walking." Taking a sip, she glanced at Angela. "What's your major?"

She sighed. "I don't know. My birth mother wants—"

"So you're adopted?"

"Yeah, why?"

Develyn shrugged. "You were saying . . ."

"My birth mother wants me to follow her into art history."

"But you don't want to?"

"If she hadn't dragged me around to so many art galleries and museums as a kid, maybe I would."

"Least you had a mom."

"Two of them, if you count the woman who raised me. Three if you count my aunt Pastora."

Develyn's black-outlined eyes opened wide. Then she looked down, hiding whatever slid through her mind.

"I had a grandmother."

Angela smiled politely, thinking she was joking. "You mean your mother was older when she had you?" Nodding her head, she snickered. "I can relate."

"No, I mean I never knew my mother, never had a mother. My grandparents raised me." She sipped from her straw.

"Why's that?"

She grimaced. "My grandparents only gave me a sketchy summary, no details. Basically, they said she died giving birth to me." She grunted. "It was like this forbidden topic. Every time I brought it up, my grandmother got teary-eyed and left the room."

"Did your grandfather ever talk to you about it?"

Develyn scoffed. "He'd just shake his head, sigh, and mumble things like, 'maybe when you're older.'"

Angela raised her eyebrows. "And I thought I had it rough."

"Why?"

Angela sighed and then licked her lips. "I knew I was adopted. It was an open adoption, for heaven's sake. I grew up with two . . . *three* . . . mothers, but recently my birth mother told me she almost aborted me."

"No." Stopping, Develyn grabbed Angela by the shoulder and turned her so they faced. "You're serious?"

"Yeah." Angela grimaced. "Talk about wondering if you were wanted."

Her eyes big, Develyn said, "I'm a survivor."

"A survivor of what?" Angela snickered, again thinking she was joking. "The Titanic?"

"No," she started slowly, keeping her eyes on her cup. "Abortion."

"What do you mean?"

She looked Angela in the eye. "My mother tried to abort me. The abortion failed. She died, and I survived."

Angela's jaw dropped. "Ohmigosh." She blinked. "Are you sure? I mean, how could you know?"

Develyn's lip curled. "My darling cousin told me one day, laid it right between my eyes in no uncertain terms." She caught Angela's eye.

Grimacing, Angela shook her head slowly. "Sorry."

Develyn tried to shrug it off. "To quote the T-shirts, 'It is what it is.'" She looked away.

In step, they turned and walked in silence, each sipping her coke, each lost in her thoughts. People passed them. Tour boats floated by.

Finally, Angela asked, "Have you ever . . . communicated with your mother?"

"Like in séances or Ouija boards?" Develyn held up her hands, shaking them as if she were scared, then abruptly dropped them and made a sour face. "What do you think?"

Angela heard the sarcasm. It was hard to misinterpret. She raised her eyebrows and was ready to back off. Then shoulders slumping, she groaned. Taking Develyn by the elbow, she stopped her.

"Look, whether you want to believe me or not, there's someone here who'd like to speak to you."

Develyn's left eyebrow and lip curled. "Yeah, right." She started off, but Angela again caught her elbow.

"I'm serious."

"And I'm Cleopatra," Develyn smirked.

"Fine, you don't want to listen, that's your business." Angela sighed. "I tried. I'm done," she said to the night.

"Who are you talking to?"

"Nobody." She sullenly sipped her coke. Then she threw back her head and groaned. "Okay, but this is the last try."

"Who the hell are you talking to?" asked Develyn.

"Ginny." Angela grimaced. "She's asking if the name Ginny means anything to you." When she was met with silence, she peered at Develyn. "Does it?"

Develyn's eyes reminded Angela of an owl's. "You're not kidding, are you?"

"Who's Ginny?"

Develyn shook her head. "Ginny only to her family. Virginia was her name."

"All right, who is she?"

"My mother."

A half hour later, they were back at the dorms. Develyn spiked two cans of coke, handed one to Angela, and sat cross-legged on the rug.

"Okay, tell me what you know."

Joining her, Angela shook her head. "I don't know anything. I just repeat what they tell me."

"They." Develyn scoffed. "I suppose you mean spirits."

Angela shrugged. "Call 'em what you want, but I can see life forces, ghosts, souls."

"You're messing with me, aren't you?" she said.

Angela grimaced and spoke to the air. "This is why I haven't mentioned it in ten, twelve years."

"What do you mean?" She looked around the room. "Who are you talking to?"

Angela changed her focus to Develyn. "As a kid, I told everyone about my 'invisible friends.'" Rolling her eyes, she took a deep breath. "At first, everyone thought it was cute, my imagination at work, but in school it was like a witch hunt. Kids thought I was weird. At best, teachers called it childish. At worst, they suggested I see a child psychologist. In self-defense, I began keeping it to myself."

"But you're telling me." Develyn raised her left eyebrow. "Why?"

"When I turned eighteen, I decided to come out of the proverbial closet. I can see souls, and I'm not going to hide it anymore, okay? This is me, weird or not." She leveled her gaze. "Like it or not."

Develyn chuckled. "Frankly, I don't trust anybody who isn't 'weird.'" She clinked her can against Angela's. "Enough with the background. What does Ginny have to say?"

Angela quieted her mind. Mentally, she invited Ginny. After a moment, she took a deep breath.

"She's here."

Develyn whispered, "What's she want?"

"She's been waiting for an opportunity to contact you." As she listened internally, Angela studied Ginny's lined, shriveled face. Then Angela stopped and shook her head. "It isn't like in the movies, where they talk in sentences." She sighed. "It's more like images that pop into my head or phrases that I 'hear' with my inner ear. Ever try tuning into a radio station when you're driving? It's something like that. I just try to make sense of the faint signals."

"Does she have anything else to say?"

Angela listened again. "Basically, she wants you to know that she's waited for this moment. Literally, waited to tell you she's sorry—"

"Sorry for what?"

Closing her eyes, Angela sighed. "Sorry for trying to abort you. Sorry for—"

"She should be!" Develyn glared at her. "A botched abortion. She couldn't even do that right."

Angela rolled her eyes. "Your attitude isn't making this any easier . . . either for her or me." She leveled her eyes at her. "Do you want to hear this or not?"

Develyn slumped. "Sorry, go ahead."

Angela tried to regain her concentration. "All I'm getting is . . ." Grunting, emoting with her hands, she struggled for the words. "I see a picture of a mother holding a baby. The feeling is a . . . a yearning. That's it. She wishes she could have been with you, could have held you, loved you." She smiled. "Love, that's the message. She wants you to know she loves you."

Angela looked at Develyn. Mascara running down her cheeks, Develyn wiped her nose with the back of her hand. Nodding, sniffling, she swiped at her cheeks, smudging the black lines of tears.

"Thank you," she said in a breathy whisper.

ILLUMINATION

*"Grace is darkness and light, peacefully
co-existing, as illumination."*

— JAEDA DEWALT

Sunday morning, Angela sat on Develyn's bed, shaking her until
she woke up.

"You awake?"

Eyes closed, she mumbled, "What do you want?"

"If we're going to be roommates, you and I have to get to know
each other. This morning, nine, wear black."

Cocking an eye open, Develyn glanced at the clock.

"Are you crazy?"

"It's ten-of, better get moving." Angela handed her a carton of
orange juice.

Develyn eyed Angela suspiciously. "We're going *where?*"

"You heard me." Angela glanced at her as she drove. "Mass at
Concepción Mission."

"I haven't been to church in years." She groaned. "Give me one
good reason why I should go today."

"I introduced you to the spirits." Hunching her shoulders, Angela
grinned. "It's only right that I introduce you to the Holy Spirit."

"If you recall, I introduced *you* to the spirits." Her lip raised in a
half-smile, Develyn eyed her until she caught on.

Nodding, Angela snickered. "The rum. Okay then, you took me to your haunts." Keeping her eyes on the road, she snickered. "Now, I'm taking you to mine."

"Haunts, I get it." Develyn grimaced. "I wanted to get to know my roommate, not find out what a dorky comedienne she is. Besides, that's two reasons. I said one."

"Here's a third. It's Corpus Christi."

"Corpus Christi?" She looked at Angela with a blank expression. "You're taking me to Corpus?"

"No, today is Corpus Christi Sunday. You know, the Feast of Corpus Christi, the Body and Blood of Christ." Angela glanced at her from behind the wheel. "And here's a fourth reason. If religion doesn't do it for you, Concepción Mission has an interesting history. It's the oldest originally built mission in Texas, maybe in the United States."

"Really?" Develyn's eyes opened wide.

Angela swallowed a grin.

During the Feast of Corpus Christi homily, the priest said, "We are what we eat. Don't we all agree? Our bodies metabolize the substances we put into them. Be it vitamins, supplements, or the Body and Blood of Christ, in a very real way, we become what we eat."

Eyes riveted on the altar, Develyn repeated the words under her breath.

"We become what we eat."

Angela glanced at her and, self-conscious about peering into Develyn's private self, quickly looked away.

After Mass, Develyn pulled Angela aside. "You mentioned Concepción Mission has an interesting history. Does it have a tour on Sundays?"

"I think it has tours every day." Despite needing all afternoon to complete her paper for Monday's class, she said, "Want to ask at the National Park Service station?"

"Yeah, I'd appreciate that."

Angela noticed Develyn's eyes were wide, but not from black liner or mascara. She saw an openness she had not seen previously. Whether from lack of time or something else, Develyn had not applied her ritual white pancake base, followed by black eyeliner, black mascara, black lipstick, and black blusher.

"Sure, I saw the Visitors Center near where we parked." Angela shrugged. *Whatever the reason, she looks softer, more approachable.*

Within minutes, they connected with one of the docents already in the midst of a tour.

"The Franciscans initially built Mission Nuestra Señora de la Purísima Concepción de Acuña in 1716 in east Texas, but they established it in San Antonio in 1731. Among San Antonio's five missions, Mission Concepción is unique because it was the only one completed as originally designed, and the only one that never collapsed. You are standing within the original walls, sharing the same space with over two hundred fifty years of history." He pointed to the mission's south window. "You see that conical shaped window?"

Angela and Develyn turned. Following the guide's arm, they saw a round window inset into thick, stone walls covered in stucco. High above the church's nave, it hung near the ceiling, above the second floor choir loft.

"This deep-set, oculus window's casement can be compared to two cones intersecting, with the window itself at the narrowest point. The external cone acts as a sunlight collector, and the internal cone acts as a sunlight diffuser. The white paint on the window's thick, inner walls increases the light's impact."

"What's its purpose?' asked Angela.

"Franciscan friars were smart. They used the sun to illustrate the Catholic faith to the local peoples. The Franciscans built symbols into their churches that didn't require words."

"I've read that the missions were sometimes used as astronomical observatories," said Develyn. "Is that the case here?"

The guide nodded. "Yes, over the centuries, Franciscan friars have used churches as solar observatories for many reasons, for instance, as a means to determine celestial events like Easter. Keep in mind, Easter's a moveable feast, so it occurs on a different date every year."

"Then they used these churches," asked Develyn, pointing, "and tools like this window to determine those dates?"

He nodded. "Easter's held on the first Sunday after the first full moon that occurs on or after the spring equinox. It's a solar event. It happens when the sun shines directly on the equator, and the length of day and night is nearly equal."

"So this window was an early calculator, using a point of light to document the passing of time and determine solar dates?" Angela cocked her head, trying to understand.

"That, but equally important, they designed this into the church as a symbol that needed no words. Concepción was built to catch the sun and bring it through the windows on days of religious, seasonal, and astronomical significance. The Franciscans used a ray of sunshine to not only illuminate the sanctuary, but to reassure the indigenous people," he looked at each of the tourists, "and us, that God's presence is all around us, always."

"Christ as the sun, Christus Sol," said Angela, staring at the sunlight streaming through the window like a beacon.

"Christus Helios," said the guide, nodding.

Angela's eyes tracked the light to where it fell on the floor.

"You mentioned astronomical significance. Ancient Aztec buildings sometimes featured solar illuminations. Does Mission Concepción have any parallels?"

Chortling, the guide held up his index finger and then pointed to the lit up portion of the stone floor.

"Funny you should mention that. You see how the window's light illuminates this area? What day is the Feast of the Assumption of the Blessed Virgin Mary?" He waited for someone to answer.

"August fifteenth," said one of the tourists.

"On August fifteenth, the sun beams through that window like a spotlight and slowly marches toward the altar. It's powerful, so intense, it hurts to look directly at the window." He grinned. "During leap year, it happens on August fourteenth, the Vigil of the Feast of the Assumption of Mary. It follows the central aisle up toward the altar, to the very center of this cruciform church."

One of the tourists raised his hand. "What's a cruciform church?"

"Cross-shaped." He made a cross of his left and right index fingers. "If you're interested, I'll tell you more about that in a minute, but first I want to show you the significance of this circular window's architectural position. It illuminates the very center of the church, at the crossing, the intersection of the nave and the transept on the Feast of the Assumption. It's really quite a sight to see."

"The fifteenth of August," Angela whispered to herself.

The docent turned toward one of the tourists. "You'd asked about a cruciform church. Think of a cross, a short top and long bottom with an intersecting piece of wood, or in the case of architecture, intersecting wings on either side." Again he made a cross of his left and right index fingers. "The long bottom part is the nave, where we're standing now, where the congregation sits. The short upper part is the altar or apse, and the crosswise 'arm' is called the transept. Where they intercept, where you see the dome, is the crossing. Make sense?"

The man nodded. "Thanks."

"As you recall," continued the docent, "the mission's full name is Mission Nuestra Señora de la Purísima Concepción de Acuña. This mission was named in honor of Our Lady of the Immaculate Conception, whose feast day is . . . ?"

"December eighth," said the same tourist.

"Exactly. Another important illumination at the Mission Concepción takes place on December eighth."

"From the same round window?" asked another in the tour.

"No, this time the light from the dome's south window crosses to the altar in the north transept." The docent pointed out the light's path with his hand. "Then, on December twenty-first, the winter solstice, the light crosses over the face and tabernacle to reach the top of the north altar. We call this the midwinter 'resurrection' illumination. Remember, the sun was a heavenly metaphor for Christ, the Light of the World."

"Christus Sol," said Angela.

He nodded. "You can view this Sun-Christ symbol here in two places. It's carved in the exterior façade above the front door, where two angels hold a chalice with a consecrated host represented as a sunburst, and it's also painted on the convento's ceiling." The docent smiled at the tourists. "So what you're doing at the winter solstice is celebrating the end of darkness. You're celebrating the coming of light, the sun, a spiritual allegory for the coming of Christ, the resurrection, and salvation."

"You mentioned a painting on the ceiling. I see quite a few frescoes," said Angela. "Can you tell us anything about those?"

"Be happy to, but that's a tour in itself," he smiled. "Are you from the area?" They nodded. "Come back next Sunday. I'm giving an artistic tour after Mass, featuring the frescoes and artwork."

"Thanks, I'll do that," said Angela.

"So will I," Develyn chimed in.

Ceren and Pastora will love it. "By any chance, is there a connection between Mission Concepción and Our Lady of Guadalupe?" asked Angela.

"Definitely," he nodded, "both through faith and art."

"Then I know at least one person who'll want to join us."

"Remember during the homily, when the priest said, 'We are what we eat?'"

"Yeah," said Angela, eyes on the road as she drove to their dorm.

"I like the way he connected taking vitamins and supplements into our bodies with taking Communion, the consecrated host and blood of Christ." Develyn stared out the windshield without focusing. "I've never heard that comparison before."

"Me, neither."

"I've always been very careful about what substances I put into my body," said Develyn. "I don't eat meat—"

"You're a vegetarian?" Angela glanced at her.

"No, vegan," said Develyn, shaking her head. "I don't do drugs—"

Angela snickered. "Other than rum."

"Other than rum . . . or tequila." She snorted. "I do like my margaritas, but I don't believe in taking any chemical substances or pharmaceuticals. I don't eat vegetables or fruit sprayed with insecticides, and I don't eat anything made with preservatives. Everything's got to be fresh. I like everything organic, natural."

"Pharmaceuticals, you mean you don't take any medicines?"

"Uhn-uh." She shook her head.

"What if you get sick?'

Develyn shrugged. "I use home remedies or homeopathic preparations, but I don't do pills or drugs of any kind—legal or illegal."

"Interesting."

Develyn turned toward her. "How about you?"

"Me?" Angela shrugged. "I take a middle-of-road approach to self control. I try to be careful about what I eat, but an occasional cookie—"

"Or rum coke," Develyn smiled crookedly.

She shrugged again, this time with a grin. "Or rum coke or aspirin's not going to kill me. Everything in moderation. That's my motto." Angela glanced at her. "You brought up the homily's topic about the consecrated host, but I notice you didn't take Communion. Are you Catholic?"

"Confirmed," Develyn turned away to look out the passenger window. "But what you might call 'fallen away.'"

"But you still want to go to Mass next week and take the tour after?"

Develyn shrugged. "Sure, why not?" She turned toward Angela and gave a twisted smile. "What can I say? I like art history."

"Then you're going to love my birth mother."

Sun-kissed

"I'll tell you how the Sun rose—A Ribbon at a time—"

— Emily Dickinson

Monday morning, Develyn studied Angela's face.

"Even without dyeing your hair black, with your creamy complexion and dark features, you're a natural for a goth girl look."

Angela raised her eyebrow. "What do you mean?"

"Friday night, you looked good." She scrutinized Angela. "But you'd look better with more shadow, less mascara around your eyes, for a smokier look." She swept a pile of clothes off her desk chair and grabbed her makeup bag. "Sit down. I want to try this look on you."

Develyn applied a pale base to her face, followed by black eye shadow, with only a thin stroke of eyeliner, a touch of black mascara, black lipstick, and black blusher. Studying Angela's dark hair, she frowned.

"You washed out the magenta streak." Getting an idea, she ransacked the top drawer of her desk. "Let's try this cherry-red hair chalk on you."

Angela skeptically glanced at her through the mirror.

"It's temporary, right?"

"Oh, yeah." Develyn sprayed Angela's hair with a water bottle and then began applying the cherry chalk to the strands, twisting as she went.

"Why are you doing that?"

"Twisting makes it release more pigment."

By the time she was finished, the lower half of Angela's long hair was bright red.

"I thought you said 'a strand.'" Angela critically gazed at herself in the mirror.

"Don't worry, it'll wash out." Develyn peered at her work of art. "This ought to get you attention."

"Yes, this Sunday," said Angela into the phone. "Can you meet us at Mission Concepción for Mass and then tour the frescoes and artwork with us afterwards?"

"Okay, Angie," said Ceren. "Did you say Judith and Pastora were coming?"

"No, Mom's attending a retreat, and Pastora's busy this week." Angela shook her head. "I'm glad you can come."

When Ceren spotted Angela in the small church, her jaw dropped. Angela swallowed, preparing herself for meeting her birth mother dressed as a goth girl.

"Hi." She gave Ceren a hug. Then pointing to her look-alike beside her, she said, "Ceren, I'd like you to meet my roommate, Develyn. Dev, I'd like you to meet my birth mother, Ceren."

They checked each other out as they politely said hello.

"Develyn," said Ceren, rolling the name over her tongue. "What an interesting name."

"It's short for Debra Evelyn, but everyone calls me Develyn." Her black lips parted in a smile. "Angela tells me you're into art history."

"That's right. I am." Eyes narrow, Ceren appraised her. "Are you an art aficionado?"

"Actually, it's my major."

"Really?" Ceren's eyes widened. "What period in particular interests you?"

"Sixteenth century."

"Really?" Ceren's expression softened.

"You've made a friend for life," said Angela, grinning. "Sixteenth century art is Ceren's specialty."

"Did you tell her?"

"Nope." Angela shook her head. "This is all unrehearsed."

Ceren turned toward Develyn. "I see your artistic cosmetology has rubbed off on Angie." Putting her finger to Angela's chin, Ceren slowly turned her head so she could better view her daughter's face and hair. "Now if you could just share your love of art history with her."

Taking a deep breath, Angela changed the topic. "So what do you think of the new look?"

Still scrutinizing her, Ceren cocked an eyebrow as she let go Angela's chin.

"It's understated."

The girls glanced at each other and laughed.

"I told you she'd accept it," Angela told Develyn as she affectionately put her arm around her birth mother's waist. "She's cool."

"So what's the name of this tour we're going on?" asked Ceren.

Develyn grinned. "You might call it the after-Mass tour."

They chuckled.

"I can see some of the old frescoes and artwork," said Ceren, appraising the painted trim. "Should be interesting." Arm around Angela, she gave her a hug. "Glad you invited me."

During Communion, Angela noticed that Develyn lined up behind her. Frowning, Angela turned toward her. "Develyn, you—"

"Don't look so constipated," she whispered with a grin. "I went to confession."

After Mass, the three hurried to the Visitors Center and reconnected with the same docent from the week before.

"Perfect timing," he said, welcoming them with an easy smile. "We're just starting the tour." He led the group to the front entrance and pointed to the twin bell towers. "Concepción's more than a church or historical mission. It's a reminder of how the Franciscans tried to teach community harmony to the Coahuiltecan natives. Some say these two towers, soaring above the nave, symbolize the fusion of the two cultures. Other historians contend there are two towers instead of one because Concepción was dedicated to a female saint—Mary, the mother of Jesus."

"Last week, you'd mentioned a Sun-Christ symbol was carved into the exterior façade above the front door." Pointing, Develyn asked, "Is this it?"

He nodded, flashing a red pointer laser at it, outlining the details.

"It's been chipped or worn away, but you can still make out its basic features. See the angel wings, the cup, the starburst at the top?"

Ceren seemed drawn to the mission's wall. She peered at the ancient wall paintings and caught her breath.

"This is the Nahui Ollin."

"You're familiar with it?" asked the docent.

She nodded. "It's the same stylized, five-part flower that's found just below Our Lady of Guadalupe's sash on the tilma." She took out her phone and snapped a picture. "I've seen this indigenous symbol in Teotihuacán, but I had no idea it was used into the eighteenth century in North America."

The docent turned to the tourists, explaining for their benefit.

"What you see here, four petals surrounding a flower's center, represents the four cardinal points of the earth."

"They can also symbolize God." Ceren met the docent's eyes. "When the natives saw this age-old symbol imprinted on the tilma, over Our Lady of Guadalupe's womb, they knew she was pregnant with God's son. It was this symbol that converted the Aztecs to Christianity and began the native conversion movement in the Americas."

The docent used his red laser to point out the faint paintings as he addressed the group.

"These are some of the fresco decorations that originally decorated the entire front of the mission. In the mid-eighteenth century, these were vivid red and blue geometric designs. To a native on the dusty frontier, this radiant church must have looked like a Technicolor mirage."

"Are there any more examples of Nahui Ollin," asked Ceren.

"Quite a few, actually. Come on inside the church," said the docent. "One of the best carvings is on the baptismal font. Originally, it had stood alone on a base, but at some point it was embedded in the baptistery's thick stone wall."

They filed into the church, turning to the right into the small chapel. There, in the wall, was the intricately carved baptismal font, complete with the stylized, five-part flower found on the tilma of Our Lady of Guadalupe. Several flashes went off before the group turned and followed the docent. Trailing behind, Angela watched Develyn lightly trace her finger over the carvings.

"The Nahui Ollin is also found in a number of frescos." Leading the group across the nave to the belfry chapel, the docent flashed his laser on the wall's faint paintings. "Look carefully inside this pomegranate blossom."

"Oh, yeah," said one of the visitors, peering closely, his flash camera going off.

"Here's another example of Nahui Ollin."

The guide led them from chapel to chapel and then stopped in front of the main altar. With his laser, he pointed out the restored border of half-Nahui Ollin designs.

"See, it's as if only the bottom half of the motif appears in the border."

One of the tourists raised his hand. "What does Nahui Ollin mean?"

"Basically, Nahui Ollin was the Aztecs' worldview. According to their mythology, the five-part or quincunx 'flowers' symbolized the fifth age. The Aztecs believed that the earth was flat and divided into the four cardinal directions: north, east, south, and west, and a fifth central point. Each direction was associated with specific colors, special gods, and certain days of the year. I'd mentioned the twin towers represented the two cultures," said the docent. "The Nahui Ollin is a wonderful example of indigenous art. As you can see, the quincunx 'flowers' appear all over the interior and exterior of the mission, as well as on Our Lady of Guadalupe's robe."

"What about the European culture?" asked a tourist. "Where's that?"

"The Spanish paintings and the Moorish dome, as well as geometrical patterns, illustrate the European influence in the mission's art and architecture." He led the tour through the church, pointing out the various works of art.

"Notice the painting over the main altar. Who is that?"

One said, "Jesus. Look at his outstretched hands."

The docent brought them in for a closer look. "It's the Virgin Mary."

"How unusual," said a tourist. "Isn't there customarily a crucifix?"

The docent nodded. "Ordinarily, but remember the name of this church, Mission Nuestra Señora de la Purísima Concepción de Acuña. It was dedicated to the Immaculate Conception. Look to your left, over the side altar on the north wall. The painting of Our Lady of Guadalupe contains not only the quincunx 'flowers,' but she's also wearing . . . what?"

Ceren gasped. "A crown. What's the date of this painting?"

"It's believed to have been painted around 1750. We're told it had hung in a private family chapel in Mexico until recently, when the mission acquired it from an art dealer in Mexico City."

"Interesting." Squinting, Ceren nodded thoughtfully. "Until 1895, nearly every reproduction showed the Virgin wearing a crown, conforming to the original artwork on the tilma. However, after the Basilica's renovation in 1895, the crown was gone from the image."

"I hadn't heard that," said the docent.

"The Codex 1548, a parchment that portrayed her without a crown and only came to light in 1995, is thought to be the oldest reproduction of Juan Diego's meeting with Our Lady of Guadalupe.

Some say the crown was painted over. Whatever the reason, it's not there now."

Develyn moved closer to the painting. As she studied it, Angela joined her.

"Do you feel a special attraction to Our Lady of Guadalupe?"

Develyn shook her head. "I never had, but the historic ties to her cloak are fascinating."

"Then you'll have to speak to Ceren. She's an art authority."

"If you'll follow me," called the docent, "we're going into the mission library."

The girls caught up with him and Ceren.

"We discussed how the twin towers represented the two cultures. As you saw, the quincunx 'flowers' are good examples, but there's something else painted on the library's ceiling. As he led them into the small room, he pointed at the fresco painting with his laser. "Look overhead."

Amid oohs and aahs, cameras flashed.

"Is it the Sun-Christ symbol?" asked one of the group.

"Christus Sol, you think so?" Shrugging, he swept the room with his hand. "Notice, there are no windows or fireplaces. At one time, this was the President Priest's original quarters. The friars had to use torches for heat and light. As a result, the ceiling was black with soot, all except for one eye of this painting peeking out from under the accumulated grime. For obvious reasons, it was called the Eye of God or All-Seeing Eye. However, a good cleaning removed the soot and revealed this curious composite of Mesoamerican and Spanish imagery. See the facial hair? Still think it's the Sun-Christ?"

"Is that a mustache?" asked one of the group, chuckling, looking overhead.

"It looks something like the el sol motif," said Ceren, craning her neck to look straight up.

"It isn't easy to confirm what this represents." He grinned. "Some say this whimsical artwork characterizes the first mestizo, a blend of the best of Native American and Spanish. And that, ladies and gentlemen, ends our tour."

Develyn pulled Angela aside. "I love that baptismal font's carvings. Before we leave, I want to get a rubbing." She reached into her oversized bag and pulled out a poster tube and box of Conté crayons.

Ceren drew alongside. "What are you two whispering about?"

"Develyn wants to get a rubbing of the baptismal font." Angela grinned. "You should relate to that."

Eyes opening wide, Ceren turned toward her. "You really are an art historian after my own heart." She smiled. "C'mon, Angela and I'll hold the tracing paper for you. Maybe some of your art appreciation will rub off on my daughter."

Develyn unrolled the tracing paper from the poster tube and placed it over the stone.

"If you'll hold this side, and you'll hold the other side, it'll just take me a minute."

As Develyn began rubbing the crayon over the thin paper from the outer edges inward, the carving's details began to come into focus.

"I see you've done this before," said Ceren with an admiring eye.

"You should see our dorm room." Angela gave a wry chuckle. "It's covered with headstone rubbings—some in charcoal, some in crayon. You'd think we lived in a paper cemetery."

"Gravestones fascinate me. I'm attracted to cemeteries." Develyn shrugged as she continued to capture the baptismal font's hollows and ridges on the tracing paper. "Actually, I'm attracted to death."

Angela and Ceren exchanged a look over her bent head.

"That's a dark view," said Ceren, raising an eyebrow.

"I was born dying. What do you expect?" Again, Develyn shrugged. "I survived the botched abortion, but my mother didn't. Inside her womb, I was literally *surrounded* by death, *her death*, as she died around me while she attempted my murder." She snorted.

"As a result, I'm attracted to it, even drawn to it. Death intrigues me. It's a spooky frontier I feel compelled to explore."

Again, Angela and Ceren exchanged a look over her head.

"There." Develyn stood up, appraising her work. She put away her crayons. "That should do it." Ceren and Angela let go the thin tracing paper as Develyn rolled it up and placed it in her poster tube.

Trying to lighten the mood, Angela suggested lunch as they walked back to their cars.

Develyn recommended a Tex-Mex bakery and restaurant.

"If you've never been there, you'll love it. It's a San Antonio icon."

As they pushed open the heavy mesquite doors, multi-colored piñatas, paper cutouts, and strings of festive, white lights drew Angela's eyes upward. The illuminated ceiling exploded with cheery color and kitsch. The wait staff wore red, green, and white uniforms, the colors of Mexico, but for Angela they lent a Christmassy glow to the June afternoon. The ambiance transported her to another time and place, a cartoon characterization of old San Antonio.

The restaurant was packed. They queued behind other hungry customers, waiting their turn alongside a glass counter displaying hundreds of Mexican pastries, flans, and galletas. By the time their waitress escorted them to their table and handed them the menus, Angela's mouth was watering.

"I'll have the Puebla chicken," said Ceren. "I love the spicy chocolate mole." She turned to Angela with a smile. "I couldn't get enough of it in Puebla, when I was pregnant with you."

"In that case," said Angela, returning the smile. "I'll have the same. What's good for the goose is good for the gosling." She closed the menu with a flourish.

"And I'll have the chile relleno," said Develyn. "Somehow, I feel drawn to it, just craving chiles."

"That's the second thing you've felt drawn to this afternoon," said Angela. She turned to Ceren. "Develyn felt a special attraction to Our Lady of Guadalupe's painting, and I told her you're an authority."

Ceren gave a self-conscious grin. "No one's ever an authority. There's too much to learn, to know, but I've been studying it for years."

"You'd mentioned how the crown had been included on the tilma until 1895. What else can you tell us about Our Lady of Guadalupe?"

Ceren tilted her head as she surveyed Develyn. "Do you know what medium was used on the tilma, for instance, ink, oil, charcoal?"

Angela eyed Develyn and Ceren, pursing her lips to keep from chuckling. She was only too familiar with her birth mother's pop quiz style of conversing. *Once a teacher, always a teacher.*

Develyn frowned thoughtfully. "Flowers, wasn't it?"

Ceren nodded. "Roses left an imprint on the tilma. Who was the artist?"

"The Virgin Mary?" Develyn's tone made it more a question than an answer.

Ceren nodded. "Last question. Has a human hand ever helped paint the image?"

Develyn shrugged, while Angela silently answered, knowing Ceren's lecture by heart.

"In 1666, Dr. Francisco de Siles and several other university professors examined the tilma," said Ceren. "They described flaking paint, where apparently silver paint had been added to the moon, tarnished black, and then flaked off. They also mentioned that the rays surrounding her had been painted gold, which later discolored. For the most part, however, they confirmed that the original colors of the Virgin's face and hands appeared untouched by humans. They said it was as if the roses' colors had been pressed into the fibers."

"Have any other studies been done?" asked Develyn.

"In the nineteen thirties, a German chemist analyzed the tilma. He concluded that the color did not come from anything animal or mineral. Since synthetic dyes didn't appear until the nineteenth century, synthetics have been ruled out," said Ceren.

"Has any study been done more recently?" asked Develyn.

"In the seventies, scientists performed an infrared study. They were unable to explain the radiance of the pigments, especially after nearly five hundred years. It seemed to them as if the image's features were formed within the twisted fibers of the material itself, not painted on or added in any way."

"Really?" Listening intently, Develyn rested her hand on her chin.

"In the sixties, Dr. Wahlig compared the colors to a photo imprinted directly onto the fabric, as if the tilma itself were the negative." Ceren asked jokingly, "Were cameras around in 1531?"

Develyn chuckled.

"Photography, as we know it, didn't evolve until roughly three hundred years after the Virgin's image was impressed on Juan Diego's tilma, so that's ruled out, as well."

"What about the rumor that the eyes of the Virgin reflect Juan Diego?" asked Develyn.

"Shakespeare said it first: 'The eyes have it.'" Ceren smiled. "Digital imagery was a natural progression from photography. Dr. Tonsmann studied the irises and pupils of the Virgin's image for over two decades. After magnifying her eyes 2,500 times, Tonsmann claimed to identify thirteen reflected images of people imprinted in them. He compared the Virgin's eyes to an ethereal photo, capturing the moment that Juan Diego first opened the tilma in front of the bishop."

Develyn leveled her eyes at Ceren, challenging her. "So is the image of Our Lady of Guadalupe real or fake?"

"That's a question for each of us to answer, not me." Ceren shrugged. "A devout person might respond that God speaks to us daily through images and events. How we interpret these visions or experiences depends on many factors, including the lenses of our life experiences."

Develyn leaned forward. "And how do you know this tilma story isn't anything but religious propaganda?"

"Okay," said Angela, taking a deep breath. "Let me step in before this becomes a heated debate. I can see the telltale signs." She turned toward Develyn. "This is where she hands you," she turned toward Ceren, "or tells you she'll email you a handout containing summaries of studies conducted on the tilma between 1751 and 1982." She turned back toward Develyn. "If you were one of her students, she'd make you write a paper on it entitled, 'Fabric or Fabrication: Is the Image of Our Lady of Guadalupe a Forgery?'"

Nodding, Ceren chuckled. "Am I that transparent?"

"Why do you think I have no interest in art history?" asked Angela, raising her eyebrow. "You've crammed this stuff down my throat my whole life."

Ceren sighed, mumbling, "Maybe I have at that."

"You've got to admit, though, it is a fascinating subject." Develyn's eyes sparkled.

"There, you see, Angie?" said Ceren. "This is the response I've wanted all along from you."

"Kindred spirits." Angela chuckled as she surveyed the two: *goth girl and middle-aged professor.*

Singing broke out at the next table.

"What's that?" asked Ceren.

"It must be somebody's birthday," said Develyn, craning her neck to see. "The waitresses sing 'Happy Birthday' in Spanish as they place a complimentary piece of birthday cake in front of you."

Angela watched the waitresses in puff-sleeved, green outfits and red aprons sing and clap their hands as everyone at the nearby tables looked on and smiled.

"What a great idea. I wish it were somebody's birthday so we could do that."

"It's my birthday next week," said Develyn.

Grinning, Angela teased her. "Think that qualifies?"

"No, but it gives me an idea. My parents are having a party for me the Saturday after next." She looked from one to the other. "You're both invited."

PARENTHOOD

"If men could get pregnant, abortion would be a sacrament."

— FLORYNCE KENNEDY

Judith found herself reluctantly driving through the Texas Hill Country toward Boerne. Her inner dialogue kept up a steady stream of excellent excuses to turn around and head home.

You're too old for this. If you were going to attend a postabortion retreat, you should have done it fifty-eight years ago, not now, when you're eighty-four. She snickered. *You're old enough to be the retreatants' grandmother . . . great-grandmother. Besides, what's the point of rehashing it? What's done is done.*

Twice she pulled off the road, intending to turn and run, but each time a mental image of Helen stopped her. *Even if I can't turn off this stream of consciousness, I don't have to listen to it.* She turned on the radio, loud, trying to drown out the doubt.

Judith turned off the sleepy main street onto a private, wooded drive. Live oaks and junipers dotted the grounds. As she neared the retreat house, she saw it was located at the crest of a hill, overlooking a rocky ravine. Limestone outcrops near the top gave way to a lush, green valley, where the eroded topsoil had accrued over decades, centuries.

Nothing's static in nature. Everything's in transit. Eroding cliffs becoming fertile land. She parked and breathed in the perfumed scented air. Looking around, she noticed a mountain laurel in bloom, its purple blossoms reminding her of lilacs. She

126

inhaled again, smelling its floral, grape-Kool-Aid scent. *This is the Hill Country at its finest. Whether the right time or not, this is certainly the right place.*

As Judith approached the limestone retreat house, a middle-aged woman, who introduced herself as Gail, welcomed her at the door.

"What a beautiful setting for a retreat," said Judith.

"Thank you. It's a donated and repurposed private estate. Come on in, and I'll introduce you around." Gail handed Judith a coffee mug containing prayer cards and hard candies and led her inside.

Her eyes taking in the decor, Judith listened to the echo of their footsteps as they crossed the limestone tiled foyer into the main room. Everything was stone, wood, or leather. The limestone theme continued with towering, dry-stacked door frames and a fireplace that took up the entire wall of the main room. Immense logs acted as beams overhead. Leather chairs and loveseats created an intimate, if not masculine, setting in front of the fireplace.

"Everyone, I'd like you to meet Judith."

Forcing a smile, Judith nodded and mumbled "Hi, hello," as each person was introduced by her first name.

Pointing to an oversized coffee table, Gail said, "Help yourself to coffee and homemade cookies. We're still expecting several others to join. Once everyone's here, we'll get started."

Judith poured a cup of steaming coffee, inhaling its aroma, and chose from the platter of tempting treats. She sat in the leather chair beside a woman who looked her own age.

The woman smiled. "I'm Ellen."

Within minutes, they found they lived in neighboring suburbs and had just become empty-nesters. They paused their conversation only when Gail introduced newcomers and then immediately resumed it. By the time Gail called the group to begin, they had exchanged email addresses and phone numbers.

"Now that all the retreatants have arrived," said Gail, "let's open with a short introduction and a prayer." Then she poured a half cup of coffee and held it eye level. "Is this heavy?" she asked the group.

People shook their heads or murmured "No."

She set down the cup. "No, it's not heavy if you hold it for a moment." Then she picked it up again and held it eye level for thirty seconds. "Do you think my arm's getting tired?"

They nodded.

"What if I held it aloft for an hour? Would it feel heavy then?"

The group murmured their assent.

"Any burden's like that. If you hold it for only a moment, it's manageable, but the longer you hold it, the heavier it becomes." Gail surveyed the group. "Guilt is like that. The longer you carry it inside you, the heavier its burden becomes." She paused, looking from one pair of eyes to the next. "How many of you carry guilt around with you?"

Judith scanned the group. Everyone's hand went up.

Then Gail pointed at a half wine barrel filled with limestone rocks.

"I want you to choose a rock and carry it with you today as a tangible reminder of all the anger, grief, guilt, regret, or shame you've been carrying with you since your abortion. Then lug that grief stone with you everywhere you go, to the restroom, the dining room, the other workshop rooms, until you're ready to relinquish your burden. It's up to you when you decide to let it go. When it's time, when you're ready, set down the stone and share why it was the appropriate time to stop carrying your burden around."

One by one, the retreatants went to the half barrel, chose a rock, and sat back down, cradling it on their laps. When it was Judith's turn, she picked through the pile and got an idea. Instead of choosing one of the local pieces of limestone with holes in it, she chose a flat, solid rock.

When Judith sat down, Ellen silently traced her finger along intersecting fracture lines in her stone.

Judith shook her head and shrugged.

Ellen again traced along the fracture lines, this time clearly delineating a cross in the stone.

Judith mouthed more than whispered, "Hadn't seen that."

When everyone had chosen a stone, Gail said, "Let's talk about letting go this burden, about healing." Again, she looked from one pair of eyes to the next. "As you can see, you're not alone. Officially, a third of all women in the US have one or more abortions by the time they're forty-five." She sighed. "Unofficially, forty percent may be the closer number. I," she gestured toward the staff, "and every one of the facilitators has personal experience with abortion and with the healing process that needs to follow."

Judith watched the stony expressions of the retreatants. Poker faces. No one blinked.

"The good news is, you don't have to carry your burden alone, anymore." Gail smiled at one of the staff. "Amy, would you like to say a few words?"

"Although God's forgiveness happens the moment you ask for it, forgiving yourself can take time, coaxing. Today, we'll invite you to participate in several spiritual exercises designed to draw out feelings that you've deeply hidden, forgotten, or never considered. You'll recognize not only your responsibility for your abortion but the roles others have played in it, as well."

Judith's thoughts flashed back to the moment she had made her decision. The sunny room of the retreat faded. As a cold darkness infiltrated her mind, she was swept back to that New Year's Eve fifty-eight years before.

She had been waiting for her boyfriend, Tim, to call. After several, nail-biting days, she was desperate and had called his house. His father had answered.

"Do you . . ." She swallowed. "Could you take a message?"

"Sorry, but I can't. He's . . . he's eloped."

"What!" She felt the color drain from her face. Tears welled up.

"It came as quite a surprise to us, too." He cleared his throat. "He'll be back in a few days. Do you want me to give him a message then?"

"Yes," Judith said, wiping away the tears. "Tell him . . . the mother of his child—"

"His child?!" The man had shouted so loudly, Judith held the receiver from her ear. "What is this? Some kind of sick joke?"

"The mother of his child is going to abort his baby, your grandchild." Her voice rising, she added, "Thanks for raising a real son-of-a-bitch!" Then she had slammed down the receiver.

Blinking as she gradually became aware of her surroundings, Judith realized she had been daydreaming, reliving the past. She looked around her. *What did I miss?*

"You'll grasp that your child loves you and forgives you," said Amy. "Let that knowledge sink in, penetrate your heart, so you can forgive yourself . . . and forgive others."

Judith grunted, the sound piercing the silence. When she felt eyes staring at her, she cleared her throat, trying to cover.

"Thank you, Amy," said Gail, her smile sympathetic as she addressed the group. "You may be struggling with an abortion you had years ago, decades ago, and have kept hidden. Or you may have experienced abortion recently, and the memory is raw. No matter the circumstances, healing is possible, and healing can begin today. This morning's portion of the retreat is designed to help those who are hurting begin to heal by entering into the grieving process." Gail cued Amy with a nod and a raised eyebrow.

"After you identify the defense mechanisms you've used to keep the abortion at a safe distance, such as denial, flashbacks, social isolation, workaholism, alcoholism, or any of a hundred other devices," said Amy, "you'll learn how the abortion has affected you and all your relationships since."

Though remaining rigid, Judith nodded internally at each device mentioned.

"The good news?" Amy said, spreading out her hands. "As you accept God's forgiveness, you can begin to forgive yourself and others."

"It's normal to mourn a lost loved one," added Gail. "Don't let guilt or denial block your grieving process any longer than it already has. Grieving is a necessary part of moving on. Accept the grief. Don't hurry past it or bury it."

"Finally," said Amy, "and perhaps most importantly, you can let go your grief so you can release your child to God's care. At the end of today's activities, we'll hold a memorial to give identity and dignity to the children who've been aborted. This will help give you closure for their loss and hope for the future."

"Today's activities are designed to help draw out any hidden conflicts, emotional wounds, or spiritual quandaries still attached to your abortion. Through these spiritual exercises, God's word, and reconciliation, you'll find peace," said Gail. "Those of you who are willing to journey through your grief will emerge free of your mental shackles through the grace of God."

At lunch time, Judith sat beside Ellen at a large, communal table. Retreatants, volunteers, and staff all merged together, chatting informally.

Over homemade soup, fresh, crusty bread, and tossed salad, Judith and Ellen got to know each other better.

"Are you married?" asked Ellen

"Widowed a year ago." Judith gave her a tight, bright smile.

"Married long?"

"Eighteen years this past time, seven years the first time, twenty five in all."

"Sounds tempestuous." Ellen's eyes smiled.

Judith shrugged. "The first time, yes, but by the time we remarried we'd grown up a bit." She swallowed a smile, recalling how he'd proposed in Puebla, Mexico, the second time. Then returning to the present, she asked politely, "And you?"

"Married nearly sixty years." Ellen smiled and splayed the fingers on her left hand, showing her wedding ring.

"First love?"

"For me, yes." Ellen made a face that morphed into a tolerant smile. "Apparently, his second."

Judith joined her as she chuckled. "Hopefully, the older we grow, the wiser." She looked into space. "Sixty years. You must have been so young. How did you meet?"

"It probably sounds trite coming from someone who's approaching her sixtieth wedding anniversary, but it was love at first sight. I was four years old, and he was ten." Ellen giggled like a girl. She leaned toward Judith, as if sharing a secret. "He'd never paid a bit of attention to me until one Christmas vacation. When I came home from college that year, his face lit up as if he were seeing me for the first time. I was swept off my feet."

"How romantic."

Then Ellen's smile drooped.

Head back, Judith scrutinized her. "From the look in your eyes, I'm wondering if there was trouble in paradise."

Ellen took a deep breath and nodded. "Our marriage was built on . . . a fluke of nature."

"A fluke of nature?" Judith smiled crookedly. "I'm not following."

"Have you ever heard of hysterical pregnancy?"

"Yes, a false pregnancy, where the woman believes she's pregnant, but she isn't?"

Ellen rolled her eyes. "Much more than that, it's where your belly swells and your breasts become tender. Where your back aches and you have morning sickness."

"That all happened to you?"

"Oh, yes." Ellen sighed. "That and more. I was so infatuated with him, that when he . . ."

"Made advances?"

"Very tactfully put." Ellen's smile was wan. "When he made advances, I . . . went along with it." She looked into Judith's eyes. "I immediately regretted it, felt so guilty, felt so scared. My period was due, so I sweated it out that weekend. But nothing happened."

"No period?"

Ellen shook her head. "I went into shock. Like I said, I began showing symptoms within days. Morning sickness was the worst. When I began vomiting every day, my mother took me to the doctor's office, thinking I had the flu. I was so uneasy in his office, he made my mother wait outside. It was only then that I confessed what I'd done. He gave me a pelvic exam, confirming my worst fears. He said my uterus was enlarged and my cervix had softened. I didn't have a clue what that meant at the time, but I could tell from his expression, it wasn't good."

"Of course, this was all before the days of ultrasound and urinalyses."

Ellen nodded. "He called my mother into the office and, in no uncertain terms, informed us I was pregnant."

"Talk about traumatic." Judith shook her head. "Unbelievable."

"It was awful." Ellen rolled her eyes. "My mother burst into tears. She grabbed me by the arm and harassed me until I told her who the father was. Then she became very still." She bit her lip, recalling. "As soon as we got home, she told my father."

"What'd he do?"

"You mean after he read me the riot act?" Ellen cocked an eye at Judith. "My father called his father and asked him and his son to stop by."

"You're kidding."

"Uhn-uh. As soon as they walked through the door, my father told them to look at me. I was mortified. Tears were streaming down my face. I couldn't stop crying. Tim took one look at my face and guessed. 'She's pregnant,' my father shouted, pointing at me, 'and she says you're the father. What are you going to do about it?'"

"A shotgun wedding?" asked Judith.

Ellen nodded. "Two days later."

"You're not the first one that's happened to, and I'm sure you haven't been the last." Judith shrugged. "Your marriage's lasted nearly sixty years. You must have worked it out."

Ellen chewed at her lip. "It was a false pregnancy. He claimed I only did this to trap him, and he's never forgiven me."

"So is that why you're here?" asked Judith.

Ellen cocked her head, apparently considering it. "In a way, it is. Our marriage was stable, but it was loveless. Tim blamed me, and I . . ." Ellen shook her head. "I just became bitter."

"Okay," said Judith. "I must be missing something. This is an abortion retreat. Why are you here?"

"It was my daughter who . . . tried to have an abortion."

Judith cocked her head. "Somehow, I'm missing the point."

Ellen took a deep breath. "Late in life, we had a daughter, Virginia. Our only child, the apple of our eyes, developed a heroin addiction. I've always thought the cold atmosphere, the loveless marriage, had something to do with that. Long story short, she got pregnant and wasn't sure who the father was."

"So you coerced her into getting an abortion."

Ellen shook her head. "Thought about it, but my husband and I talked it over and decided . . . *offered* to take her in during her pregnancy, help her kick the addiction, and keep the baby."

"What happened?"

"One night, when she was seven months along, she snuck out. A 'friend' took her to a back-alley butcher, who botched the job." Ellen's eyes took on a glassy look. She swallowed. "The 'friend' drove her to the hospital's emergency entrance, literally pushed her out of the car, and drove off, wheels screeching, leaving her screaming after him in the driveway. Luckily, someone saw Ginny collapse. They brought her into the OR, found our phone number in her purse, and called us at four in the morning."

"Were they able to save her?"

Ellen shook her head.

As Judith murmured "sorry," she reached over and squeezed Ellen's hand.

"What they called us about was the baby. Somehow, it survived the saline abortion."

Judith squinted. "I'm not familiar with saline abortion. How does that work?"

"They use a long needle to siphon the amniotic fluid and then replace it with a strong salt solution. The salt's corrosive, so it burns the baby's lungs and strips away its skin. From what I've read, it usually takes about an hour and a half for the baby to die." Ellen looked into Judith's eyes. "If the abortion's successful, the mother delivers a desiccated, dead baby."

Judith grunted at the thought. She shook her head, trying to rid her mind of the image.

"It sounds antiquated."

"It is. It was developed in the thirties."

Judith's eyes opened wide. "But you said this baby survived? How?"

"Whoever did the abortion had no training, no knowledge." Ellen swallowed. "Instead of injecting the salt solution into the baby's amniotic sac, they injected it into Virginia's bladder and bloodstream. The doctor said she was hemorrhaging when she arrived. By the time they got her into the OR, they couldn't stop the bleeding. Not even transfusions could keep up with the blood loss, and she slipped into a coma. That's when they discovered the baby was still alive."

"It was too late to save your daughter?"

Tears starting at the corner of her eyes, Ellen nodded. "They kept Ginny alive until we got to the hospital. When we asked about the baby, the doctor explained that a C-section would put additional stress on Ginny's already compromised system. Point blank, they asked us what we wanted to do, save Ginny or save the baby. We asked about the odds of Ginny's survival. Either way, they couldn't guarantee the outcome, but they said they had to work quickly if we wanted to save the baby."

"What did you do?"

"My husband and I looked at our daughter, lying there so pale, looked at each other, and made our decision."

"They performed a C-section?"

Tears running down her face, Ellen caught her breath as she nodded. "They delivered the baby as Virginia slipped away."

Judith handed her the Kleenex box. "What a burden for you and your husband." She looked at her. "But it wasn't your fault."

Eyes bloodshot, Ellen glared back. "How can you say that? It was! We pushed Virginia. We had her so late in life, she was all we had. All there was to our marriage. We put so much pressure on her to succeed, she crumbled. Heroin was her escape, and this was the result."

"All your eggs in one basket," said Judith. "I understand. That's how I feel about Angela Maria."

"Your daughter?"

"My adopted daughter." Judith gave her a half-smile. "So where's your daughter—"

"Granddaughter," corrected Ellen.

"Where is she now?"

"She's starting at the University of Texas this summer."

"Austin?

"No, San Antonio."

"Really?" Judith snickered.

"Why?"

"Small world, that's where Angela Maria's going to school."

HEART OF STONE

"A new heart I will give you, and a new spirit I will
put within you; and I will take out of your flesh the
heart of stone and give you a heart of flesh."

EZEKIEL 36:26

Driving back home from the retreat, Judith glanced at the flat, solid rock that bore the incision of a cross. *The symbol of my burden, the mill stone around my neck.* She had not been able to set it down until she had gotten in the car, until she was alone with her thoughts about her long-aborted baby. Then she had taken a deep, cleansing breath, feeling calmer than she had in years. The guilt seemed less formidable, less palpable.

When she arrived home, she took the stone to the lantana rock garden in the back yard and propped it against an aged, live oak. She righted it, so the cross was straight, and buried its bottom edge in the soil. As she stood up, she surveyed it. *How appropriate. It even looks like a headstone.* Now I have a place where I can visit with my daughter, a place where I can remember her, even if I can't see her.

Suddenly, she felt the buzz of her cell phone on her belt.

"Angela, how good to hear from you."

"How did your retreat go?"

"It went well. I still have to synthesize what I heard with what I've felt for fifty-eight years, but," she looked at the stone, "I definitely feel better." She told Angela about the stone and its meaning.

"I'm glad. Next time I come home, maybe I can visit it with you."

"How about next weekend?"

Angela hemmed. "My roommate's invited me to her birthday party in Austin. How about I come home after the party, say six o'clock, and then go back to San Antonio Sunday afternoon. Will that work?"

℘

After she hung up, the phone vibrated again.

"Ellen?" Judith smiled to herself. "What a pleasant surprise."

"I'd meant to ask you today at the retreat, but there was so much going on, it slipped my mind. How'd you like to come to our house Saturday afternoon? We're having a few people over, and I hope you can join us."

"Actually, that'd work out well," said Judith. "My daughter's got something going on, and I'll be on my own until six o'clock."

"Good. We seemed to hit it off, and I wanted to get to know you better," said Ellen. "You have our address. Why don't you come by at two?"

℘

Judith brought out a lawn chair, placed it in the shade, and sat in front of the stone, contemplating her aborted daughter. In the stillness, she could hear mockingbirds flitting through the trees overhead. A summer breeze bathed her in the scent of freshly mown grass.

"Helen," she whispered. "How could I have let you go? I'd never have guessed how much I'd miss you . . . especially since I've never met you."

As the shadows lengthened, then disappeared, and the stars began to twinkle, Judith rose and walked into the house just as the kitchen phone rang.

"Faith," said Pastora's voice over the phone. "How did you like your retreat?"

Judith smiled at her sister's use of her childhood name.

"All things considered, it went well."

Pastora's breathing was audible in the silence. Finally, she asked, "That's it? That's all you have to say?"

"I met a woman that I'm staying in touch with, in fact, getting together with next week."

"I'm glad," she sighed uncomfortably, "but didn't you receive any insights?"

Judith told her about the rock in the lantana garden, about her guilt being less blatant.

"That's good, but what about forgiveness?"

"Forgiveness of whom? Tim?"

In an instant, her mind flashed back to the moment she had made her decision, when she had given his father a message: "The mother of his child is going to abort his baby, your grandchild." *It's all his fault. I made this decision in anger, retaliation for him deserting me. How can I ever forgive him?* She sighed. *No, it's my fault. I'm the one that did it.*

Then Pastora's words penetrated her thoughts. "More importantly, forgiveness of yourself. You've internalized your guilt for so long, you don't realize you've been living under a cloud. It's followed you wherever you've gone. Whatever you've done to compensate for it, this self-imposed cloud of shame has overshadowed you."

"What do you mean, 'compensate for it?'"

"Your drive, your determination, and, to some extent, even your adoption of Angela Maria. All these things you did to compensate for your feelings of unworthiness," said Pastora. "You've managed to avoid your guilt without confronting it."

"I've always had a full life."

"You mean a full schedule. Filling your life with agendas, trying to make up for not having it filled with God's grace, isn't the same. You've tried, but, you have to admit, you can't work off or bury your guilt. At some point, you have to acknowledge it or remorse will consume you." She took a deep breath. "And I think this may be the time. Give yourself this gift."

"What gift?"

"The gift of forgiveness. Reconcile with yourself." Pastora sighed. "Life's too short to squander it with regrets. Tear off this defensive 'Band-Aid' of busyness. Expose your wounds. Acknowledge them. It'll hurt for a moment, but then the guilt will drain away, and you'll begin to heal."

§

Saturday afternoon, Judith found her way to a gated community in the Hill Country. She felt she had entered Tuscany. Second floor, arched doorways with lattice-work balconies drew her eyes upwards. Earthy-red, terra-cotta tiles topped the limestone mansion. The entrance to Ellen's house had arched, double doors made of mesquite, set off by an overarching stone portico.

"Come on in," said Ellen, as she opened the door.

"Your home is gorgeous. Looking around the limestone-block foyer, she said, "It's a starter castle."

Ellen laughed. "First, let's get you a drink. Then I'd like you to meet my granddaughter, the birthday girl."

As they entered the great room, Judith saw the double staircase, curving its way to the second floor. Immense mesquite beams and rafters supported the two-story cathedral ceiling. Massive window walls lit up the interior. People milled about everywhere but were dwarfed by the size of the room.

"I take it back," said Judith. "This *is* a castle."

Ellen winked. "Yeah, but it's difficult to dust."

Limestone columns supported archways that divided the entry from the sitting room to the right and the dining room to the left.

"Seriously, Ellen, this looks more like a hotel than a house. It's stunning."

"I'm not kidding about the dust." She grinned. "Limestone disintegrates."

Walking around the central table, topped with a fresh floral arrangement of Stargazer lilies and giant white hydrangeas, they passed between the double staircases on their way to the solarium.

As they approached the bar, someone entered from the sitting room that Judith recognized, yet didn't. She stopped, stared. She blinked.

The black-haired, black-lipped person dressed in black spoke to her.

"Mom?"

"Angela?"

"You two know each other?" asked Ellen.

"I thought we did." Judith eyed Angela's goth girl outfit.

"What are you doing here?" asked Angela.

"Ellen's the person I mentioned that I met at the retreat. What are you doing here?"

"Develyn's my roommate. This is the party I'd mentioned."

Judith shook her head, chuckling. "It's a small world, but this is ridiculous." She studied Angela's dress, a crisscrossed bodice over a short, gathered skirt. She reached out to fondle the magenta streak in her hair.

"Is it permanent?"

"That was my first question." Angela smiled. "No, it's temporary color. I'm just trying out the look." She posed. "What do you think?"

Judith struggled to be tactful. She took a deep breath as she examined the makeup, hair, and dress.

"Different."

Angela chuckled. "You diplomat, you, skirting the issue."

"You sound like your Aunt Pastora." Judith gave her a wry smile.

"And here's the birthday girl," said Ellen, introducing them as Develyn approached.

"Roommates?" *There's the influence.* Judith scrutinized Angela's cookie-cutter twin as she consciously arranged her mouth into a smile. "I can see the resemblance."

Glancing from Judith to Develyn, Angela said, "I believe there's someone else here you know."

"Really?" Judith scanned the solarium. Then her eyes opened wide as she saw a dark-haired, middle-aged woman, wearing a business suit. "Ceren?"

As Ceren approached, she said, "I hadn't realized you were invited, or I would have picked you up."

Judith turned to her host. "Ellen, how do you know my friend, Ceren?"

Ellen shrugged. "I don't." She held out her hand. "I'm Develyn's mother, Ellen."

Develyn said, "Sorry, I thought you two had been introduced. This is Angela's mother, Ceren."

Ellen's brow creased. "I must have misunderstood." Turning to Judith, she said, "I thought you were Angela's mother."

Looking from Ellen to Ceren and back, Judith grinned. "I am. I'm Angela's adoptive mother, and Ceren's her birth mother."

Ellen nodded. "There must be a story there." She smiled warmly. "I hope to hear it one day." She spotted a person and called out to him. "Tim, there are several people I'd like you to meet."

A balding, portly, pretentious man approached, dressed in a tweed jacket with leather elbow patches. Swallowing a sneer, Judith instantly categorized him. *A stereotype of a professor. Bet he's got a pipe in his pocket.* Then she took a second look, blinked, and shut her gaping jaw.

"Judith, you've known two of the last three people you've met today. By any chance, have you ever met my husband, Tim?"

Past, Meet Present

"The strongest of all warriors are these two—Time and Patience."

— Leo Tolstoy

Judith struggled to show no recognition, no emotion. "Did you say 'Jim?'" she asked innocently.

"No, *Tim*," responded the man, blandly extending his hand. "How do you do, Judith, is it?"

She smiled. *Ah, my name's changed. Even if he recognized me, this will make him rethink.* "Yes, Judith Brannon, how do you do?" She gave his hand a curt shake, quickly extricating her fingers.

"Judith Brannon," he repeated slowly, as if trying to recall information. "You're from Kyle, on the Library Board, if I recall correctly."

Judith shook her head.

"On the Wimberley-San Marcos border," corrected Ellen. "Judith's the mother of Develyn's roommate, Angela."

He squinted as he turned toward Ceren. "I thought—"

"Ceren's her birth mother," Ellen interjected, "and—"

"I'm Angela's adoptive mother." Judith stared him down.

"A pleasure to meet you," Tim said, waving to a man at the door. "Now, if you'll excuse me, ladies. Stephen appears to be in desperate need of something."

Judith breathed a sigh of relief that he had not recognized her. *Thank God.*

"What?" She turned toward Ellen.

"I said, let's get you that drink."

"Sounds good." *I could use one.* "Nice to meet you, Develyn. Angela, maybe I can give you a ride home and save your roommate the trip."

"Okay." Angela nodded. "I'll catch up with you later."

"Ceren, did you want to join us?" Ellen gave her a warm smile. "I see your glass is nearly empty."

Ceren was watching Tim greet the man at the door. "What?" She paused as if replaying Ellen's offer and glanced at her glass. "Oh, no . . . thanks, I'll just nurse this a while." She smiled stiffly. "Actually, I believe I see," she caught her breath, "an acquaintance."

As she walked off, Ellen turned to Judith. "This party seems to be a gathering of old friends."

"Yes, doesn't it, though?" Judith gave a nervous laugh.

"Would you like a glass of champagne, or would you prefer something stronger?"

"Actually, I'd like a shot of tequila." Judith gave a bright smile. "An old friend of mine taught me to sip and savor tequila."

Ellen poured a double shot into a glass for Judith and picked up a flute of champagne for herself.

"Cheers," she said, clinking glasses. Then she looked into Judith's eyes. "Have you done any soul-searching since the retreat?"

Judith snorted as she glimpsed the back of Tim, still talking at the door.

"Yeah, I have, but I get the feeling it's only begun."

Ellen nodded. "I know what you mean." She looked at her daughter, chatting with Angela. "Develyn confided something this morning that's put all of last week's exercises into a different perspective."

"Really?" Judith sipped her tequila, rolling it on her tongue as Father O'Riley had taught her. "What did she have to say?"

"Apparently, your daughter has a gift."

Judith narrowed her eyes, sensing what was coming. "What do you mean, 'a gift?'"

"Develyn said your daughter spoke to Ginny, her mother, who died of an ab . . . who died." Ellen gulped her champagne. Then she put her fingers to her mouth, as if gathering her thoughts. "From what Develyn tells me, Angela told her Ginny loves her." She looked into Judith's eyes. "It was the first time Develyn's spoken of her mother since she was a very small child. Maybe . . . I think Angela's good for her." She smiled. "I'm glad our children are friends, roommates."

Judith gave a bland smile. *I'm not so sure.*

As the pause lengthened, Ellen asked, "Don't you agree?"

"I'm sure Develyn's a lovely girl, but I've barely said five words to her." Judith shrugged. "I don't know her yet. But, if she's your granddaughter, I'm looking forward to spending time with her today."

"I'd like that," said Ellen. "I'd like both our families to get to know one another better."

Ohmigosh! Judith mumbled a banal response as she focused on her glass.

When Ellen deftly picked up the conversational ball, Judith studied her, looked hard at her. *Why did Tim marry her instead of me? What did she have that I didn't?* Eyes narrowing, her resentment grew by the millisecond. Judith scrutinized the posh surroundings, the tufted leather furniture, the signed artwork, all the trappings of success. *Was it money? Was that why he married her?*

Then she recalled Ellen's words at the retreat: they had grown up together. *I don't recall Tim being wealthy.*

Ellen had said hers was a false pregnancy. Judith groaned inwardly. *There was nothing false about mine. My pregnancy was only too real. In this conjugal game of 'musical chairs,' why was I the one left out, left standing alone, the one who had to get an abortion, the one who had to make her own way? What's so special about her?*

As Ellen chattered on about their granddaughter, Judith's eyes glazed over. *Ellen has had Tim all these years. She not only married him, she's had a family with him. She never had to experience abortion . . . at least, not firsthand. Why? Why did he choose her over me?*

Without warning, her mind flashed back to their first date. She had been walking across the university campus one late September afternoon. She could almost smell the earthy scent of the fallen leaves. She could see their vibrant red and gold colors juxtaposed on the ground, glorious in their second encore. She could hear the sighing boughs above. Mentally shivering from the late autumn crispness in the air, a chill shot down her spine.

"How's your dissertation coming along?" Tim had asked casually, coming up from behind and catching her off guard.

What had started as an intellectual conversation turned into an extended discussion over coffee. That was followed by an intense brainstorming session, which led to dinner.

Dinner. She smiled inwardly. It had been a greasy spoon student joint and Dutch treat, at that.

The party chatter woke her from her musings. As Judith became aware of her surroundings, she studied the present-day Tim, talking to someone at the door. She sniffed. Fat, balding. Age had not been kind to him. *What did I ever see in him? But, oh, I loved him. Gave him everything—my body, my baby, even my fertility. What did he do? Turned his back on me . . . for her.* Judith squinted as she focused on Ellen, tuning in just in time for her punch line.

"So when I asked Develyn why she wore these black clothes and all this black makeup, she said, 'Good Goth, Grandma, how do you want me to dress? Like a nun?' I shrugged and said, 'It'd still be black.' Ellen laughed merrily, her eyes crinkling at the corners.

Despite feeling contempt for her long-ago rival, Judith could not help but chuckle along with the woman standing across from her. Though she may have been her unwitting adversary, Ellen was hard to dislike.

Ellen glanced at the girls and then looked Judith in the eye. "What do you think? Do you approve of this goth girl look?"

Choosing her words carefully, Judith answered more than one question. "It's all so new to me." As her eyes swept the room, she glanced at Tim, then looked away and studied the goth girls. "Tell you the truth, I haven't had time to process how I feel."

Ceren stood in front of a bluebonnet landscape, pretending to admire the oil painting. Positioned obliquely to the door, she could view the two men talking and catch every third word of their conversation without to appearing to eavesdrop.

"Stephen, this isn't a good time." Tim gestured toward the people. "Can't you see we have guests?"

"But this'll only take a minute. Just sign here, and—"

The host shook his head. "We've been over this. No." He handed him back the manila envelope and tried closing the door. "This isn't the time. Make an appointment through the department's secretary."

Ceren eyed the guest's silver-shot head of hair. *Could it be?* She moved a step closer, still pretending to regard the artwork.

Propping the door open with his foot, the man turned back. "This paper would at least let me retire, not—"

"Not what? Stoop to look for another job? Stephen, I only allowed you to lecture here one semester as a favor to you. You let me down . . . royally. No, you've had your chance, and you blew it. Now, please leave." Again, Tim tried closing the door.

Eyes narrowed, Ceren scrutinized the person named Stephen. She noted the nearly-white hair and deeply-lined face, but the name was wrong. *Yet, those high cheekbones. I know that face. Could it possibly be?*

Before Tim could close the door on him, the doorbell rang, and two guests greeted him with hearty handshakes. As Tim played the genial host, Stephen crept past them, unnoticed by everyone but Ceren.

Even at a distance, she could smell the stale cigarettes. Her nostrils curled in distaste.

Still positioned in front of the painting, she swiveled slightly to her right, keeping an eye on him as he crossed the main room. When he sauntered between the staircases toward the bar, she cut through the dining room and peered at him from behind one of the columns.

Closer now, Ceren could see flecks of dandruff on his shoulders and bushy, gray hairs sprouting from his nose and ears. He took a champagne flute from a tray at the bar, downed it in a gulp, looked around furtively, set down the glass, and picked up another. He then ran his hand through his unkempt hair, as if making himself more presentable for the party.

Ceren was only too well acquainted with that characteristic gesture. *Jarek!* She went cold.

Three plans of action raced through her mind. Confront him and tell him what a miserable excuse he was for a man. Ignore him but lurk, listening for more details of what hinted to be yet another scandal, and then gloat. Point him out to Angela so their daughter could see the spineless slug that was her birth father.

She caught herself. Each plan seemed less charitable than the previous. Instead, she decided to tell Judith. Let her observe this 'Stephen' and confirm her suspicions that he really was Jarek, not a look-alike. Then she would decide her course of action.

Ceren spotted Judith speaking with Ellen, only feet away from him. She waited until he downed a second glass of champagne and picked up a third, turning his back for a moment. Then she casually crossed behind him and joined the women.

"Ceren, your glass is empty. Let me get you a refill." Ellen whisked away her glass, leaving her alone with Judith for a moment.

"Do you see that man at the bar?" At Judith's nod, Ceren asked, "Does he look familiar to you?"

Judith waited until he turned around. Then she gasped. "Jerk."

Before they could say more, Ellen returned with a fresh glass of champagne for Ceren.

"Was that person who you thought he was?"

"Still not sure," she glanced at Judith, "but I'm fairly certain he is."

"Isn't this a small world?" Ellen sipped her champagne.

"Ghosts from the past," said Judith, "just when you'd thought you'd laid them to rest."

"Coming back to haunt you." Ceren's lopsided sneer was sour.

Ellen shuddered. "All this talk about ghosts lately is giving me goose bumps."

Ceren smelled his stale cigarette reek before she heard him. "He's here," she mouthed more than whispered to Judith.

"Ellen, how good of you to invite me to your party." Glass in hand, he joined the trio, posing as a guest.

"It's Steve, isn't it?" she asked, obviously struggling to cover her unfamiliarity with him.

"Stephen," he corrected her.

Ellen smiled graciously and turned to introduce him. "Judith, I'd like you to meet my husband's associate, Stephen."

Judith had to admire her style. *She's smooth. I'll give her that.* She met his smile with a smirk.

"So, Stephen, you say, haven't we met before? You remind me so much of someone I knew named Jerk . . . uh, Jarek." She took pleasure in watching the man's expression droop before her eyes. "By any chance, do you have a brother by that name?"

Blinking in apparent disbelief, he opened his mouth to speak, but his voice failed. Then glancing at Ceren, his eyes bulged. He threw back his head, downed his drink, and promptly began choking.

"Stephen, are you all right?" asked Ellen, patting him on the back, each tap releasing bursts of stale cigarette stench from his jacket. "Come over to the bar. Let's get you a glass of water."

Judith turned to Ceren. "Does that answer your question?"

"Who was that?" asked Angela, joining them, her eyes focused on the drama at the bar.

Judith kept her voice as matter-of-fact as possible. "He said his name was Stephen."

Angela's eyes narrowed. "There's something about him that's familiar. Do I know him?"

"I don't believe you've ever met him." Ceren exchanged a look with Judith.

"Can't put my finger on it," Angela watched him, "but there's something I recognize about that man." She scratched her ear. Then her eyes widened. "Be right back."

Before either woman could stop her, Angela approached the bar.

Daddy?

*"It is easier for a father to have children
than for children to have a real father."*

— Pope John XXIII

"Hi," she said, staring hard at his prominent cheekbones, his cerulean-blue eyes, trying her best to keep her voice from trembling.

"Hello," he said back with an affable smile, despite recovering from his choking spree. He cleared his throat and sipped his water. "Are you one of Dr. Barona's students at the university?"

"I go to UTSA." She shook her head. "Why, are you a colleague of his?"

He arched an eyebrow and snorted. "I used to be."

"Where are you lecturing now?" She searched his face for clues.

Sighing, he took a drink of water. "I'm . . . retiring." He looked at Tim, talking with a group of guests. "Actually, the decision's just . . . come to me."

"Then you must be looking forward to spending time with your family." She watched him closely, trying to read his blue eyes.

He glanced at Ceren's narrowed, suspicious eyes watching him and quickly looked away.

"Not really." He sighed. "I don't have a family."

Angela's ears perked. "No children?"

With a half-shrug, he said, "I heard . . ." He started over. "I have a daughter, but she's grown."

Covering her gasp, Angela clapped her hand over her mouth. She struggled to keep herself together, but she felt tears stinging her eyes.

"Excuse me." Mustering her composure, she walked back to Ceren and Judith, her spine straight. With her back to him, she brushed away her tears.

"What did he say to you?" Ceren put her arm around her.

"He's my father, isn't he?"

Ceren started to shake her head no, but Judith said, "You might as well know." She glanced at him. "He's your biological father."

"Not your dad, not 'daddy,'" said Ceren, tight-lipped. "That would imply a man who helped raise you. Sam was your father and your dad." She jerked her head in his direction. "He's simply the person who impregnated me."

"I'm going to talk to Ellen about asking him to leave." Judith started toward her.

"Her husband already did, but he snuck back in," said Ceren, her mouth downturned in disgust. "Tell Tim he's making a nuisance of himself."

Judith turned pale. She opened her mouth to protest, but Angela lightly touched her arm.

"No," she said, "not yet. There's something I need to do." Angela took a deep breath and walked back to him.

Looking into his blue eyes, she said, "I'm Angela. I'm your daughter."

"I suspected it, especially when Ceren put her arm around you." His voice broke, and he cleared his throat. "How . . . how did you know? Had you seen pictures?"

She smiled. "No, I've never seen a picture of you." She glanced at Judith. "My mother never asked for any from Ceren, and, even if she had, I don't believe my birth mother kept any pictures of you."

He looked from Angela to Judith to Ceren. "So—"

"Ceren gave me up for adoption. Judith is my mom."

His Adam's apple bobbing, he looked at his shoes. Sighing, he raised his eyes.

"Then how did you know me?"

"When I was very little, I recall Ceren telling Mom that I had your high cheekbones. Recently, she mentioned your electrifying blue eyes. Those tips clued me, along with . . . intuition." She shrugged. "Somehow, I just knew."

He moved toward her, as if to hug her, but Ceren started toward him, scuffling her feet in the process. He looked toward the sound and saw Judith put a restraining hand on Ceren's elbow. Instead of hugging her, he reached for Angela's hand and kissed it.

Feeling elated on one level but uncomfortable on another, she motioned to two chairs.

"Let's sit down, where we can get acquainted."

He blinked. His eyes took on a humble, wistful look as he followed her. His behavior not lost on her, Angela felt the grown-up with her father the dutiful child. When they sat beside one another, she turned toward him.

"Where have you been all these years?"

His eyes clouding over, he looked down at his shoes. "Here, there, this university, that college." He shrugged.

"Have you ever tried to contact me?"

He looked up at her and then quickly looked away, eyes misting. In that moment, she saw the emptiness behind his eyes. *A lost soul.*

After an awkward silence, she said, "Never mind. It doesn't really matter now. It's enough that we've met."

A look of gratitude came into his eyes as he reached for her hand.

"It's more than that. It's a magic moment." He swallowed. Then, hoarsely, slightly off-key, he began singing the Drifters' "This Magic Moment."

Again, she felt the adult in the situation. With Ceren, Judith, and several other bystanders watching curiously, Angela tried to mentally blot them out, focus on her father. When he finished the chorus, she smiled, squeezed his hand, and let him go.

"Thank you, that was sweet."

"Thank *you*." He gave a half-smile, emphasizing where the gratitude lay. "This has been a . . . a tough week, but seeing you, meeting you, makes it bearable." He glanced toward Judith and

Ceren, then turned back to her. "Judith's done a wonderful job raising you." His eyes took in Angela's appearance. "You're a grown woman . . . a lady." He swallowed again. "I know I haven't been a good father to you." Shaking his head, he groaned. "There are many things I regret about my life, but you . . . Can you ever forgive me?"

With a nod, she looked him in the eyes. "I forgive you." She gave him a wry smile. "Let's put that behind us. I want to enjoy the time I have with you."

"There'll be other—"

"No, there won't." She stared evenly into his eyes. "You know it as well as I do." She took a deep breath. "This is our time together. We met here today for a reason. It was no coincidence." She shrugged. "Maybe it was to find closure to this unwritten chapter in our lives."

Again, he stared at his shoes.

After several minutes ticked by, Angela sensed their interval had ended. Putting on a bright smile, she made a concerted effort to be charitable.

"What girl wouldn't want to meet her dad?"

The sound of approaching footsteps made her look up. Tim strode toward them, red-faced and scowling.

Jarek jumped to his feet. "I was just leaving." Then turning one last time toward Angela, he dipped his head in an awkward bow. "Thank you."

As Angela watched Tim usher him out, she felt his humiliation. No matter their brief history together, she pitied the empty husk that was her father. He had never tried to contact her. She knew that, even without his ability to admit it. She had heard Ceren's story, seen his hollowness firsthand, yet he was her father.

She had always wondered about him, daydreamed about meeting him, and now she had.

Slouching, her expression grim, Angela rejoined Ceren and Judith.

"I'm glad Tim put an end to that." Ceren's eyes narrowed as she watched Jarek being escorted out the door. Then she turned to Angela. "What did he have to say for himself?"

"That he was sorry."

She said it with such humility that Judith and Ceren asked no more questions. Instead, they exchanged a look over her head.

Then Ceren inhaled deeply.

"I feel I've been holding my breath since I saw him." She shook her head, as if to rid herself of the image. "That was unpleasant."

"Considering our academic circles," said Judith, shrugging, "I'm surprised it hasn't happened more often."

"Apologies, ladies," said Tim, joining them. "Apparently, Stephen had a little too much to drink."

Angela's eyebrow shot up, but she kept silent.

"I hope he wasn't annoying you."

Angela shook her head while Judith sipped her tequila, studying his face.

Ceren said, "For a moment, I thought he was our musical entertainment."

Tim chuckled politely. Then glancing at their glasses, asked, "Can I get you ladies anything to drink?"

Angela shook her head. "No, thanks."

Ceren held up her half-full flute. "I'm good."

"Judith, I see your glass is empty. Can I get you a refill?"

Realizing she'd have to answer him, she looked at her empty glass.

"Better make it a soft drink. I'm driving."

"That's right," he said, reaching for her glass. "You live between Wimberley and San Marcos, Ellen said. Anywhere near the Devil's Backbone?"

She nodded but was unable to meet his eyes. When he did not respond, she peeked and saw he was watching her expectantly.

"Purgatory Road," she added as she looked away.

"Gotta' love those Texan names." He chuckled as he reached for a fresh glass. "Mixer okay?"

"Mmm-hm." She kept her eyes averted, not wanting to make eye contact.

"Here you go."

She turned toward his voice and saw he was holding out a glass to her.

"Thanks." With a polite nod, she returned to Ceren. "Where'd Angela go?"

"Develyn wanted to show her something."

"Maybe it's just as well." She sighed.

"Why, what's wrong?"

She shook her head. "Before I go into that, I want to hear how you're doing." Judith nodded toward the door.

"You mean after seeing Jarek." Ceren rolled her eyes. "It was a shock. Worse was watching him chat with Angie. The man can't be trusted." She took a deep breath. "I've tried to forgive him over the years, but seeing him again, face-to-face, is unnerving." She shook her head. "I don't think I can ever excuse him after . . ." Not completing her thought, she finished her champagne in one gulp.

Judith nodded. "I can understand."

"No, you can't." Ceren scowled at her. "You were there, but you didn't go through it."

Judith gave a wry chuckle. "Oh, I beg to differ."

"What do you mean?"

"You're not the only one who had to deal with pregnancy outside of a happy marriage." She raised her eyebrow. "I had an abortion fifty-eight years ago."

"That's right." Ceren bit her lip. "Sorry, Judith, I'm a little self absorbed this afternoon." She snorted. "But at least he didn't show up here to ruin the party for you."

Judith gave a wry grin. "If only that were the case."

Ceren looked her in the eye. "You mean, he's here?" Judith nodded. "Where?" Ceren searched the men within eyeshot. "Ellen's husband."

"Our host?" Ceren's eyes widened as her jaw went slack. "Really?" Again Judith nodded. "I must say you're taking it well."

"That's because he doesn't recognize me." She crinkled her forehead. "Inside, I'm a nervous wreck. I don't want to think about my blood pressure."

Ceren glanced at their hostess, chatting with another group. "Does Ellen know?"

"Nope." She pressed her lips together as she shook her head. "Neither did I until she introduced him to me."

Ceren blinked. "How can you be sure it's the same guy? After nearly sixty years, people change."

Judith touched her face by her left temple. "Did you notice his mole?"

"No, but a facial mole wouldn't prove anything. A lot of people have them."

"A lot of people by the name of Dr. Tim Barona?"

Ceren groaned. "I see your point." She worked her lips, as if thinking. "You're sure he didn't recognize you?" Judith nodded. "What about your name?"

Judith's mouth twisted into a half smile. "When he knew me, I was Faith Truman, not Judith Brannon."

Ceren scanned her face. "And you have no distinguishing facial features. At least, no moles or beauty marks that I can see." She shrugged. "Maybe you can pull this off by simply ignoring the situation."

"It's like a waking nightmare, something I've dreaded happening, and now here it is." She grimaced. "I actually feel queasy."

"Try to relax. Take a deep breath."

Judith grunted. "I can't explain why, but it's as if I'm ashamed."

"He's the one who left you, so let go of any guilt. Hold your head up." Ceren gave a lopsided smile. "Own the room."

Judith twisted her mouth into a wry grin. "Angela's the one who's outclassed us. Gracious, empathetic. Wish I could muster that instead of these negative feelings." As she shook her head, she gestured with her right palm. "On the one hand, I'm embarrassed." She glanced toward Ellen, then toward Tim. "On the other, I'm resentful, angry. Either way, I'm stressed."

"Do you want to leave?"

"Yes." Judith snorted. "But I also want to see how this plays out." She winked. "Think I'll stay around a while."

Driving back home, Ceren mentally replayed the chance meeting with Jarek. *How could I ever have married that . . . loser? What does it say about me? Naïve? Definitely, but how could I have been taken in by his lies?* She shook her head and groaned. *What a stupid kid I was.* Then she recalled the cerulean blue eyes of her father that she had seen again in Jarek. *A father figure, pure and simple. Jarek reminded me of him. Even so, how could I have been so gullible?*

Her mind jumped to Justin, comparing him to her first husband. She snickered. *No comparison, only stark contrast.*

Then she recalled how Angela had responded to meeting her father, forgiving him. *Thank God, growing up she had a dad, a real father in Sam. He and Judith did a fine job raising her. Despite the bad seed, she's growing into a strong, straight tree. Angela shows a lot more maturity at eighteen than I did at twenty-six.*

Her mind returned to Justin. Smiling, she recalled their honeymoon.

PUPPIES AND PYRAMIDS

"I believe in my mask— The man I made up is me.
I believe in my dance— And my destiny."

— SAM SHEPARD

Two hours later, they pulled in to Teotihuacán. Even on the approach, they could see the tops of the Pyramids of the Sun and Moon, glistening in the setting sun. Their hotel was just outside the perimeter of the archaeological site, minutes from the highway. Justin opened her door and offered her his hand.

"Well, Mrs. Garcia, after we check in, would you like to go to dinner? I understand there's a restaurant within walking distance that's a converted cave."

Accepting his hand, she swung out of the car and into his arms, enjoying the warmth of his protective embrace.

"Sounds romantic, Mr. Garcia."

She took her eyes off Justin long enough to notice the name of their hotel: Tonantzin Resorte de los Sueños, Tonantzin's Resort of Dreams. Raising her eyebrow, she turned back to him, silently questioning.

"Since your project with Judith was about Tonantzin, I thought I'd surprise you. I hope you'll enjoy staying here."

Dreams of Tonantzin. She recalled the dreams when she had been pregnant. As if a word association game, her first thought was Angela Maria. Now that part of her was gone. Angela Maria had been given away.

Like an ice cream headache, a brain freeze, the memories came swiftly—tiny knives stabbing her mind. The pain of separation palpable, she pressed her fingertips into her forehead, trying to stave off the sudden headache.

Justin responded to her changing expressions. "Would you rather stay somewhere else?"

Lifting a corner of her mouth in a weak smile, she shook her head. "Not on a bet. I just . . . had I ever told you about the dreams?"

"No."

"Twice, actually, three times, I dreamt Tonantzin was the daughter I carried, Angela Maria."

He lifted his eyebrows skeptically. "They were just dreams."

"I know it sounds implausible, but, at the time, the dreams seemed very realistic, especially the last one." Her voice dropped to a whisper. "Angela Maria's gone. Yet here . . . and here," she touched her womb and her heart, "I feel her like a phantom, amputated limb."

"Dreams can seem real, and memories can be tangible." His eyebrows knitted together sympathetically as he drew her toward him. "Ceren, I love you. I can't make up for past hurts, but I promise I'll do everything I can to make you happy from now on." He glanced at the hotel and then back to her. "This is our first night together. If this place isn't everything you wanted, everything you imagined for our honeymoon, we can leave—"

She put her finger to his lips, seductively silencing him. "It's perfect." She smiled, meaning it. "As long as I'm with you, where it is doesn't matter." Standing on tiptoe, she kissed him lightly on the cheek.

"Did I tell you we have the bridal suite?" He raised and lowered his eyebrows in his Groucho Marx imitation. "Doesn't that deserve another kiss?"

The tension headache fading, she chuckled. This time, eyes closed, she kissed his lips slowly, promising more.

His mouth softened into an easy-going smile. "Maybe we don't need to go out to eat—"

"Food first. I haven't eaten all day. I need sustenance, Mr. Garcia."

§

They walked to a hundred-year-old restaurant, located in an ancient cave the Aztecs had used for food storage. It incandesced with vivacious reds, yellows, oranges, indigos, and chartreuse. Multicolored tablecloths, napkins, brightly painted, high-backed chairs, and flickering candles brought the cave to life.

"It's a cavern tavern," quipped Justin as he ordered margaritas.

A trio of guitarists and a harpist strolled over and strummed "Guantanamera" as the waiter brought the drinks and a salad made with quelites.

"How do you pronounce this?" Ceren asked the waiter, trying to read from the menu.

"Kay-LEE-tayz," he answered phonetically. "It's an Aztec word for this green herb."

Tossed with a dressing made from the prickly pear cactus fruit, the salad looked like discarded weeds, but Ceren found its taste surprisingly appetizing.

As she and Justin shared a platter of squash blossom and mushroom quesadillas smothered with melted cheese, the strolling musicians stopped at their table and broke into a rendition of "Besame Mucho."

She leaned in to him and whispered, "They're good, but nothing tops the night you serenaded me."

Justin gave her hand a squeeze. Then he tipped the musicians enough to play tableside until the waiter asked if they wanted dessert. Full from the quesadillas, they only groaned, paid their tab, and got up to leave.

They strolled back along the cobblestone road as it began to drizzle. Stray dogs and feral cats dozed or played in front of the souvenir stands lining the way.

Under one shop's eaves, a man wove a vibrant tablecloth on a handloom. The cotton weave contained fifteen columns of color, burnt orange and rusty red filling every other row, with cobalt blue and loden green interspersed. The shuttle clacked rhythmically as it raced back and forth. The sound attracting their interest as much as the colors, they stopped to watch and inspect the fabric.

"Remind you of anything?" he asked.

Ceren nodded, smiling slowly, remembering. "Our first date, tying up life's loose ends." She squeezed his hand. "That's what we're doing with our marriage—making a tightly knit fabric from loose threads."

"The woof and warp of life," he said, repeating one of their first conversations.

She squeezed his hand. "You know, to the ancient Nahuatls, spinning and weaving represented life, death, and rebirth. Tonantzin, as Ix Chel or Tlazolteotl, was known as the Great Spinner of the Thread and Weaver of the Fabric of Life." She gestured with her other hand. "Like thread winding around a spindle, Tlazolteotl represented a pregnant woman, growing big with child. Then, in the process of weaving, as the thread unwound from the spindle, the spindle shrank in size, but the thread was reborn into cloth."

"Makes sense."

"Something I didn't tell you on our first date, I can share with you now. The intertwining of threads also symbolized," Ceren paused as she shyly leaned into him, "the coming together of a man and woman, so, to the ancient Nahuatls, spinning and weaving were closely linked to pregnancy and childbirth."

Justin pulled her against him in a warm embrace.

As if on cue, a puppy's high-pitched woof drew their attention. They turned and saw an exquisite double rainbow, the colors more brilliant than the loom's tablecloth.

Ceren drew in her breath.

It filled the sky from horizon to horizon, one end touching the ground just in front of one of the pyramids, a translucent fan of color through which Ceren could see the ancient structure. It was an aura, shimmering over all, but emanating from that pyramid.

"A sign if ever I saw one," she said, mesmerized. Then she turned toward Justin. "Let's visit that site tomorrow."

"Ix Chel," said the weaver, wearing a tongue-in-cheek smile, "the moon goddess, also called Lady Rainbow, is blessing your visit."

The rain progressed from light to steady, and they ducked into a souvenir stand to wait it out. Ceren saw a small, white puppy sitting at the entrance, whimpering, watching them. It approached, nuzzling Ceren's legs, inviting her to pet it. She laughed, and, as she petted the puppy, the two bonded.

The rain let up a few minutes later, and they resumed their trek back to the hotel, the white puppy following at a distance, unobserved. As they walked, they looked up in awe at the enormous double diadem still vibrant above them, like a multicolored tiara crowning the heavens. It reminded Ceren of the verse from Isaiah, "a royal diadem held by your God."

The next morning, they walked to the pyramids. The stroll through the hotel's gated entrance took them past thick adobe walls, painted in pastel shades of aqua and lilac. A private Toltec ruin had been excavated in the front, while a regal row of organ cacti lined the front perimeter like spiny sentinels, keeping intruders and locals out of the gated grounds as austerely as the uniformed entrance guards.

Just as they reached the pyramids' entrance, they noticed a group of five men, dressed in traditional red-and-white embroidered clothing, gathering around a tall pole. Hands cupped above their eyes, shielding them from the intense sunlight, they watched as the men climbed the pole. One perched at the top and began playing a flute as the other four attached ropes to their ankles.

"The Aztecs believed their culture had to be renewed every fifty-two years," said the announcer. "La Danza de los Voladores, this ancient dance that you're watching, the Dance of the Flyers, symbolizes that belief. Each man ties a rope around his ankle, jumps off the 150-foot pole backwards, headfirst, flies upside down, and slowly spins thirteen times. Four men times thirteen revolutions equal fifty-two, the number of years in a sacred series."

Ceren took their new camera from its bag, focused, and set it to record.

The four voladores swooped down in ever-widening circles, like giant raptors. Ceren and Justin stood riveted, unable to take their eyes off the pole flyers, as the flute piped its haunting melody, and a drum tattooed a mournful cadence.

A woman's scream interrupted the announcer as the rope of one of the voladores slipped. The crowd gasped and held its collective breath as the flier plunged head-first toward the pavement below. Midair, the man grinned at the audience, adjusted his rope, and resumed his graceful descent in perfect formation with his compadres. Realizing his trick, the crowd now laughed at the man's brazen joke.

"Give Juan a big hand," said the announcer, and the crowd applauded. "This ritual honors the earth and the march of time, according to the Aztec calendar," continued the announcer. "These four men represent the four corners of the earth, the four winds, the four elements, and the four seasons."

When their feathered headdresses swept the pavement, the four fliers righted themselves and stepped off their virtual merry-go-round to an applauding crowd. Wearing a wide grin that exposed several missing teeth, the young daredevil passed his hat among the crowd.

"Gracias," he nodded when Justin tossed in several pesos.

"That 'flight' will get your heart racing," Ceren said as they made their way into the Teotihuacán Archaeological Park.

Justin shook his head. "You couldn't pay me to climb that pole, let alone jump off."

"Originally, that the pole represented Tlazolteotl, the goddess of fertility, another name for Tonantzin."

SACRED GIFT

"I'd heard the fliers performed as a sacred rite to Quetzalcóatl, but the announcer didn't mention either of those connections." She shook her head. "The pantheon of Nahuatl, Aztec, and Mayan gods is immense—and confusing." With a self-effacing chuckle, Ceren added, "I've been researching the Mesoamerican gods for over a year and still don't have a handle on their genealogy."

Barely inside the park, she stopped to inspect the ancient wall paintings and caught her breath.

"This is the Nahui Ollin." She bent down to examine it.

"The what?" Justin squinted at the painting.

"The Nahui Ollin. It's a stylized, five-part flower that's found just below Our Lady of Guadalupe's sash." Jaw slack, Ceren looked up at him. "I can't believe we're seeing the same emblem here that's found on the tilma." She took a picture and then another.

"Now that you mention it, it does look familiar," he said, head cocked to one side as he studied it.

"Sure, you've probably seen it a hundred times on the Stone of the Sun and its replicas." She drew a picture in the air, her hands depicting the huge, round stone unearthed in Mexico City. "I knew this indigenous symbol was ancient, but I had no idea its origin was this old . . . or it could be from an even earlier period."

"What's it mean?" He looked to her for the answer.

Careful not to touch the painting, keeping her fingers an inch away, she pointed out the features.

"See the four petals surrounding the flower's center, like a primrose?" He nodded. "Those petals represent the four cardinal points of the earth. They can also symbolize abundance, the universe, God." She met his eyes. "When the natives saw this age-old symbol just below Our Lady of Guadalupe's sash, over her womb, they knew she was pregnant with God's son. This symbol was what converted them to Christianity."

"That really is amazing." Justin drew in his breath. Then he pointed at the artwork. "But these buildings and this particular flower precede the tilma by what? Five hundred years?"

She nodded. "At a minimum, no one knows for sure." She noticed another symbol several feet away. "And look at this." Kneeling, not directly touching the stone so the oils of her skin would not damage it, she pointed, again tracing its features in the air. "See how this symbol's edges are curved."

"I can barely see the paint," he said, squinting. He got down on his knees to look more closely. "It's so faded."

She nodded and drew its outline just in front of it.

"This is another stylized flower. See, this one's almost heart shaped. It's very similar to other flowers adorning Our Lady's tunic." She looked up at him. "Remember the Aztec themes, flower and song. Flowers played a tremendous part in their imagery. Look closer. Inside the flower, its details almost look like a human face. Can you see?"

"Barely, but I can use my imagination to fill in the blanks." He chuckled.

"Heart shaped flowers with a face symbolized a change of heart in a person. They signified a person's willingness to rethink his perspective—"

"To convert," he said, nodding. "I see your point." His eyes met hers. "You really do enjoy your line of work, don't you?"

"Art history's so interesting. I just love it." Both of them crouching on their knees, she wrapped her arms around his neck. "I'm so glad we came here for our honeymoon." She Eskimo kissed him on the nose and sighed. "I'm so glad we're married."

"Me, too," he said, returning her Eskimo kiss, then rising to his feet and helping her up. "Did you know these symbols were here? Is that why you wanted to honeymoon here?"

"I'd heard there were some parallels, but," she glanced down at the painted flower, "it's mind-boggling to discover them for yourself."

Hand in hand, they turned onto the Avenue of the Dead and began walking toward the Pyramid of the Moon.

"Do you know of any other similarities between Teotihuacán and Our Lady of Guadalupe?" he asked.

"Only generalities. For instance, I've read that the Teotihuacán Great Mother goddess was the precursor of Tonantzin, which some believe was the predecessor of Our Lady of Guadalupe. Or that Ix Chel, who the weaver said was also known as Lady Rainbow, was sometimes confused with the Virgin Mary."

"Is that true?"

She shrugged. "They're theories." She glanced at his face. "Keep in mind, I'm simply interested in the artistic representation on the tilma. I'm concerned with these theories of the goddesses and the historical image of Our Lady only to the extent that they involve the artwork." She shook her head. "I'm not making any religious equations."

He nodded. "Understood, yet the native Nahuatls accepted Our Lady of Guadalupe and converted to Catholicism so quickly after her appearance, it makes you wonder," he said.

"That same theory suggests the natives identified Our Lady of Guadalupe with their already existing Cosmic Mother."

"The transition did appear seamless."

She shrugged. "Who knows?"

"Máscara, señora, máscara?" asked a dark-eyed, preadolescent girl, holding up a stone death mask.

Ceren fingered the mask's glazed patchwork of stone, molded into a face with holes for the eyes and mouth.

"Cheap," said the girl, "for you, a special price."

Ceren looked at Justin, who groaned. "We'd have to carry it all day."

The girl's expression drooped.

Ceren smiled at her. "If you can give us a very special price, we'll take it."

"Okay," said the girl, a hopeful smile lighting up her face.

"You softy," whispered Justin, his eyes twinkling as he pretended to scowl.

"Oh, come on, it's art, and you know how I love art, almost as much as I love you."

After they chose a mask, Ceren linked arms with him, and they continued toward the Pyramid of the Moon.

"Besides, death masks are a specialty of Teo."

"Really? Why?"

"Death is an integral part of the Mexican culture. People celebrate death here almost as a prerequisite to life."

"I've heard of the Day of the Dead," said Justin, "but, transferring here in February, I haven't celebrated it yet. Have you?"

She took a deep breath. "Celebrated isn't quite the word, but yes, I've certainly experienced it."

Her tone made Justin look. "Why the long face?"

"On Dia de los Muertos, the Day of the Dead, I went into Mexico City, intending to abort Angela Maria."

He breathed in sharply. "Sorry, I—"

"You didn't know." She smiled briefly through thin, tight lips. "I told you about going to the basilica, but I didn't tell you any of the . . . details." She rolled her eyes. "Sugar skulls and painted, clown-white faces with black eyelids and black 'stitched' lips still haunt me." She shivered, recalling the Calavera Catrina and Catrine faces. "I literally saw the face of death that day."

A deep 'V' appeared between his eyes. "If you'd rather not talk about it, I'd understand."

"I'm fine." She flashed him a wider smile, hoping to convince him. "Some people believe that the Day of the Dead is a thread, a direct link, leading back to the ancient rituals of the Teotihuacán, Toltec, Olmec, or even older civilizations."

Justin snorted. "That reminds me of a Mexican saying. 'Life is like a snake crawling out of its old skin.'"

"If not rebirth each time, it certainly is reinvention," she said, as they strolled along the Calzada de los Muertos.

On their descent from the Pyramid of the Moon, Ceren looked at her watch. It was eleven thirty.

"I'd really like to see the Pyramid of the Sun by noon, so we don't get shadows in the pictures."

"In that case," he said, "we'd better get moving."

"Did you know, the Pyramid of the Sun is the third largest pyramid in the world, after Egypt's Cheops and Cholula's pyramid?"

"Is that a hint you'd like to visit Egypt next?" Justin asked, his eyes tipped up at the corners in a teasing smile. "You've already talked me into seeing Teo and Cholula."

They laughed as they raced across the Avenue of the Dead but, at seven thousand feet above sea level, were panting before they approached the base of the stairs. Catching their breath, they began the series of ascents. At each of the five levels, the view changed significantly.

Watching the changing heights and perspectives, Ceren said, "Let's stop and record the sights from each tier."

"I don't know if we can," Justin said, looking around at the crowded platform. "There's really no room."

Ceren looked behind them at the single file line of people spurring them forward. Camera in hand, she said, "Okay, but on the way down I'm going to photograph the scenes from each level. I know Judith will find it interesting."

When they reached the penultimate tier, they noticed two people sitting on the rim of the pyramid, their feet hanging over the ledge, gazing at the Pyramid of the Moon.

Gasping for air, Justin said, "Oh, that looks good."

Ceren looked at the relaxed couple, wanting to join them, sit down, rest, and fill her lungs. Then she checked her watch: five minutes to twelve. Too out of breath to speak, she shook her head and tapped her watch.

With a resigned groan, he nodded. They each took a deep breath and pushed on. Climbing over the broken stones, they reached the top just as the sun reached its zenith. Not to miss a moment of the bright, white light, Ceren began snapping pictures, the views more astounding in each direction.

From the crest of the pyramid, they could see the layout of Teotihuacán. The Avenue of the Dead, what had once been the city's main street, extended for more than a mile on a north-south axis, although, as they gazed southward, they could make out half-buried bits and pieces of it beyond the citadel.

Just past the wall and fences, Ceren saw the souvenir shop they had ducked into the night before. As she turned to look back at the Temple of the Moon and to the right to see the modern building alongside the pyramid, she got her bearings.

"Justin, the museum next door is the building the rainbow indicated. Let's go there next."

"Sure. Look, you can see our hotel." Approaching her from behind, he cuddled her as he pointed with an outstretched arm.

Ceren leaned into him as her eyes followed the line of his extended arm, seeing the half-hidden, half-imaginary continuation of the avenue. Their hotel was directly aligned with it, right along the archaeological zone.

"I'll bet those excavated ruins on the grounds were once part of this complex."

She looked though her lens, but the camera did not do the long shot justice. She continued circling the top tier of the pyramid, taking pictures from all four cardinal points. Capturing the views on film, she was mindless of the time, heat, or altitude as the sun's delicate descent angled and cast subtle shadows.

When the shadows lengthened, they realized an hour had passed, and the heat of the day had apparently dissuaded climbers.

"The crowd's definitely thinned," she said, taking a deep breath, "along with the air."

Justin chuckled. "Finally, room to sit down."

They sat on two of the rounder rocks, facing the Pyramid of the Moon, and took long drinks from their water bottles. Tangerine colored Monarch butterflies, outlined in black lace, floated by in a breezeless dance. She tried to capture them on film, but they swung away in a do-si-do—square dancers following a soundless caller's directions.

Taking a protein bar from her backpack, she noticed the white puppy at her side. She looked around, but no other person was on the pyramid. At over two hundred feet above the ground, the puppy had made an astounding climb—apparently unguided.

"You're the one we met last night," she said, affectionately scratching the puppy's head and neck, feeling the soft bristles of the glossy coat. "Are you thirsty, girl?"

Ceren poured some water into her hand, and the puppy gently lapped it up.

"Are you lost?" she asked, pouring more water into her hand for the puppy to drink. It lapped with a pink tongue as soft as goose feathers until it had had enough. Then Ceren fed her bits of her protein bar as they looked north at the Pyramid of the Moon, sharing the view.

She kneeled down to pet the puppy, and it stood on its hind legs, straining to kiss her. Ceren kept her neck high, so the kisses could not reach her face. Then, putting her arms around the puppy, she felt the glossy smoothness of her coat, and Ceren lost the struggle, giving in to the puppy's kisses on her neck and chin.

"Oh, what a cutie you are. Who could resist a little girl like you?" Opening her eyes almost as wide as the puppy's, she looked to Justin. "What do you think? Should we start our family on our first full day of marriage?"

Subduing a smile, he tried to raise his eyebrows sternly. "Do they even allow dogs in our building?"

"Yup, the people on the first floor have one." As the puppy continued to lick her, she had to giggle. "She tickles."

"She's such a little dog, perrito," he said, scratching the puppy's neck.

"That's a great name. Perrito, it is." She turned toward Justin. "Did you know the Toltecs believed white dogs symbolize faithfulness and fortitude on spiritual journeys?"

When she looked up at him, the glaring sunlight behind him blinded her. Shielding her eyes, she saw orange and saffron-yellow butterflies sashay between them, seeming to enjoy the white heat.

"Does that apply to puppies, too," he asked lightly, "and what about these butterflies? Were these symbolic to the Toltecs?"

"Yes," she said, leaning against him and placing his arm around her shoulders. "To them, butterflies symbolized transformation, metamorphosis, as they moved from the earth to the sky."

"Is that so?" he asked, absent-mindedly petting the puppy on her lap.

She nodded. "They believed butterflies symbolized souls, here to remind us life is a fleeting source of pleasure and shouldn't be taken too seriously. Do you realize you're looking north?"

"Really?"

"To the Toltecs, white represented the energy of the north—a purifying energy."

"So?"

"The puppy's white. You're facing north. Butterflies are circling above." She stopped, considering her next words. "Do you sense anything?"

"Only that, at seven thousand feet above sea level and the two hundred plus feet of this pyramid, we're above seventy-five percent of the earth's atmosphere. With the ozone layer this thin, I can feel the ultraviolet rays scorching the back of my neck."

She sucked in her breath when she saw his neck. "It really is getting red. You wouldn't want to get heat stroke up here. Maybe we should climb down and get in the shade?"

A glint in his eye, he asked, "You're not prejudiced, are you?" To her blank stare, he added, "Are you sure you don't judge people by the color of their . . . necks?"

She grinned. "Watch your step on the way down. Some of those stairways are pitched so steeply, they're nearly vertical."

"I'll lead, so I can break your fall if you slip."

Ceren started after him but saw the puppy was not following. She turned back and called, "Come on, Perrito."

"Are you coming?" Justin's voice hailed her from several steps down.

"Be with you in a minute. Just want to make sure this puppy gets down safely."

She picked up the puppy and nestled it in her camera bag, leaving only its head sticking out so it could breathe in the thin air. Removing the camera, she carefully descended, only pausing on each level long enough to photograph the changing scenery.

Back on the ground, Ceren scratched the young dog's head.

"How's our puppy doing?"

Ceren gently pulled open the front flap of her camera bag so they could peek in.

"She's still sleeping." A sense of maternal satisfaction coming over her, she smiled. "Poor thing, she must have been exhausted after climbing all those stairs."

Following the path behind the temple, they saw the museum. As they entered, Justin whispered, "It's so quiet."

Looking around, Ceren said, "Except for a few guards, it's downright deserted." She gave his hand a friendly squeeze.

Hand-in-hand, they walked from one room to the next, gazing at the compilations of pottery shards, incense burners, braziers, and other assorted artifacts. They stepped into a two-story, glass-walled room and were confronted with the Pyramid of the Sun.

Ceren caught her breath, whispering, "It's breathtaking. The pyramid fills the entire window wall."

Then they looked at the transparent, Plexiglas floor. Beneath their feet lay a diminutive diorama of the city. On tiptoes, they gingerly tested the floor. When it proved solid, they strolled across it from one miniscule temple to another.

"Look at the miniature city of Teotihuacán below our feet." Justin said, chuckling. "We can walk its perimeter in seconds instead of hours."

Finally, they moved from the sunlit room, with its imposing view of the Pyramid of the Sun, into a dark chamber barely lit by red lights. As their eyes adjusted to the low light levels, Ceren felt more than saw a burial chamber of eighteen children's skulls. Transfixed, she stared and stumbled toward the area, open except for a low Plexiglas wall with signs reading "No Tocar!" Don't touch!

A lump rose in her throat, and she gasped. Inexplicably, she began trembling. The plaque by their small skulls read, "Found at the Temple of Quetzalcóatl, it is unknown whether these were intended to be sacrifices of decapitated children or if it is a concentration of skulls removed from other graves." She couldn't comprehend why, but she was drawn closer and closer until she was leaning over the low, Plexiglas barrier.

Suddenly, she felt Justin's strong hands on her shoulders, pulling her back.

"What's wrong?" he said.

Almost in a trance, she looked at him as if waking from a dream. "I don't know."

"You were so close to the edge, I thought you were going to fall in."

She breathed deeply. "I saw the tiny skulls of those babies and it . . . it reminded me . . ."

Justin took her in his arms. "Flashbacks?"

"The skulls remind me of the day I nearly aborted Angela." She looked back at the remains. "The way these tiny lives were snuffed out so long ago, I nearly ended my baby's life." She shook her head. "The culture of death, both the ancient and modern versions, both cultures killed . . . kill . . . children."

"But you didn't abort Angela," he said softly.

"That's true, but I nearly did. You have no idea how close I came." She looked up into his eyes, baring her soul. "If it hadn't been for—"

"The point is, you didn't."

She sighed. "In some ways, the result's the same. I gave her up. She's a part of me, yet she's apart from me." She put her arms around him. "I miss her so much."

Their movement woke the puppy. As she shifted and whimpered, the camera bag seemed to come alive. The wriggling puppy and bag made Ceren chuckle, despite the topic of conversation.

"You've got this baby for now," Justin said, reaching in to pet the puppy. "If it's God's will, we'll have a child of our own soon."

Squeezing her arms around his waist, she drew him toward her in a hug.

"I do love you."

Wordlessly, he wrapped his arms around her, his embrace echoing her sentiments.

A LIFETIME IN MY HEART

"Before I formed you in the womb, I knew you . . . ."

JEREMIAH 1:5

Ceren took the indicator into the bedroom to show Justin. The best she could manage was a tight-lipped smile.

"It's negative."

"Next month," he said gently, taking her into his arms.

"It's been a year." She put her arms around his neck. "Don't you think it's time to see a fertility specialist?"

He scratched his head. "Maybe it is."

She nodded. "I'll make an appointment tomorrow."

They heard the thump-thump of the dog's tail and then a whimper. The dog looked at them with sad eyes.

Justin patted the bed, "Okay, Perrito." With a quick bark, the dog jumped on the bed and put her cold, wet nose between them. "You've got this baby for now."

Ceren smiled crookedly, recalling he had said that a year ago.

After her lecture, Ceren stopped by the outreach center to help Pastora with the postabortion ministry.

"Hi," she said absently, setting down her books.

"Hel-lloo!"

Pastora's enthusiastic greeting made Ceren look twice. Pastora's smile spread from cheek to cheek.

"You look like you're about to explode," said Ceren. "You're absolutely beaming." Then she noticed Pastora was standing at an angle, concealing something in the crux of her arm. "What're you hiding?"

"It's a surprise." Turning toward her, Pastora said, "Look what showed up on the church steps this morning."

Ceren gasped. "A baby!" She held out her hands hungrily. "Oh, could I hold it?"

"Of course." Pastora's smile widened as she gently transferred the bundle into Ceren's waiting arms.

"What a precious little doll," said Ceren, fondling its little fingers and toes. "Is it a girl or a boy?"

"A baby boy," said Pastora, "practically a Christmas baby."

"And a newborn. His eyes aren't open yet." Her mouth suddenly set in a thin, grim line, she asked, "Why would someone leave this adorable little boy?" Then she caught Pastora's eye, and the memories of her own pregnancy answered her question.

"The baby also has . . . what some might call a defect," said Pastora.

"Where? I don't see anything wrong with him." Ceren looked over the baby. "Ten fingers, ten toes, eyes are still closed, but they'll open."

"That's just it. Look more closely at the eyes." Pastora's voice lost its lilt. "The doctor thinks he has Down syndrome."

Ceren felt a knife plunge into her chest. She looked at the baby and recalled how her doctor had considered that grounds for aborting Angela.

"Are they sure?" She suddenly felt sick to her stomach. "I mean, was this just an initial opinion, or have they done any blood tests to make an actual diagnosis?"

"So far, just a visual appraisal," said Pastora. "The tests are scheduled for Friday, but the pediatrician thought he heard a slight heart murmur through the stethoscope, and his eyes appear to slant upward."

Ceren grunted indignantly. "Well, that doesn't prove a darn thing." Ceren pursed her lips in a tight, white line.

Pastora chuckled. "You sound and look as if you're defending the baby."

Ceren laughed at herself. "You're right. I do." She sighed. "I just can't stand the thought of labeling this sweet little baby, when they haven't even tested him. His eyes aren't even open, for heaven's sake." She hugged the baby to her chest. "Poor little thing."

Pastora watched her closely. "The problem is, we don't have a facility to care for babies." She shrugged and held up her hands in resignation. "We're simply not designed for it. We don't have the resources, and I don't know what to do with him until the authorities enter him into the system."

"Well . . . maybe . . . what I'm thinking . . ." Ceren tripped over her words until she looked into Pastora's mischievous, laughing eyes. "Oh, you shrewd woman, you set me up, didn't you?"

"So Pastora said we'd have to fill out the paperwork to be foster parents," said Ceren. One arm holding the baby, she emptied the grocery bag with the other, putting away the baby bottles, baby formula, baby shampoo, baby lotion, baby powder, and diapers she had bought. Perrito dogged her every movement as she skipped about the kitchen.

"So—"

"Oh, before I forget, Pastora said that she'll put in a good word for us with the foster board, or whatever it is they call it here."

"So—"

"Here," she said, handing him to Justin, "would you hold the baby while I put these away?" She stopped momentarily, gasped, and looked at him. "The baby—don't you just love the sound of that?"

Jaw slack, Justin quickly dumped his armload of paperwork on the table and awkwardly accepted the baby. Woofing at the commotion, the dog sniffed at the baby.

Calling over her shoulder as she put away the new baby supplies, Ceren asked, "What do you think of the little tyke?"

"He's—"

"Isn't he adorable?"

"I—"

"He's such a little doll, don't you think?"

Back from the storage closet, she held out her arms. With a subdued smile, just his dimple showing, Justin handed off the baby to her. She wrapped her arms around the bundle and cuddled him to her chest.

"You're awfully quiet tonight," she said, finally taking her eyes off the baby to look at Justin.

He chuckled.

"What do you think of this little sweetie?"

"He's a cutie." Justin gently stroked the baby's downy head. "How long have you had him?"

She checked the clock. "About three hours, why?"

"It's fair to say you two have bonded." His smile fading, his eyes narrowed. "You realize, don't you, that it's dangerous to get too attached."

Automatically tightening her grip on the baby, she looked at the bundle in her arms and chewed her lip.

"The authorities could place him before we even turn in the paperwork to foster him." His eyes softened, "Let alone adopt him."

Ceren lifted her eyes from the baby to him. "You read my mind." She stared at him with a mixture of love, gratitude, and wonder. *Oh, I love this man.*

He shook his head. "I read your body language." Justin gave her a wry grin. "You're pretty much an open book."

"You'd consider it? Adoption, I mean. We haven't even discussed it."

"We both want to start a family, and this little guy needs a home." He shrugged. "It's not rocket science to figure it out." Then his expression became serious. "We're going to have to fill out reams of paperwork and jump through all kinds of hoops, but—"

She stopped him with a kiss. "Thank you!"

"Before you thank me, just realize this isn't a done deal. Even after the paperwork and hoops, there could be another family that's in line to adopt him first."

"I know." She sighed, hugging the baby closer to her. "I just feel he's somehow meant for us."

"And there's something else we need to discuss. What if he does have Down syndrome?" Raising his eyebrow, his expression challenged her. In the silence, she could hear the dog sniffing the baby.

"This little guy hasn't even been tested." She caressed the baby fuzz on his head. "Even then, tests can be wrong. I remember how prenatal testing 'proved' Angela had Down syndrome, and I nearly aborted her." Squinting, setting her jaw tightly, she said, "I don't care how much paperwork it'll take. I don't care whether or not he has Down syndrome. I know now how Judith felt. This 'throw-away' baby won't make up for the one I gave away, but adopting him would be a start toward atonement. Plus, I love him already. I want this baby." Then looking at Justin, she added, "Anyway, that's my take on it. How do you feel about adopting this baby if he has Down syndrome?" She looked up to Justin, tense, waiting for his opinion.

"Who knows if God will ever give us this chance again? Even if . . . when we get pregnant, there's no guarantee that baby would be genetically perfect, either." He took her in his arms. "I look at this baby as a gift."

Tears beginning to fill her eyes, she hugged Justin while the dog pranced, sniffed her abdomen, and softly woofed for attention.

Reaching down to pet her, Ceren laughed. "Perrito, it looks like you won't be an only child anymore."

"Where did this little one come from?" asked the doctor, chucking the baby on the chin. "Aren't you here for fertility testing?" Checking his chart, he chuckled. "Maybe you don't need my services, after all."

Ceren cuddled the baby to her chest. "Justin Jr. is a gift, but he needs a brother or a sister." Sighing, she added, "Even if our dog thinks that's her responsibility."

"Come in," said the doctor.

"Here are the results of the urinalysis." The assistant handed him a printout.

As the doctor read the paper, he scratched his head. "How long have you and your husband been trying to get pregnant?"

"Twelve months." When he didn't say anything, she became concerned. "Why?"

"I was right. You don't need my services, after all." He smiled and passed her the printout. "Congratulations, Mrs. Garcia, you're going to have a baby." Then his eyes rested on the baby in her arms. "Another one."

LIFE LINES OF COMMUNICATION

"If there is to be reconciliation, first there must be truth."

— TIMOTHY B. TYSON

A chill passed over Ceren as she drove home, and she turned down the car's air conditioning. *Justin's so different now. He used to be spontaneous, fun. Now, he's so cold, distant. We never talk anymore . . . haven't since . . .* She swallowed, recalling how it had started. Her mind slipped back to the drive home from Angela's First Communion. *Was that eleven years ago?*

They had gotten a late start on their way back. Justin was driving, and the sun had nearly set. As they were driving along the highway, a six-point buck jumped out in front of the car ahead of them. The car swerved to avoid it, and Justin veered to avoid the careening car, but a third car, coming up fast from behind, had forced them off the road and into the ditch.

When they came to a neck-jolting stop, they assessed the damages. A quick check showed the boys were shaken but fine. Ceren and Justin had only bruises and contusions to show for the accident, but the car was badly damaged. Justin got out, pulled the crimped fender away from the front wheel, and discovered the car was still drivable. They were only a few miles from home, so they decided to continue. On the way, Ceren felt a pinching sensation in her stomach. The pinching quickly escalated into cramps and then contractions. Justin rushed her to the emergency room, but it was too late. She had miscarried.

The following months were a blur. She recalled the deep depression. She had taken off the summer semester but felt listless when the fall semester had begun. Sometime during those first months, Justin became aloof, distant. He took care of the boys and the house as she tried to climb out of the depression, but she felt as though she had lost her best friend along with her baby.

She silently blamed him for the accident, for losing the baby. She blamed him for being non-communicative, for locking himself in his office and being detached, unapproachable. She felt she had had to bear the loss alone, and for that she resented him.

Self-help books became her companions. Ceren read every page printed that dealt with the grief of a lost child. She joined support groups and talked with others, but she and Justin had never once discussed the death of their baby. Never once. *It's as if he never cared, as if the baby never existed.*

By the time Ceren drove into their garage, she was unsure who she resented more: Jarek or Justin. Her first husband had been the reason she had given up Angela for adoption. Her second husband had been the reason their last child had miscarried.

She walked into a silent house. With the sun setting, she turned on the kitchen lights.

"Hello?" *Guess no one's home.* She rolled her suitcase down the hallway and noticed the light on in his office. "Justin?"

"You're home early. I thought you were staying in Austin until tomorrow night." He looked up from his computer screen and half turned in his chair. "How was the conference?"

She shrugged. "Okay."

He turned back toward the screen. "Anything interesting happen?"

She wanted to tell him about Jarek and Angela, but, seeing his back, she changed her mind.

"Nope. You?"

Eyes on the screen, he shrugged. "Not really."

Grunting, she turned away and continued on into the bedroom. As she began to unpack, memories flooded her. Instead of her suitcase, it seemed she was unpacking her mind. Thoughts about the early years of their marriage tumbled through. *How happy we were. What happened?*

Then she remembered the miscarriage. And the resentment. And the blame. *Esteban.*

Then she recalled Angela's words. "I won't say Esteban's spirit is earthbound, but it's stretched between heaven and earth. He says your feelings for him interfere with his ability to move into the spiritual realm." *He can't move on.* She sat down on the bed, head in her hands, and let the tears fall. *Esteban.*

Hearing a tap on the open door, Ceren looked up. Justin stood in the doorframe, watching her. Taking off his glasses, he came around to the side of the bed.

"What's wrong?"

Sniffing, she swiped at her tears. *What do I say?* "Oh, nothing." *Everything.*

"Nothing, huh?" Wearing a wry smile, he sat down beside her. When she kept silent, he said, "I know things haven't been right between us for a while now—"

She scoffed. "That's an understatement."

"There's no need to get snippy." Grunting, he stood up. "Look, if you'd rather be alone, I—"

She reached for his hand. "No, I'm sorry, Justin." She sighed. "Snapping at you has become a pattern, a bad habit." She looked up into his eyes. "I apologize, and I'd really appreciate it if you'd talk with me a while."

"Sure." Watching her, he sat down. "Something's evidently happened. Want to tell me about it?"

"Actually, I do." She shared the unexpected meeting with Jarek and the way Angela had recognized him, forgiven him. Finally, she gave him a brief description of the spiritual encounter with Esteban. When she finished, she looked up at his eyes. "What do you think about it?"

Justin took a deep breath. "Wow." He gave a wry chuckle and scratched his receding hairline. "I don't know where to start." Then his face took on a no-nonsense expression. "I'm a lawyer, so let's approach this chronologically. The first thing you mentioned was running into Jarek. How do you feel about that?" He watched her closely. "Any old feelings for him resurface?"

"No!" Her jaw fell open in shock. Then she snorted. "If anything, just the opposite. I can't imagine what I ever saw in that man. He's such a . . . loser. It's the only word I can find to describe him. It's so obvious now." She looked up at his face. "No, trust me, no feelings of that sort, at all."

"Then how did you feel?"

"Schadenfreude." She glanced up with a shy grin. "I enjoyed his misfortunes a bit too much. Have to admit, a part of me was glad to see him beg for a job and get thrown out of the party."

"Understandable. Anything else?"

"Repulsion. He literally reeked of cigarettes." Justin's steady gaze made her search deeper. Looking into the distance, she gathered her thoughts. "Something else." She glanced up at his face. "I couldn't help comparing him to you. I could've been stuck with him."

His businesslike expression morphed into a sour smile. Tongue-in-cheek, he said, "That's a left-handed compliment if I ever heard one."

She winced. "That didn't come out quite right. What I meant—"

"That's all right." He waved off her explanation. "I get the general gist."

"No, what I meant was how lucky I am I met you." Scoffing, she shook her head. *Why hasn't that occurred to me before?* She looked at him, waiting for a response, some encouragement.

After a pregnant pause, he said, "Anything else?"

It wasn't the reaction she had wanted. She took a deep breath. Then her thoughts returned to the baby. Despite blaming Justin for the miscarriage, she still hoped they could get past it, move on. *It's been so long since he's held me.* Sitting so close, she wanted to reach out to him, but his polite, aloof smile held her at bay.

He shifted his weight as if he were going to stand. "Well, if there's nothing else—"

"Actually, there is." She swallowed, screwing up her courage to broach the subject they had avoided for eleven years. She thought of what Angela had told her and debated how much to divulge.

He stifled a sigh but stayed seated. "What is it?"

"It's just," she grunted, "I'm hesitant to bring up this topic." She shook her head. "It's always caused us such bitterness, started so many fights. We've never talked about it, but I think it's time we did." She took a deep breath and began. "The miscarriage." Once she started, the words began pouring from her lips. "We've never discussed what really happened, how the baby's death affected us, but it's become a wedge that's driven us farther and farther apart."

"Further and further," he corrected, a half-smile playing at his lips.

His grammatical pet peeve. She had to chuckle, despite the topic. "Fine, have it your way." Then her smile drooped. "But the fact is, it's come between us."

He nodded solemnly, his head bent.

She went on. "According to what Angela told me, Esteban is what . . . *who* has come between us. He's only wanted our attention so he could tell us not to blame ourselves. He wants us to release him, to forgive each other and let him go—let his spirit rest."

By the time Ceren finished, she was in tears. Justin pulled her to him and put his arms around her. Tears running down her cheeks, she sobbed against his chest, letting the ache melt away. He held her gently yet tightly against him until she took a deep breath and sniffed.

"Need a Kleenex?"

She nodded as he reached for the box and handed it to her. After she wiped her eyes, she looked into his bloodshot eyes and realized he'd been crying along with her. The sobs had been theirs, not just hers.

"I thought you didn't care."

"That's not true," he said, wiping his eyes with his fingers. "I cared very much, maybe too much, but I saw how broken you were by the miscarriage. Ceren, you were falling apart. Our boys needed us, and you were so distraught, you . . ." He looked down.

"I wasn't there for them." The realization brought on a new round of tears. She moved closer, sobbing against his chest, tasting her salty tears along with the ribbed cotton of his polo shirt. Then she remembered having to deal with the grief by herself. "But I thought Esteban, the pregnancy, the miscarriage hadn't meant anything to you. You never once cried, never showed any emotion at all . . . until now."

"I wanted to," Justin looked into her eyes, "but I felt I had to be strong for you. I thought you understood. I hid my emotions—buried them so we could go on as a family, go on as man and wife."

She started crying.

"I'm sorry, Ceren."

Speaking through her tears, she said, "No, I'm the one who's sorry. I don't know why I couldn't see that. Why I couldn't let go of the grief. I just . . ."

His grip tightened. "We just didn't communicate. You thought I didn't care, and I thought you understood."

Catching her breath, she said, "There's something else." She focused on his collar, unable to meet his eyes. "I've always," she swallowed, "always blamed you for that accident."

"Don't you think I haven't blamed myself, as well?" He held her out and stared at her until she met his gaze. "But we can't play that 'what if' game? What if I'd swerved the other way? What if we'd left five minutes earlier or later?" He shook his head. "We can't do that to ourselves."

"Not anymore." She watched his dark eyes. "What are we going to do?"

"What did Angela suggest?"

"According to her, Esteban's spirit can't move on until I . . . until *we* let go. She said his umbilical cord stretches from this world into the next."

"Then I recommend we say a prayer together. Tell Esteban how much we love him, that we love him enough to let him go, and that we release him from our grasp to God's care."

STONE HEART

*"The pain of having a broken heart is not so much as to kill you,
yet not so little as to let you live."*

— ANONYMOUS

As Develyn's birthday party wound down, Angela climbed into Judith's car.

"I'll pick you up tomorrow afternoon on the way back to San Antonio," said Develyn, seeing her off.

"Better idea," said Angela. "Why don't you come by tomorrow morning? Come to church with Mom and me."

Develyn shrugged. "Okay, see you nine thirty-ish?"

"Perfect." Angela waved as Judith drove off.

"Why did you invite her to Mass?" Judith's smile was quizzical. "I'd hoped to have you to myself until later in the afternoon."

Angela bit her lip, trying to put her thoughts into words. "I sense a hunger in her. She's searching for something . . . maybe . . ."

"What?"

"Just had an idea." She turned toward her mother. "Let's go to the mission for Mass tomorrow. It's a beautiful drive, and something tells me it'd be good for Develyn."

Judith nodded and then turned toward Angela. "How did you feel meeting your birth father?"

Angela took a deep breath. "I felt it was a gift."

"A gift?" Judith scowled her disbelief.

Taking in her expression, Angela snickered. "I know he's never taken an interest in me, never been a part of my life." She swallowed. "Ceren told me what he'd done before I was born, but I didn't want to make any assumptions. When I saw him at the party, I recognized him almost immediately. I felt some sort of connection, and I wanted to hear his side of things."

"Did you?"

Snorting, she shook her head. "Not really. He was so remote, almost out of touch with reality." She shrugged. "I don't know. He just seemed a lost soul."

"Did he tell you anything?"

"Other than when he was singing?" She chuckled. "No, I'd hoped to ask him questions about his DNA, or if there were any inherited diseases or physical traits."

"You've got his high cheekbones."

She nodded. "It was that and his incredible blue eyes that made me guess who he was."

"But you'd thought of meeting him?"

Angela heard the sting in her voice. "You're my mom, and Sam was my dad. Ceren and Pastora have been my aunties, but I have to admit." She took a deep breath. "I'd always been curious about my birth father."

Judith's forehead crinkled as she grimaced. "I guess that's understandable." She glanced at her daughter. "Was your curiosity satisfied?"

She looked into space, asking herself the same question. "I'd hoped to hear a reason, even an excuse, why he never tried to get in touch with me, *something*, but he gave very little. I don't think he has anything to give. All I saw in his eyes, in his spirit, was emptiness."

"Did he share anything about his life?"

"He said he regretted many things and asked me to forgive him, but there was no revelation, no emotional disclosure."

"Do you think you'll hear from him again?"

"No," she sighed. "That chapter's closed. While I was talking with him, I had an image of two circles intersecting. Just like geometric circles, the overlap of two social circles can also meet."

Grimacing, she pressed her lips together. "No matter how short lived it was, I'm glad we connected."

Judith and Angela stayed up late, watching an old movie, eating popcorn, and catching up.

When the alarm went off at eight o'clock, Judith hit the snooze button and rolled over.

At eight thirty, Angela knocked on Judith's door. "Coffee's ready."

At nine fifteen, Angela knocked again and cracked Judith's door open. "Develyn's going to be here in a few minutes. Don't you want to get dressed for church?"

Judith groaned. "The spirit's willing, but the flesh is weak."

"Is that a 'no?'"

"Why don't you and Develyn go to the mission, then head straight back to San Antonio? I'll just go to a later Mass here."

Develyn and Angela drove through the Hill Country north of San Antonio, passing arroyos, rolling bluffs, and overlooks on the winding, ever-climbing roads. The closer they got to the mission, the more spectacular the sweeping hilltop vistas.

They passed an old cemetery nestled beneath gnarled, live oaks.

"Ohhh . . ." Develyn's eyes widened as she noted the crooked headstones. "Maybe we should stop and take a rubbing. It'll just take a second."

Angela checked the time. "Mass starts in ten minutes. Can't it wait until afterwards?"

"I guess." Develyn shrugged. "Sure." Then, catching her breath, she pointed to a street sign. "Look at that."

"Dead End." Angela started laughing. "Now that's appropriate." Still chuckling, she looked at her friend. "Why are you so fascinated with cemeteries and tombstones?"

"I told you." Develyn glanced at her. "I was born dying."

"Yeah, I can see how that might influence you initially, but why do you like them so much?"

Develyn shrugged. "Death intrigues me. From my earliest memories, I've always wondered what it would be like to be dead. You know, like mother, like daughter, following in dear old Mom's footsteps." She snorted. "My cousin always said I had a death wish."

"Do you?"

"No." She rolled her eyes, dismissing the thought. "Cemeteries are interesting, that's all. Tombstones have these quirky sayings carved into them that distill a person's whole life into a couple words. I love to read the stones and guess the stories."

"Like what?" Angela turned toward her.

"I saw one Depression, thirties-era headstone for a little boy," said Develyn, her eyes on the road. "It looked homemade—concrete embedded with the boy's marbles."

"Couldn't afford marble, so they used marbles." Angela grunted, thinking. "That and the fact that they'd probably been his toys."

"While the cement was wet, someone used a stick to write 'His Soul in Stone.'"

"Must have been the parents, certainly someone who cared."

"That's what I mean." Develyn glanced at her. "Cemeteries hold memories and history. They're so much more than final resting places. There's something almost alive about them."

Angela snorted. "Ain't that the truth?" Then she turned toward her friend. "Maybe sometime you'd like to visit your mother's grave with me?"

Develyn nodded, her eyes on the road. "Maybe I would at that."

Minutes later, they parked beneath a caliche cliff. Fossilized shells poked out of the chalky rubble, their white remains gleaming in the morning sun. To Angela, it was an open invitation. Surveying the stony smorgasbord, she teased out a calcified, heart-shaped clam. As she turned it in her hand, Develyn leaned over to take a look.

"Oh, you found a bivalve."

SACRED GIFT

"A little souvenir of today's visit. Not a tombstone, but a permanent marker of this shellfish's life." Angela smiled. "Want it?" She held it out to her.

Develyn shook her head. "Thanks, I've got some at home. Love those fossilized hearts, though."

"Hard hearts." Angela chuckled as she tossed it in her purse.

They chatted quietly as they climbed the stone stairs to the open-air chapel. Birds chirping, a summer breeze ruffled their processed, black hair. The peppery, floral scent of sage filling the air, Angela breathed deeply. A few feet from the church, they saw a sign asking for silence.

Turning toward each other, they shrugged but walked on. As they approached, the native limestone and cedar, open-air chapel began to take shape: octagonal. Wood and flagstone tiled the floor. Cedar shakes crowned its roof.

Inside, a vaulted ceiling with cedar rafters and crossbeams lifted their eyes toward the crucifix, hanging between knotty pine louvers. The architecture was more an open-air pavilion than a church. No glass windows or screens interrupted the birds' songs. Their chorus rang from the juniper branches only inches from the paneless 'windows.' Fans overhead moved the cross-draft breezes, providing a comfortable temperature, even in July. They took their seats at hand-fashioned, pine pews topped with carpet samples.

"They look like picnic benches with backrests," Develyn whispered.

Angela nodded but kept silent. She looked at others around her. No kneelers, people had set the remnants on the flagstone floors and were kneeling on them. Following their example, she placed a carpet square in front of her, knelt, and prayed.

The fresh, country air and birds' warbles buoyed her spirit. She felt freer than in a four walled church—less confined, less on display. From the corner of her eye, she peeked at Develyn. Also on her knees, her eyes were closed in prayer.

When the priest began the homily, he told the parable of the seeds that fell on different soils. Then he searched the faces of the congregation.

"You come to Mass on Sundays. You listen to the word of God. He puts seeds in your heart every week, but are His seeds taking root in you? Is your heart trampled soil, hard as concrete from the feet of the travelers, or 'fertile soil'? A seed can't grow in rock. God's word can't penetrate a stone heart. When you listen to His word, does it sink in, take root, or does it wither and die? God's love can only penetrate a hard heart when the person's open to it. Let His seed take root in you and flower."

After Mass, as they walked back to the car, Develyn gestured to the well-worn caliche trail. "This is just like the footpath in the homily."

As if in answer, birds landed along the perimeters of the walkway in front of them, pecking at seeds and insects.

"There's your proof." Angela smiled

Develyn turned to her. "Do you still have that bivalve?"

She nodded. "Why?"

"Mind if I have it? After thinking about it, you're right. It would make a good souvenir of today's visit to the mission."

"Sure." Angela dug in her purse, found the fossil, and handed it to her. "You didn't want it before. What changed your mind?"

Develyn sighed. Narrowing her eyes, chewing her lips, she seemed to search inwardly for the answer. Finally, she shrugged. "I don't know, just the joke you made about hard hearts. Then, when the priest started talking about seed falling on the trampled soil of a footpath, I thought of that fossil. Suddenly, his words made sense. I think this fossilized heart would be a good reminder."

"Of what?"

Develyn took a deep breath and made a futile gesture. "To soften my heart, to be fertile ground for God's word to take seed. Something along those lines." Shaking her head, she laughed. "I'm getting so philosophical these days." She gave Angela a friendly nudge. "You're a bad influence on me."

Quote-Along

*"If they substituted the word 'Lust' for 'Love' in the popular songs
it would come nearer the truth."*

— SYLVIA PLATH

When they got back to San Antonio, Develyn's answering machine was blinking. She pressed the button.

"Dev . . . you there? Pick up. It's me."

"Develyn, give me a call when you get back."

"Dev, it's Travis. There's a Quote-Along at the Draft House this afternoon. Want to go? Call me."

Listening to the third message, Develyn's eyes lit up. "A Quote-Along."

"What's a Quote-Along?" Angela crinkled her forehead.

"It's where they play an old movie and everyone knows the lines. Then you quote along with the characters. Plus, they have props, games, food . . . and beer. It's fun. Want to go?"

Angela grimaced. "I really should work on my paper."

"When's it due?"

"Friday."

She rolled her eyes. "That's then, and this is now." Develyn picked up the phone and dialed. "You've got plenty of time to . . . Travis, it's me. I'm back. Got a friend for my roommate?" She put her hand over the phone and whispered, "He's asking." She nodded to Angela and removed her hand. "What's playing?" She nodded. "Mmm-hmm. Mmm-hmm. Okay, see you then."

Angela read the marquee. *Indiana Jones and the Last Crusade.* As they approached the box office, Develyn waved, and two young men joined them.

"Angela, this is Travis, and . . ." Develyn looked to her friend to finish for her.

"This is my roommate, Kio," said Travis.

They got tickets and found their seats. Travis led Develyn by the hand. Angela followed her, and Kio brought up the rear, so the two girls were seated next to each other.

When they ordered, the waitress checked their IDs. Everyone but Angela was twenty-one.

"Sorry," the waitress said to her, "got to be twenty-one."

"I'll just have a coke."

"In that case, I will, too," said Develyn. When the waitress left, she whispered. "No worries, I've got a flask in my purse."

The attendants handed out kazoos and toy whips. When the theme song played, everyone kazooed along. When Indy used his whip, everyone whipped along. In between, they munched on potato skins and deep-fried mozzarella sticks and quoted the lines along with the characters.

Halfway through the movie, Develyn began sharing more of her time with Travis, her head resting on his shoulder, his arm around her.

As the movie began rolling credits, Kio leaned over and said, "Hey, you two, come up for air. Movie's over."

"Already?" Develyn broke away from Travis and stretched her back.

As they began filing out, Travis waited for Kio as Develyn took Angela aside.

"Travis and I have some unfinished business." Her smirk turned into a grin. "Do you mind if Kio drives you back to the dorm?"

"Develyn," she said uncomfortably, "I don't know the guy."

"He's an astronomy nerd." She snickered. "You're safe." She winked. "He's also Travis's roommate, so if you could take the long way home, I'd appreciate it."

Angela groaned.

"C'mon, Angie, I'll owe you one."

Calling her by Ceren's nickname for her softened Angela's resolve. Rolling her eyes, she sighed. "All right, but you owe me big time."

Develyn gave her a quick squeeze. "Thanks!" Once in the lobby, Develyn paired up with Travis, waved, and said, "See ya."

Blinking, working her jaw, Angela turned to Kio. What she saw in his eyes was fear, which gave her courage.

"Do you feel as uncomfortable as I do?"

He chuckled nervously. "I think awkward's a better word, at least from this side of things." He grimaced. "Sorry."

She shrugged. "It's not your fault."

"Travis said to get lost for a while, but I can take you straight home and then kill time on the River Walk." He raised an eyebrow, as if getting an idea. "That is, unless you'd like to walk with me?"

She looked into his eyes and knew. *I can trust this guy.*

"What do you want to do?"

Shrugging, she smiled. "It's a good night for a walk."

MEA CULPA

*"The passion of hatred is so long lived and so obstinate
a malady that the surest sign of death
in a sick person is their desire for reconciliation."*

— Jean de la Bruyere

When Judith got back from Mass, the phone was ringing. By the time she answered, all she heard was a dial tone. Ten minutes later, it rang again.

Caller ID read "Private Number." Debating whether or not to pick up, she let the answering machine get it.

"Judith?" said a voice that sounded vaguely familiar, yet she did not recognize it.

She picked up. "Yes?"

She heard someone take a deep breath and then pause.

"Who is this?"

"This . . ." He cleared his throat. "This is Tim." As if an afterthought, he added, "Tim Barona."

Judith caught her breath. She moistened her dry lips and asked in a cold monotone, "What is it you want."

"There's something I need to ask you." Again he took a deep breath. "Are you . . . do you know anyone by the name of Faith Truman?"

Her heart stopped. Confronted ear-to-ear by her past, she froze. Seconds ticked by. She debated whether to hang up or tell him off. *How do I respond? Fifty-eight years, a lifetime . . . several. This is my chance. Tell him what I think of him for deserting me, for causing my abortion.* She wracked her brain to remember her well-rehearsed speeches, but nothing came to mind. She was at a loss for words.

"If you don't want to talk to me, I can understand, but . . ." He took another deep breath. "Please let me say something to you, something that's been on my chest for years, that . . ." He grunted. "I'm sorry. I'm so deeply sorry for leaving you, for not explaining . . ." He sighed. "Can you ever forgive me?"

It was Judith's turn to sigh. "I've tried. Over the years, I've even told myself I do forgive you, but the resentment, the hatred, the hurt always come back to haunt me. I don't think I ever can."

"Even now, when I'm asking you to forgive me?"

"This is all so surreal." She shook her head, wondering at the situation. "Meeting Ellen, and then finding out you're her husband. She's the reason—"

"I left you?"

"Exactly." She scoffed. "Why? Why did you run off with her? What made you desert me without so much as a goodbye?"

She heard him swallow, hem and haw. The waiting irritated her. It reminded her of the hours of waiting for his call all those years before, the call that never came.

"I'm listening. You're the one who called me, remember? If you've got something to say, spit it out." Her anger rising, she added, "Try to be a man for once."

"I don't know where to begin."

"Try Christmas vacation fifty-eight years ago, when you were supposed to come home with me, meet my family, so we could announce our engagement. What happened?"

He started slowly. "I don't want to sound . . ." He groaned.

"You're not sounding anything. Except weak." Judith found her voice. "If you don't have anything to say, I'm hanging up." She silently counted to three. "Okay, have a nice life."

Before she could put down the receiver, he said, "Wait, please. The reason I didn't call was because I was forced into marrying Ellen."

Her laugh was sharp. "Forced into marrying." She scoffed. "What'd she do, hold a gun to your head?"

"It's complicated." He grunted. "My father worked for hers. She and I grew up together, but there was always this . . . call it 'class boundary' between us. Then, that winter break, my father talked me into asking her out. One thing led to another, and we . . . got together."

"You mean, you got her pregnant."

He gave a mirthless laugh. "Not really."

"Oh, that's right." Judith recalled Ellen's story from the retreat. "She mentioned she'd had a false pregnancy."

"Hysterical pregnancy is more descriptive." He snorted. "Her father badgered mine, intimidated him, threatened him. My father pressured me, telling me it was my duty. She was crying. I was expected to—"

"Do the right thing," finished Judith. She sighed, believing him. Ellen had given her a similar story from her own perspective. She started to soften, seeing his side of it. Then she got angry with herself for being so easily placated. "What about me?" Her voice came out louder than she had intended. "Why couldn't you at least have been man enough to call me and tell me what had happened?"

He grunted. Then sighed. "I'd meant to. Things just happened so quickly that I put it off until the next day, and then the next."

"What you're trying to say is that you were a coward." She snorted. "You weren't man enough. You left me to deal with your aftermath . . . alone." The bitterness welling up, the memories began flooding her. She remembered the fear of discovering she was pregnant and then the trauma of hearing he had married someone else. "How could you do that to me? How could you have left me to deal with your baby, with the abortion?"

He groaned. "I didn't know you were preg—"

"I told your father I was pregnant. When he told me you'd run off with someone else, I warned him I'd abort his grandchild. Yet you did nothing. You never contacted me." She shook her head, suddenly choked up, reliving the events all over again. She swallowed the lump in her throat, swallowed the pain. "How could you be so heartless?"

"He never told me."

"How could you . . . What?"

Tim repeated his words.

"What do you mean?"

"My father never told me about your phone call, not until years later."

In a small voice, she asked, "You didn't know about the baby?"

He grunted. "Not until my father was on his deathbed. Then he confessed the secret he'd carried all those years."

Judith opened her eyes wide. "When was that?"

"Twenty-one years ago, roughly the same time our daughter Ginny died. It was one of the reasons I was compelled to bring up Develyn. Ellen was too old to have more children, and with Ginny gone, I felt such a void. Then, when my father told me of your pregnancy, I had hoped I had another child somewhere in the world. I did search for you then."

She sneered. "You mustn't have looked very hard."

"I kept up with your published papers, your books. I traced you to the university and through a mutual acquaintance learned you had no children."

"Mutual acquaintance?" She snorted. "You don't mean Jarek."

"Yes, we've known each other a long time."

She mumbled, "I knew there was something about him I didn't like."

"What?"

"Birds of a feather. Go on. You still haven't told me why you never contacted me."

"I learned you didn't have any children, and so many years had passed . . . that . . ."

"You chickened out." She said in disgust. "You're a coward. The only reason you considered looking me up was for your own selfish motives. You wanted an heir." She laughed bitterly. "The irony of it. Long after our baby was dust, you wanted our child. You never cared about me."

"That's not true, Judith." He cleared his throat. "I cared very much for you. I did love you all those years ago, but you're right that I was too cowardly to explain what had happened, why I didn't marry you. I simply couldn't face you."

"So why this sudden change of heart?"

"I'm eighty-seven. I've been carrying this guilt with me nearly sixty years." She heard the pain in his voice. "When you showed up at the party, I realized it was a gift, probably my last chance to ask your forgiveness."

"Right." She sniffed. "How did you ever find my phone number, anyway?"

"Yesterday, Ellen mentioned you lived between Wimberley and San Marcos. Then, when I asked if you lived near the Devil's Backbone, you said you lived on Purgatory Road." He gave a dry laugh. "That was all I needed. The Internet's a wealth of information." He took a deep breath. "Judith, meet me for a cup of coffee. I really would like to apologize in person."

"What?" She scoffed. *Who does he think he is? Who does he think I am? The same naïve girl I was at twenty-six?* "You're really too much, you know that? You expect to snap your fingers and after fifty-eight years I'll come running. Is that it?"

"No—"

"Well, I'm not the wide-eyed grad student I was when I met you." She groaned. "What were you thinking? Were you planning to sneak around behind Ellen's back the same way you crept around behind mine?"

"No, I—"

"Do you have any idea what you put me through? The misery, the guilt? You're the reason I aborted our baby." She groaned in her anger. "You make one stinking phone call after all these years, say you're sorry, and expect everything to be just hunky-dory."

"That's not what I—"

"Well, mister, you can take your sanctimonious apology and put it where the sun doesn't shine."

She slammed down the phone. Trembling with anger, she took a container of hibiscus tea from the refrigerator and poured a glass. Her hands shook so much, she dropped it. The glass shattered, scattering the shards and red tea across the floor.

Blood. It looks like blood.

Her mind flashed back to the recovery room in the abortion clinic. With a sinking heart, she recalled feeling the flow of blood between her legs. *Not menstrual blood, but Helen's blood.*

She began wiping up the mess and, in the process, sliced her hand on the broken glass. *More blood.*

Wrapping gauze around her hand, she left the mess and staggered to the lantana rock garden in the backyard. Stopping in front of Helen's makeshift memorial, she saw the stone propped up against the live oak where she'd left it. Helen's place. Covering her eyes with her hands, she began sobbing. *Helen.* The sobs shook her body as the tears began.

He asked me to forgive him, but I don't believe him. I can't believe he's truly sorry.

A breeze blew through the tree, rustling its leaves overhead.

Forgive.

Judith flinched. She looked around quickly to see who was there but saw no one. *It must have been the wind.* She took a deep breath, trying to still her rapidly beating heart. Closing her eyes to compose herself, she willed her mind quiet. Then she tried to communicate.

Helen, how can I forgive him? I can't even forgive myself.

Again a breeze blew through the tree, rustling its leaves overhead.

Forgive.

I heard that. "Who's there?"

Judith's eyelids flew open just in time to glimpse the crocheted, white hem of a dress slip behind the tree. *The giggling girl? Did I imagine that?* Her mind flashed back to the Basilica of Our Lady of Guadalupe, where she had seen the giggling girl nearly nineteen years before.

She stepped behind the ancient tree but knew, even before she saw, there would be nothing, no one. Then she heard a crash. Judith rounded the tree in time to see Helen's headstone fall forward, cleanly breaking in half.

A breeze blew through the tree a third time, rustling its leaves overhead.

FORGIVE.

This time, Judith got the message. A shiver ran down her spine despite the oppressive July weather. Squaring her shoulders, she strode back to the kitchen, took the phone off the hook, and dialed *69. As it rang on the other end, she felt butterflies in her stomach. *What if he hangs up? What if he answers?*

A recorded voice spoke. "Leave a message after the beep."

She mustered her resolve and swallowed. *If not for you, for Helen.*

Her voice a ragged whisper, she struggled to mean her message. "I forgive you."

STARRY-EYED

"I am but a firefly caught in his jar and when he looks at me,
I can't help but glow."

— KELLIE ELMORE

Kio parked near the River Center, and they entered the procession. Filled with lights, laughter, and the promise of excitement, the River Walk bustled with people. Parents pushing baby carriages strolled past them. Children followed, twirling light sticks in the twilight. Couples of all ages walked by, some hand in hand, some single file. Young adults on the lookout for Miss or Mr. Right watched each passerby expectantly. Angela could almost sense their hormones and pheromones infusing the night. The air tingled with electricity, and the anticipation was contagious.

Restaurants, outdoor cafes, and bars lined the River Walk, their sizzling specialties adding to the mélange of scents and sensations. The heady aromas of barbeque, grilled brisket, hot dogs, fajitas, roasted peppers, and caramelized onions mingled and melded. Table after table of people dined al fresco under multicolored umbrellas. Strains of live jazz and mariachi music wafted onto the sidewalk, subtly changing the ambiance as they walked by, adding to the party-like atmosphere.

To keep from getting separated in the crowd, they held hands. Logistically, it made sense, and it only seemed strange for a moment. After the initial jolt, it seemed natural. Angela's hand fit into his, and it felt right.

The only problem was the noise level.

"Ever been on the Museum Reach?" Kio turned toward her as he raised his voice above the hubbub.

She shook her head.

Smiling, he said, "Follow me."

Half of her balked, wanted to turn back. *Though noisy, there's safety in numbers.* The other half trusted him, was curious about him. She suspended judgment.

"Okay."

They turned right at the "Museum Reach" sign post. Immediately, the crowd thinned. The decibel level lowered. Within minutes, very few people even passed by. They could talk. They could hear each other. More, without the surrounding canyon walls of the high-rises, the twilight breezes seemed to blow through that branch of the river, cleansing the air.

As if she had removed a tight bra, Angela could fill her lungs. She took a deep breath, feeling free from the noise, the crowds. Here, it was just Kio and Angela.

Acting as her personal guide, he directed her attention to the knobby cypress knees, the majestic palms, and the pecan trees that lined the river. Fingers to lips, he shushed her as they passed a row of sleeping ducks perched on the rocky stepping stones just offshore. He silently pointed out their bills, tucked beneath their wings to keep out the fading light. His eyes, crinkling at the corners, caught hers in a gentle smile.

He called her attention to the landscaping. Hibiscus, angel's trumpet, and lantana lined the landscaped banks along the meandering path. Night blooming jasmine began releasing its scent. Yellow-crowned night herons fished in the shallow waters beside them. The more they talked, the farther they walked. Suddenly, a huge concrete structure loomed in front, straddling the river.

"Is that a dam?" she asked.

Nodding, he pointed. "Texas' only river lock and dam makes the nine-foot water level conform to the river's new section. As the lock gates close, water rushes in or out, raising or lowering the boat. The whole process takes less than five minutes. Want to watch?"

They stood on a bridge overlooking the lock and watched a river taxi progress through it. Farther ahead, they passed a rock grotto, walking behind its waterfall. Angela shuddered and laughed aloud as errant drops sprayed her neck, sending goose bumps down her spine.

As they approached the Jones Avenue Bridge, Angela listened. At first, it sounded like a video arcade. Then it sounded like animals.

"What is that?"

"That's sound sculpture."

"What?"

He chuckled. "Sequenced speakers under the bridge pitch 'sound art' from a blend of recorded broadcasts. It's called 'Sonic Passage.'"

"Ceren would love this. She likes anything to do with art."

"Who's Ceren?"

She told him about her birth mother and the open adoption while they meandered along the winding path.

"What does the name mean?"

"Ceren?" She looked up at him. "It's Turkish for young gazelle or fawn." Then Angela cocked her head. "I've never heard of the name Kio before. Is it a family name, or does it mean something in another language?"

He grinned. "It's the Chinese name for Spica, the brightest star in Virgo. The constellation shows a goddess holding sheaves of grain. Spica marks the grain in her hand. In fact, the star's so bright, it was used to discover the precession of the equinoxes." His eyes twinkled.

"Really?" She looked at his eyes and smiled. "Are you Chinese?"

"One-sixteenth. My great-grandmother was half Chinese."

"Interesting. So the stars must have predestined that you'd be an astronomy major."

He shrugged. "There may be some truth to that."

"Why?"

"My father's an astronomer."

"Then he named you?"

"Not really. My great-grandmother said the Chinese believe Spica's a lucky star. Since my birthday's in September and I was born a Virgo, she said I was—"

"Born under a lucky star." Angela spoke the words along with Kio, and they laughed.

As twilight began to fall, they passed beneath a colorful school of larger-than-life fiberglass fish dangling from the Interstate 35 overpass. By the time they reached the Pearl Brewery, it was nearly dark.

"Want to take the rio taxi back to the River Center?"

She nodded. "It was great walking while it was light, but I wouldn't mind sitting down for a ride back."

"We walked a good mile and a half, maybe two. Besides, twilight's supposed to be the best time to see the bridge art works."

They caught an open-air river taxi just as the moon began to rise. Passing under the Lexington Street Bridge, they saw reflective, suspended prisms dancing in the breeze, scattering flashes of color. As they passed beneath the McCullough Bridge, glittering, steel mesh panels pulsed to life with an array of ever-changing hues.

Sitting beside each other, Angela could sense the rise and fall of Kio's breathing. In the quiet of the early evening, the only sound was the wash of the water against the boat. Though there was no crowd to separate them, she continued holding his hand. She liked the connection.

With his other hand, Kio pointed out the summer sky. "With all this light scatter, it's hard to see the stars, but do you see those three?"

"Yeah."

"That's the Summer Triangle: Vega, Altair, and Deneb." He brought his hand down. "You can't really see them in the city, but three constellations are associated with those stars: Lyra, the Harp; Aquila, the Eagle; and Cygnus, the Swan."

Then he pointed to the Big Dipper and traced his finger downward towards a bright star on the right. "Arc to Arcturus." He continued to curl his finger down and to the right until he pointed to the brightest star. "Then spike to Spica."

"Your star." She smiled up at his face. "As an astronomy major and a 'lucky star' in your own right, of course, you'd know that." Then she remembered the mission tour. "I learned something interesting at Mission Concepción recently. By any chance, have you heard about local solar illuminations?"

"Oh, yeah." Even in the dark, Angela could see his eyes light up. "Both Missions Concepción and Espada have them."

"Really?" She turned toward him, brushing against him in the close proximity of the river taxi. "What can you tell me about them?"

He reacted to her touch, drawing nearer, but Angela sensed it was their intellectual rapport, the meeting of their minds, that prompted his response. His eyes opening wide, his face became animated as he shared his knowledge.

"Mission Concepción has three illuminations." He thought for a moment, adding, "Five if you count the analemma."

"Count the what?" Squinting, she cocked her head to the side.

"An analemma's a graph of the sun's position measured at the same time of day from the same place, something like time-lapse photography. It's not an object. It's the path the sun takes over the course of twelve months." He looked at her, his gaze challenging. "Can you guess its shape?

She shrugged. "The earth's path around the sun is elliptical, so I guess it'd be oblong, oval." She looked up for confirmation.

"Not exactly. An analemma looks like a lopsided figure eight." She shook her head. "Can't picture it."

He scratched his neck and tried again. "Think of a flat bowling pin. It's got a large, oblong bottom and a short, oblong top."

"Okay, that makes sense."

"What we'd see if we took a snapshot of the sun's position every day and then graphed it on a chart would be the outline of a big bowling pin. From earth, it looks like the sun loops back on itself, crossing its own path, and then repeating it a second time in a lopsided figure eight."

"One end would be the winter solstice, and the other would be the summer solstice."

"Right."

His nod encouraging, she pushed further. "The earth rotates around the sun, and it's in a different position each month. You're saying that, during the analemma, the sun's rays spotlight the very same place on earth twice a year since those two days share the same sunrise and sunset."

"Exactly." Leaning toward her in his enthusiasm, he held out his closed hand for a fist bump.

His response struck her as funny. As she bumped fists with him, she started chuckling. Though she tried to curb it, she couldn't.

"What's so funny?" Blinking, he lost the glimmer in his eyes. As her chuckles turned into giggles, his smile faded. Finally, he said in a monotone voice, "Sorry if I'm boring you with this."

"No, not at all." Looking into his wounded eyes, she saw she had hurt his feelings. She lightly touched his arm. "I'm sorry. It's just that when you said 'exactly' it sounded like a sigh of relief." She hunched her shoulders. "Am I that hard to teach, that dense?"

She watched the light return to his eyes. "No, just the opposite." His mouth curled into a shy grin. "I'm just glad we were connecting, relieved our conversation's making sense to you. I'm not used to talking about the sky with anyone but my father and other astronomy nerds."

She nodded. "Astronomy's obviously important to you." She grinned. "I'm glad because solar illuminations are something that captured my imagination, too. The docent at the mission said that on Assumption, Aug—"

"August fifteenth the sun illuminates the altar."

Her jaw dropped. "You know about that?"

He nodded. "We studied it last semester." His face lit up. "In fact, it's something I'd really like to see."

"So would I." Caught up in his enthusiasm, she nodded, seconding the motion.

They looked into each other's eyes and blinked. He swallowed. "Would you like to go together?"

Raising her eyebrow, Angela gave a slight shrug. "Sure." She felt his hand gently squeeze hers.

LIKE A HORSE AND CARRIAGE

"First best is falling in love. Second best is being in love. Least best is falling out of love. But any of it is better than never having been in love."

— MAYA ANGELOU

On August fifteenth, Kio picked her up early. When they arrived at Concepción Mission, they found seats in the front pews, almost under the dome, along the center aisle.

"Front and center." Angela stood on tiptoe to whisper in Kio's ear. "We've got a good view."

As the docent entered the area in front of the main altar, beneath the dome, he asked, "What's an illumination?"

A woman sitting in the pew across the aisle raised her hand. "It's when the sun appears to light up or even move across an object. For instance, in Chichen Itza, during the spring equinox, the sun seems to slither down the pyramid, like a snake, connecting with a stone carving of a serpent's head at the stairs' base."

The docent nodded. "Good example, would anyone else like to describe an illumination?" When no one else raised their hand, he said, "For our purposes, an illumination occurs when the sun's rays enter a church and appear to move across an architectural feature, such as a transept crossing, altar, or carved plaque, or across portable art, such as a painting or statue. On special days of seasonal, religious, and astronomical importance, the rays illuminate specific areas. What's the significant day today?"

Members of the group said, "The Feast of the Assumption."

He nodded. "Today's illumination is my favorite. It's the only one whose path starts in the pews, as if touching us with the finger of God. It's the only one you can stand in and be blinded by the sun's radiance."

One of the group raised his hand. "You mentioned that the illumination moves across a feature or work of art. What do you mean?"

"'Moves across' isn't quite the right term." He grimaced, as if concentrating. "It's what we see, what we perceive. The reality is that the feature or artwork is stationary on earth, but earth is revolving through the fixed beams of the sun."

"You mean, like sunrise?" asked someone.

He nodded. "That's a good example. The sun doesn't actually rise. What we see isn't really what's happening. The earth moves, not the sun. Our place on the earth's surface is constantly rotating around the sun, rotating into the sun's rays. We're basically riding a spinning ball, tilted at an angle, traveling in an elliptical orbit around the sun."

The docent stepped into the illumination's rays. "Concepción was designed to catch those sun beams and bring them in through the windows. During Assumption, the illumination moves across the floor and passes under the center of the dome, which is an architectural feature of importance."

"Why's the dome important?" asked a tour member. "What's special about it?"

"The meaning may have been lost through time." The docent shrugged. "Or it may have a symbolic significance. For instance, the Brunelleschi dome on the Florentine cathedral built during the Renaissance was considered symbolic of placing man and his abilities at the epicenter of the world."

"Does this solar illumination happen every year, every Feast of the Assumption?" a woman asked.

He nodded. "This is just one of five illuminations. They're all annual phenomena, but this one's especially symbolic because the light crosses the center of this cruciform church." He pointed at the circular window above the choir loft. "Watch how the sunlight's focused through that window, falls on the floor, and makes its way to the center of the church, right beneath the dome."

Angela turned toward the incoming light and winced. "Oh, that's bright."

"Really intense," said Kio, shading his eyes.

The docent squinted as he peered up at the incoming light. "It's like looking into a high-powered spotlight."

The group watched the beam of light crawl across the pews, across the flagstone floor. When it reached the center, beneath the dome, the docent called everyone to come forward for a better view of the two-foot wide sun spot.

A Hispanic woman crossed herself. "Es un signo de Dios."

"Sign from God," whispered Angela, looking at the circular window, the beam of light streaming from it, and the spot under the dome where the sun's reflected light illuminated it. *As if God Himself is highlighting this spot.*

"The Assumption's the second major feast of the Virgin," continued the docent, "so the illumination's appropriate. In fact, astronomically, it's the only feast day that could occur through a west facing window in this part of the world."

Kio murmured and nodded his head, agreeing.

"Concepción is four point two percent off the true cardinal points. The sun's altitude is twenty-one point eight degrees, and the azimuth is two hundred and seventy-four point one degrees. True west is—"

"Two hundred and seventy degrees," said Kio.

"Precisely," said the docent. "So who had the mathematical know-how to construct this solar observatory? Was it the Franciscan friars or the Free Masons who built it?"

"Franciscans," said Kio, his arms crossed.

The docent nodded. "It probably was the Franciscans. There's substantial evidence to support the Franciscan siting and construction of the missions in California as solar observatories, so why not here, as well? After all, the friars had access to the ten *Books on Architecture* by the Roman Vitruvius, and recently church documents were uncovered that actually specified this particular style of alignment architecture."

Tongue-in-cheek, Kio whispered to Angela. "And detractors say the Church is anti-science."

She rewarded him with a lopsided grin.

"Solar geometry," said the docent, "means the mission churches were positioned so that sunlight would stream through the windows and illuminate a feature, artwork, or tabernacle on a particular date, usually the feast day of the saint spotlighted. In today's case, it's the Feast of the Assumption. On August twenty-ninth, we're blessed with a second illumination." He chuckled. "I call it the Last Judgment, and that one crosses over the main altar tabernacle with another story all of its own. Thank you, folks, this concludes today's illumination demonstration, but I hope to see you all again in two weeks."

"However," the priest quickly added, "I invite you to stay for the Mass that follows. Sacred geometry is what inspired the Franciscan friars to synchronize the sun's path with the church's architecture, but it's God's word that inspired them to build this sanctuary."

"Want to stay for Mass?" asked Angela.

With a nod, Kio agreed. "Might as well. We're here." Then he grinned. "But first, let's see if we can get a better view of the illumination from the choir loft." He grabbed her hand in his. "Quick, before it moves away."

After church, they went to the River Walk for dinner. Finding an open-air table beneath one of the multicolored umbrellas, they watched the flat-bottomed tour boats float by.

Savoring their smoked shrimp enchiladas and chicken fried steak fajitas, Angela felt something flutter against her neck. She turned just in time to see a grackle swing around the side of her head, swoop down, snatch a taco chip from her plate, and fly off, chip in beak.

Chuckling, she turned to Kio. "Did you see that? The little thief's wings brushed my neck as he did a U-ie and stole my chip."

Overcome with laughter, all he could do was nod as he held his sides. Finally, with tears in his eyes, he said, "Best dinner show ever."

They strolled along the River Walk after dinner. As the lights began shimmering in the dusk, Kio asked, "How would you like to take a carriage ride?"

Her eyes opening wide, she looked at him, seeing him in a new light. *What a romantic. I never would have guessed.*

"I'd love it."

They climbed up the stairs to street level. Parked at the corner was a dappled-gray draft horse hitched to a Cinderella-pumpkin carriage. The carriage frame was festooned with blinking, white LED lights.

"This one all right?"

"Oh, yeah." Angela nuzzled the horse, gently stroking its velvet-soft mouth.

Then Kio held out his hand as he helped her into the carriage. As she nestled against him, the horse and carriage began moving. She rested her head on his shoulder, listening to the clip-clop of the horse's hooves on the pavement.

The sound reminded her of two hearts beating together, separate yet connected. A new concept entered her mind as she peered up at him through her eyelashes. *His heart and mine? Maybe.* She breathed a contented sigh, enjoying the ride.

SACRED SPACES

"We all make choices, but in the end our choices make us."

— KEN LEVINE

Freshly showered, Angela sat in bed, reading. Develyn burst in the door.

"Want to go to a party?"

"Are you kidding?" She checked the time and snickered. "It's eleven o'clock. I don't want to get dressed and go out at this hour."

Develyn shrugged. "Suit yourself." She kicked off her heels and, reaching under the bed, felt around for a pair of flats. "But you're only young once."

It was Angela's turn to shrug. She returned to her book as Develyn put on her flats and moved to her desk.

She spoke to her reflection in the mirror as she applied fresh eyeliner.

"How are you and the astronomy nerd getting along?"

"Kio?" Angela looked up from her book and grinned. "Great, in fact, you might call it illuminating."

Pencil poised in hand, she did a double take. "Huh?"

Angela chuckled. "He took me to a solar illumination at church. Then we had dinner on the River Walk and went for a carriage ride."

Putting down her makeup pencil, she paused, looking off into space. In a quiet voice, she said, "Sounds like fun."

"It was." Angela nodded. "How's it going with Travis?"

"Oh, you know." She sighed.

"I thought you went to a party with him." Angela looked at the clock. "An earlier party. What happened?"

"Oh, you know." She shrugged.

"No, I don't. What happened?"

"The party was boring. Loud and boring. Blaring music and trippy freshmen." Scoffing, she shook her head. "It's getting old."

"What is?"

She sighed. "Everything, party after party, night after night. I don't know. It just feels like something's missing."

"Weren't you there with Travis?"

"Yeah." She brushed her hair listlessly.

"Don't you like being with him?"

She sighed. "I guess." Then she snickered. "That is, when he's not sniffing around, flirting."

"I thought you two were a couple."

"I s'pose."

"You're coming in at three o'clock every morning." Raising her eyebrow, Angela looked pointedly at her. "There must be something you like about him."

Develyn snickered. "Yeah, one thing." Then she flicked back her hair from her face. "But even that's getting old."

"From all the nights you've been spending with him, I thought you lov—"

Her lip raised in a sneer, she snorted. "Yeah, right."

"Well, if you don't love him and you're not enjoying it, why do you keep sleeping with him?"

Develyn turned to look at her. Her eyes bloodshot, she looked as if she were in pain.

"I'm so lonely, I can't stand it. I feel empty." She banged her chest with her fist. "Don't you hear a hollow thud?" She sighed. "There's nothing inside me. I just feel dead, except when I'm . . . with Travis. It's the only thing that makes me feel alive."

Angela grimaced. "Maybe if you started seeing other guys, you'd—"

"I don't want to sleep around."

"I didn't mean that." She sighed and started again. "I just meant . . . If you keep on thinking what you've always thought, you'll keep on getting what you've always got."

"That actually makes sense." Develyn gave a wry grin. "If you keep on thinking what you've always thought . . ." She paused, waiting for the line.

"You'll keep on getting what you've always got."

"Where'd you hear that?"

"From my Aunt Pastora."

"She sounds like a smart lady."

"She is." Angela got an idea. "Would you like to meet her?"

Develyn shrugged. "Sure."

"I told her about the illumination at Concepción, and she wants to see it. Want to come with us?"

"Okay, just let me know when." She applied lipstick and stood up. "See ya."

"Where're you going?"

"The party."

Angela let out an exasperated sigh. "I thought you said—"

"Yeah, it's boring, but I can't stand being alone with my thoughts. In case you haven't noticed, I don't much like my own company." She snorted. "At least the noise will keep my mind occupied."

Angela muttered.

"What?"

"Busyness." She shook her head. "You just fill your time with busyness. You're not enjoying what you do. You're not accomplishing anything, and yet you keep on doing it anyway. I don't get you."

"Neither do I." She grimaced and shut the door behind her.

"Are you ready?" Angela called through the door.

"In a minute," called Develyn.

"Hurry up. We have to pick up Pastora and get to church. We don't want to miss the illumination."

Develyn grunted.

Five minutes later, Angela knocked on the bathroom door. "C'mon, we've got to go."

As Develyn opened the door, Angela stared. *Can't put my finger on it, but something's different.* "Are you all right? You look so pale," she said. Angela's eyes narrowed as she scrutinized her.

"I'm fine." Develyn grabbed her purse as if in a trance. "Let's go, already."

"Are you sure you're up to it?"

"Yeah."

Angela noticed the bloodshot eyes and smudged mascara.

"Have you been crying?"

Develyn rolled her eyes and then, sneering, focused a pained expression on her.

"Get real."

Angela parked in front of the convent. Nuns wearing habits were chatting in small groups, entering and leaving the building.

Develyn sat up straight, looking. "What is this place?"

"This is where Pastora lives. Back in a minute."

"Your aunt's a nun?" Develyn's eyes opened wide.

"Uh-huh." She nodded.

"Really? You might've mentioned it."

"Why?"

Develyn fastened her blouse's top button, covering her tattoo. "I don't know." She mumbled uneasily. "For one thing, I would've dressed differently."

"Relax, Pastora's great." Angela grinned. "She's never met a person she didn't like."

Then Develyn's eyes took on a wistfulness as she spoke with her hands.

"I've always felt an affinity for nuns," she squinted, as if searching for the right words, "a respect for them, a connection, but from afar, you know what I mean? Always wanted to sit near them, talk to them, but, until now, I'd never had the opportunity. This is the first time I've ever actually met one."

"Don't worry. Pastora's the most down-to-earth person I know, and she always seems to say just the right thing." Angela grinned. "You can try if you like, but it's not possible to feel uncomfortable around her. She'll put you right at ease."

A few minutes later, Angela spotted Pastora seated in the main room, her back to the door. Putting her arms around her shoulders, she gave her aunt a quick hug and then moved around to the front.

"Angela, I knew it was you before I saw you." Pastora smiled warmly, her clouded eyes sparkling. "I recognized your scent, Vanilla Missions."

"Nana's scent."

"Nana's scent," Pastora repeated, nodding. She leaned toward Angela and breathed deeply as they walked out the door. "It takes me back."

Angela smiled at her favorite aunt. "Ready to view the illumination?"

"Illumination," repeated Pastora with a chuckle. "Funny you should phrase it that way." She surveyed her niece. "There's something I need to discuss with you, something that may be long overdue."

"Okay." She scrutinized her aunt's face. *Wonder what this is about?*

As they approached the car, Develyn jumped out of the passenger seat and held the door open.

"This is my roommate, Develyn," said Angela, gesturing toward her, "and this is my aunt, Pastora."

"Pleasure to meet you." Develyn gave a nervous laugh.

"What a remarkable name."

"I was baptized Debra Evelyn, but everyone calls me Develyn."

"So tell me, Develyn." Cataracted eyes twinkling, Pastora smiled her little girl grin. "Are you a little devil?"

For once, the girl was speechless, but Angela noticed a wry smile tug at the corner of her mouth.

Inside the mission, the three women sat in the front pews along the center aisle, near where Angela had sat with Kio.

"It's got the best view." Angela smiled as she followed Pastora into the pew. Trailing, Develyn sat on the aisle. Even as they took their seats, the illumination was beginning to slowly move across the main altar.

Pastora cocked her head and listened. "Do you hear that?" she whispered.

Angela nodded, but before she could answer, the docent welcomed them with a smile.

Directing their attention to the altar, he said, "I call this the Last Judgment."

From the corner of her eye, Angela saw Develyn flinch.

"As you can see," said the docent, pointing, "the illumination lights the tabernacle. This actually occurs on two dates: today, August twenty-ninth, and again on April thirteenth. This is the most complex of the illuminations, and it requires an understanding of three things." He counted them off on his fingers. "The analemma, the solar identity of the two dates, and the friars' apocalyptic belief."

As he gave a technical description of the analemma, Angela traced the outline of an infinity symbol on her hand. "Think of a figure eight," she whispered to Pastora and Develyn.

"The second thing you need to understand," said the docent, "is the solar identity of the two dates." He held up two fingers. "The sun rises and sets at the same time on only two days: August twenty-ninth and April thirteenth. This is important because they occur at the analemma's center."

"Where the figure eight crosses," Angela whispered, again tracing the outline of an infinity symbol on her hand and pointing to its narrowest point.

"These illuminations all fit into the Franciscan friars' devotion to Mary and their apocalyptical world view." He pointed to the round window at the back of the church and then used a laser pointer to trace the path of the sun's rays. "The Last Judgment illumination comes through that window and crosses the tabernacle at the main altar."

"This might sound like a dumb question," said one of the people in the tour group, "but what's significant about the main altar?"

"It's a great question. In fact, it's such a good question, I'm going to give you two answers." The docent grinned. "Let's start with the painting above the altar. Who's the central figure with the outstretched hands?" When no one answered, he asked, "Is it a painting of Jesus?"

Nods and murmurs agreed it was.

"Look more closely. It's a painting of the Virgin Mary." The docent winked. "It's not a painting of Jesus or the expected crucifix. It's a painting of the Holy Mother. Why?" His eyes took in the group. When no one answered, he asked, "What's the name of this mission?"

"Concepción."

"The Franciscans were devoted to Mary, and this solar illumination underscores the importance of the Immaculate Conception. That's the first answer." Again he counted on his fingers. "The second answer is the tabernacle. What do they keep in the tabernacle?"

"The Holy Eucharist," said another of the group.

"Precisely. The tabernacle, placed on the main altar, is the focus of the entire church. Jesus is the focus, the center of the church, the center of Christianity. So there, my friends, are the two answers. Jesus and Mary are the foci of the Last Judgment's illumination."

"Why do you call it the Last Judgment illumination?" asked Develyn in a small voice.

"As you recall, I said you need to understand three things: the analemma, the solar identity of the two dates, and the apocalyptic belief of the friars. We've covered the first two. Now, to discuss the Franciscans' apocalyptic belief, we need to walk to the back of the church."

"What do you mean when you say 'apocalyptic belief?'" called someone from the back.

"It's a belief that the world will end very soon, even within a person's own lifetime. If you'll follow me, I'll show you two chapels." He led them beneath the choir loft. "To the right, they had a Chapel of Gabriel to sound the trumpet."

As they walked inside, a man pointed out the rope hanging from the ceiling.

"What's this for?"

"It rings the church bell." The docent grinned. "Okay, normally Gabriel sounds the trumpet, but, in Concepción's case, he may just ring the bell."

The group chuckled as he led them to the chapel to the left.

"The Franciscans also had a Chapel of St. Michael the Archangel to defend them, so they were prepared for the end of the world. They had Gabriel to warn them and Michael to defend them."

The same man spoke up from the back. "I still don't understand why you call it the 'Last Judgment' illumination."

Develyn repeated under her breath, "Last Judgment."

"It's the apocalyptic view that the world's going to end. The message to us is to prepare for judgment, which brings us to the winter solstice, December twenty-first," said the docent. "On that day, the shortest day of the year, Concepción has another illumination. Christ, as the Light of the World, appears as an illumination."

"Does it also come from the circular window?"

"No." The docent pointed to the dome. "The sun comes through the south dome window during the month of December and crosses over the face of the altar on the north wall. This is the midwinter 'Resurrection' illumination, proof that Christ rose from the darkness, rose from death, and resurrected."

As they filed out of the St. Michael Chapel and the docent led them toward the library, Angela noticed Develyn was not behind them. She glanced around the church and saw her kneeling in front of the Our Lady of Guadalupe painting. When she saw that Pastora was listening to the docent, engaged with the tour, Angela decided to wait at the front pew for Develyn to finish her prayer.

Finally, Develyn stood and turned toward her. As she did, their eyes met, and Angela saw her mascara and tear streaked face. Develyn looked away, swiping at her tears, and Angela hurried forward.

"What's wrong?"

"Nothing." Her voice caught, and she cleared it.

"Yeah, I can see that." She pointed to her cheek. "You missed a streak."

Her hand to her face, Develyn shook her head. "Actually, I've missed a lot of things, and, for the record, everything's wrong."

Angela put her arm on her shoulders and led her to the pew. "C'mon, sit down and tell me." She glanced over her shoulder. The church was empty. "Everyone's still busy with the tour. What's going on?"

"To start with, this." Develyn pulled three crumpled hundred dollar bills from her pocket.

Angela looked at the damp, green papers. "What's it for?"

Her narrowed eyes were the color of flint. "Payment for services rendered." Her voice sounded like gravel. Again, she cleared it.

"Travis?"

"You guessed it."

"As long as I'm guessing, you're pregnant?"

"Two for two."

"And this is his subtle suggestion to get an abortion."

Her face contorted as she spit out the word. "Bingo."

What can I say? Angela took a deep breath. "How can I help?"

"You can't. No one can. This is something I have to figure out for myself."

"What about your grandmother?"

Develyn rolled her eyes. "She went through this with my mother. She won't want to go through this again with me." Her shoulders slumped. "Besides, we've never been very close."

"Then what are you going to do?"

"I don't know." She sighed. Pressing her lips together, she glanced at the painting. "Been wondering that myself."

Angela followed her glance and then looked at the crumpled money. "Besides giving you this 'tip,' did Travis have anything to say?"

"He wanted to know why I was so stupid as to get pregnant." Angela raised her eyebrow.

"Let me guess again. You don't believe in taking—"

"I don't do pills or drugs of any kind, including birth control pills." Her eyes narrowed. "He knows that. He always used protection. Then he asked if it was his baby."

Angela took a deep breath. "Nice guy." She shook her head.

"Yeah, real gem." Develyn snorted.

"Don't worry." Angela tightened her grip around her shoulders. "Even if Travis isn't there for you, you've got me. We'll figure something out."

"Figure what out?" asked Pastora, suddenly appearing at the end of the pew.

"Nothing," said Develyn, swiping her eyes and looking away.

Pastora glanced at her niece. Angela felt it disloyal to share Develyn's confidence, so she pursed her lips and looked down.

"Tell me." Looking from girl to girl, Pastora asked, "Does this 'nothing' have anything to do with a boy?"

The girls exchanged glances.

Pastora swallowed a wry grin. "I'll take that as a 'yes.'" Her grin fading, she looked at Develyn and sighed. "It's not the first time I've seen these telltale mascara streaks. Are you pregnant?"

Again the girls exchanged glances.

As if she were asking the time, Pastora quietly said, "How far along?"

Develyn bit her lip, glanced at Angela, and shrugged. "Seven or eight weeks."

"How's the boy taking it?"

Develyn rolled her eyes. Then she held up the three damp bills.

"I see." Pastora took a deep breath. "What are you going to do about the baby?"

"I'm not ready for a baby. I haven't even finished school."

Pastora's eyes drilled into hers. "What I asked was, 'What are you going to do about the *baby?*'" When she didn't answer, Pastora added, "Babies don't always come along at opportune moments. Ready or not, in about seven months that baby's going to need a home and a lot of attention."

"I can't wait seven months. I don't have that kind of time to wait around, doing what? Crocheting booties? I have to finish school."

"What's stopping you from attending school while you're pregnant?"

Shaking her head, Develyn grunted in frustration. "Oh, I don't know. Money? A place to stay?"

"Can your parents help with that?"

Develyn exchanged a glance with Angela. "Not really." She leveled her eyes at Pastora, challenging her. "I don't have parents. My grandparents raised me after my mother died trying to abort me."

Pastora responded as if she had been slapped. With a gasp, her head snapped back, and her face went pale.

"Besides," said Develyn, scowling. "It's not like it's a baby. It's more like a ... a ... weed growing inside me. Something I just want to rip out by its roots and be done with it."

"Weed ..." Pastora repeated the word. Then, in a gentle voice, she asked, "Are you familiar with the Parable of the Weeds?"

She rolled her eyes. Then, frowning, Develyn shook her head.

"A farmer sowed wheat seed in his field," said Pastora. "While everyone was asleep, his enemy sowed weeds among the wheat.

When the wheat sprouted, the weeds also appeared. The workers suggested pulling up the weed seedlings, but the farmer advised patience, saying, 'Let both grow together until the harvest. At that time, gather the wheat. Then collect the weeds and burn them.'"

Develyn leveled her narrowed eyes at Pastora. "So what's that got to do with me?"

"At this stage, it's too early to tell the wheat from the weed."

"If we're talking about 'seed,'" she hissed, "it's bad." Grimacing, she rolled her eyes. "Trust me. Travis's sperm isn't capable of sowing anything but 'weeds.'"

At her words, Pastora blinked but otherwise appeared unruffled. "The moral of the parable is patience," she said. "Don't rush to judge. Don't make any snap decisions. Have you ever had a bad opinion of someone and found out later you were wrong? Whenever we don't have the full picture, our judgment can be flawed, and it's difficult to separate the blessings from the curses. What's wheat can look like weeds. Aren't we lucky God's got the bigger picture?"

"So you're telling me to carry this baby to term, deliver it, and then see whether it's weed or wheat seed?" Her lip raised in a sneer, her tone was sarcastic.

"I'm asking you to be patient, and not just with this decision about your baby. Be patient with yourself, too. In fact, be as patient as God is with you. Whatever you lack, He'll provide for you. Remember, your baby—*and you*—are still works in progress."

"You're telling me to 'judge not that ye not be judged.'" Develyn pointed to the illumination still barely visible on the wall. "But the whole theme of tonight's illumination is the 'Last Judgment.'" She tapped her chest. "I'm not the one judging so much as the one being judged. God's not providing for me. He's judging me, just like my grandparents have always judged me." Swallowing, she looked Pastora in the eye. "They've always blamed me for my mother's death. Even though I survived a botched abortion, they somehow held me accountable for her death."

228

"Then you of all people should realize how 'bad seed' can produce good results. You survived and thrived." Pastora's eyes remained calm. "Don't let others' judgments color your views. Don't do to your baby what was done to you. Don't pronounce a death sentence on the seed developing inside your body."

"And how would I live for the next seven months?"

"Your grandparents have nurtured you all these years," said Pastora. "I can't believe they wouldn't help you now. Talk to them."

Develyn curled her lip. "Disowning me would be their 'Last Judgment.'"

"You're worried about what they'll say?" Pastora glanced at the painting of Our Lady of Guadalupe, and her face lit up with her little girl smile. "I know of another unwed mother."

Develyn followed her glance. "Mary?"

Pastora nodded. "Don't you think she also wondered what people would say? God took care of her, just as He'll provide for you and your baby. Give Him a chance. Let Him work His miracles through those around you."

Develyn grimaced. "I'll think about it." Then she looked around until she spotted the poor box. "But first, there's something I have to do." She strode to the alms box, stuffed the damp, hundred dollar bills through the slit, and took a deep breath.

"Who's up for dinner?" asked Angela as they left the mission's parking lot.

"Sorry, but you'd better count me out." Develyn scowled. "Food and I don't get along very well anymore. Besides, I don't think I'd be very good company."

"We can go to your favorite Tex-Mex bakery and restaurant, where you took us when Ceren was here." Angela watched her response in the rearview mirror.

Develyn sneered. "Oh, yeah. As I recall, I was craving chilies that day. Should've guessed then I was—"

"C'mon, it'll be fun." Angela tried to coax her through the rearview mirror.

"Thanks, but no thanks. Just drop me off at the dorms." She took a deep breath. "I need to do some thinking."

Visibility of the Invisible

"Some people can't see the color red.
That doesn't mean it isn't there . . . ."

— Sue Grafton

After Angela drove Develyn home, she took her aunt to their favorite restaurant, a quiet bistro with tufted, overstuffed booths where they could talk. Sitting across from each other, Pastora leveled her eyes at Angela.

"Develyn could use a friend right now."

"I'll do all I can," she said. "Just not sure what to do."

"Sometimes people let a clue slip into their conversation," said Pastora. "Has she ever hinted about a leaning, an inclination toward anything?"

Angela started to shake her head no and then recalled Develyn's conversation outside the convent.

"She did say she felt an affinity," she grinned as she looked at her aunt, "toward nuns."

"Really." Pastora's face lit up. "In that case, there's someone I'd like her to meet, who I think might be able to reach her, relate to her. Can you arrange a time for us to chat?"

"Sure, what about Sunday Mass at the Mission of Divine Mercy and then talk afterwards?"

"Perfect."

Angela smiled at her aunt. "Now that we have a game plan, what was it you'd wanted to discuss earlier?"

"Your cologne."

Angela squinted, wondering if she had heard correctly. "My cologne?"

Pastora folded her hands. Hunching her shoulders, she smiled her impish grin and nodded.

Angela raised her forehead skeptically. "You want to wear Vanilla Missions?"

Pastora giggled like a young girl. "No, I want to tell you what inhaling the scent of Vanilla Missions has done for me."

"This ought to be good." Angela's smile was dubious.

"You know it was my mother's scent."

She nodded. "Nana's."

Her face beamed. "It's lifted the veil for me."

"Okay." She studied her aunt. "In what way?"

Angela watched Pastora's face lose its animation, as if a shadow passed over her.

"I'm going to confide something to you that, except for my spiritual advisor, I haven't told anyone else in decades."

"Wow." Angela raised her eyebrow. "What's brought this on?"

"You've opened my eyes, lifted the wool, you might say."

"I have?" Angela blinked. "How?"

Her aunt squirmed. "When I was a young girl, I saw," she took a deep breath, "spirits."

Angela felt her jaw drop. "Wait a minute." She snickered. "Aren't you the person who said there's no such thing as spirits?"

Pursing her lips, she nodded.

Angela caught herself before she rolled her eyes. "Aren't you the same person who lectured me about the cult of spirits being nothing but a substitute religion?"

Her lips still pursed, she nodded and heaved a sigh.

Angela held up her hands, palms upturned. "I give up. What happened to change your mind?"

Pastora fixed her childish grin on her again. "You."

"Me? How?"

"As I said, you've opened my eyes. Actually, my nostrils." Smiling, she leaned toward Angela and inhaled her fragrance. "Remember that day you, Judith, and I met for lunch?"

Angela nodded.

"Your scent brought back not only memories of my mother but," she took a deep breath, "my mother's spirit."

"Let me get this straight. You saw Nana's spirit?"

"Uh-huh."

Angela inhaled through her nostrils. "Really? When?"

"After our lunch, I did some soul-searching. I talked to my spiritual advisor about it, and he recommended several books. I read Saint Thomas Aquinas' *Summa Theologia* and Saint Bernard of Clairvaux's *Sermon on the Beatific Vision*, but what spoke to me was the *Spiritual Exercises* of St. Ignatius of Loyola." Pastora looked at her as if she had explained everything.

"Sorry." Puckering her brow, Angela shook her head. "I'm not familiar with those writings."

"According to St. Ignatius, there are eight rules." She smiled gently. "I'll spare you the treatise, but the seventh rule spoke to me. To paraphrase, it said good angels touch those who go from good to better." She grinned. "I especially like his analogy of good—like a drop of water being absorbed by a sponge—but evil is like a drop of water rolling off stone."

Angela hunched her shoulders. "I'm glad you're not against seeing spirits, but . . ." she scratched her ear, "I'm just not following. What happened to change your attitude?"

"I prayed about it for weeks. Finally, last Saturday, while I was showering, I saw my mother."

"In the shower?" Angela winced, unable to stop her knee-jerk response.

Pastora nodded. "It's not as odd as you might first think. When a baby's *in utero*, it's constantly bathed, rinsed with warm water. The shower's similar—relaxing, healing, refreshing, like—"

"A mother's womb." Angela nodded.

"While there, I had a vision of my mother." She looked up. "Only for a moment, mind you, a fraction of a second, but it was enough to convince me that what I saw, the spirits I had seen as a child, were not evil, but good."

"Wait a minute." Angela held up her hand. "You saw spirits as a child?"

"Yes." Pastora nodded shyly. "Actually, quite often."

Angela shook her head. "Then what made you so critical about me seeing them?"

"Don't get me wrong." Pastora lifted her left eyebrow. "I'm against necromancy, as in the Witch of Endor conjuring up Samuel's spirit for Saul, but I've prayed enough, read enough, that I'm convinced not all spirits are evil. They can also be God's messengers."

"So why were you against me seeing them?"

Angela watched the thoughts pass through Pastora's mind, as if clouds were sweeping across her face. Suddenly, she looked her age. The lines showed on her forehead. The creases between her eyes deepened.

"When I was thirteen," said Pastora, "I saw spirits often, nearly every week. Although I welcomed it initially, it began to scare me. I couldn't talk to my mother about it. She was too ill. Instead I talked it over with my CCD teacher. She quoted Second Corinthians, chapter eleven, verses fourteen and fifteen."

Angela shook her head. "I'm not that familiar with scripture."

"Basically, it says the devil can disguise himself as an angel of light, and that his demons are fallen angels masquerading as gentle spirits." Pastora pressed her lips together and sighed. "From our talks, she convinced me that all spirits were diabolical. No matter how benign they might appear, she urged me to banish them from my mind, from my sight."

"You mean you had this incredible gift and you hid it, suppressed it all these years?"

Pressing her lips together, she nodded.

Squinting, Angela shook her head. "How were you even able to do that? When spirits come to me, they come when they're ready. I don't call them. They just . . ." she shrugged, "appear."

"When spirits came, I asked them to leave," said Pastora. "After a while, I began denying their existence."

"But you were obviously sensitive to them. Didn't they keep trying to contact you?"

"Yes, I struggled with that for decades." Pastora's eyes met hers. "It became my cross to bear, my penance, but I wouldn't allow the devil into my mind."

Angela winced. "But spirits aren't all evil."

Pastora gave her a wan smile. "Thanks to your stubborn streak, I realize that now."

"You mean, thanks to my perfume." She chuckled. Then she studied her aunt. "When I was a small child, I never hid my gift. It never occurred to me. Why pretend not to see something I thought was obvious to everyone, something I thought everyone could see? When I talked about Abby, Toci, or Nana, Mom called them my invisible friends."

"I remember." Pastora nodded. "I wondered, worried, prayed about it even then."

Angela took a deep breath. "At first, people seemed to think it was cute, my imagination at work, but once I started school, I was branded weird. At best, teachers called my encounters childish nonsense. At worst, they suggested I see a child psychologist. To protect myself, I began keeping quiet about my gift, but . . ." she leveled her eyes at her aunt, "I promised myself that once I turned eighteen I wouldn't hide my light under a bushel basket. God gave me a gift, and I'm never going to hide it again."

"It truly is a gift, isn't it?"

Angela smiled, glad she was finally able to share her thoughts with her aunt. "Something else. At Concepción tonight, you asked if I heard something. What did you hear?"

Pastora's face brightening, she gave her little girl grin. "Gregorian chant."

Angela nodded knowingly. "I had a feeling you'd sensed that."

"You heard it, too?"

"Heard and saw it."

"Saw?" The word a wistful sigh, Pastora's jaw fell open. "What did it look like?"

"A monk stood near the painting of Our Lady of Guadalupe, chanting."

Pastora groaned. "Maybe someday that sacred gift will return, but I've suppressed it for so long, I'm afraid I may have lost it."

"All things are possible with God. Just leave yourself open to His graces." She grinned. "Don't block the flow."

WOMAN ON A MISSION

"Every story of conversion is a story of blessed defeat."

— C.S. LEWIS

Sunday morning, Angela drove them to the mission. As the car climbed the steep roads near Canyon Lake, she gazed at the hilltop and valley panorama through the windshield.

"Have you spoken to your grandmother yet?"

Develyn shook her head as she stared out the window. "Not sure how to broach it." She snorted. "Waiting for an opportune moment, I guess."

"Maybe Pastora will have some ideas."

Develyn turned toward her. "That's right. You said Pastora would meet us there." Her expression softened. "I like your aunt. She may have heaven on her mind, but her feet are firmly planted on the ground."

Angela glanced at her friend. "Good characterization. She's probably the holiest person I know but never holier-than-thou, always down-to-earth."

They turned into the caliche parking lot.

"There she is now," said Develyn, pointing to two sisters in black habits.

Angela parked alongside them. Then Pastora greeted the girls with hugs and smiles as she introduced them.

"This is my dear friend, Mother Mary Agnes."

"Please call me Mary Agnes," she said with an easy smile.

They chatted as they climbed the stone path to the open-air chapel until they approached the sign asking for silence.

ℰℊ

After Mass, they gathered at picnic tables in the open-air pavilion for fellowship and a potluck dinner. Pastora and Angela sat on one side. Develyn and Mary Agnes sat across from them.

"What prompted you to become a religious?" asked Angela.

Mary Agnes shared a smile with Pastora. "Did you coach her?"

With a grin, Pastora shook her head.

"What?" Angela looked from one to the other. "I'm just making conversation."

Pastora said, "I asked Mary Agnes to join us because I feel she and Develyn share something in common."

"Really?" Develyn turned toward her. "What?"

Mary Agnes blinked, looked down, seemed to gather her thoughts, and then met Develyn's eyes. "Pastora told me a little of your background. Years ago, I, too, found myself pregnant and unmarried."

"Were you a nun then?" Develyn's eyes widened.

She shook her head. "No, that was before I was called. Back then, I had a boyfriend in college that I believed I loved."

"Did you?"

She tilted her head and gazed off in the distance. "Not really, not by the standards I use to define love now." She turned back toward Develyn. "But I found myself in a position similar to yours, pregnant and unsure what to do next. My boyfriend pressured me to get an abortion. Despite not having the answers, I knew that wasn't it."

'What did you do?"

"After a lot of soul-searching, I decided to carry the baby to term and then choose whether I wanted to give up my child for adoption or raise it as a single parent. During those months, to help with the bills, I worked at a free health clinic that specialized in women and children's care." She shrugged. "Maybe because I was pregnant, I was drawn to the birthing center."

"Maybe God drew you there," said Pastora gently.

Nodding, she agreed. "Maybe that was the beginning of God's call to me." She turned toward Develyn. "One day, a woman came in with abdominal cramps. Two hours later, she gave birth to a tiny baby weighing less than a pound, less than a can of corn. A breach baby girl, her tiny backside slid into one hand, while I caught her head in the other. She was so premature, her skin was nearly translucent. I could actually see her tiny heart beat." She winced. "Beat isn't the right word. It was more a fluttering than a rhythmic heartbeat."

"How old would you guess she was at birth?" asked Develyn.

"The mother had no idea, said she didn't know she was pregnant. She went into the clinic for cramps, thinking it was appendicitis." Mary Agnes frowned at the irony. "The closest we could figure, the baby was about twenty-two, twenty-three weeks."

"So young." Develyn shook her head.

"So small, so still." Mary Agnes raised her eyebrow. "I placed her frail body in an incubator. Since her lungs hadn't had time to develop, each shallow breath was a gasp. I put a bag-mask over her tiny mouth and nose and began giving her gentle puffs of oxygen, hoping to expand her lungs, help her breathe."

"That must have been tough." Develyn's eyes met Mary Agnes's. "Especially when you were pregnant yourself."

Mary Agnes nodded solemnly.

"What happened?"

Mary Agnes sighed. "We weren't equipped with a neonatal intensive care ward. We were a free neighborhood clinic, a simple birthing center. I could see her skin turning gray, her chest heaving with every labored breath. I knew we were losing her. Using a few drops of water, I named her Mary Agnes and baptized her in the name of the Father, the Son, and the Holy Spirit. The size of a newborn kitten, she fit in the palm of my hand. Then I kissed her little forehead and whispered, 'It's all right. Go to sleep.' A moment later, she stopped breathing." Mary Agnes held up her hands and studied them. "Mine were the first and the last to hold her." Folding her hands, she added, "I consider it a sacred gift."

"You named her Mary Agnes," said Angela. "Was that baby what prompted you to become a religious?"

Mary Agnes nodded. "God works His miracles through others. We're all part of His plan."

"And your baby," asked Develyn, "what happened to her . . . him?"

"My cousin and her husband adopted him."

"All things work together for good for those who love God, who are called according to his purpose," said Pastora.

"Adoption." Develyn looked off into space, as if thinking. "So then what? How did you go about becoming a sister?" asked Develyn, leaning forward, her chin pressed into her fist.

Mary Agnes exchanged a gentle smile with Pastora and then turned toward Develyn.

"First and foremost, I prayed about it. Becoming a religious is not synonymous with running away from the world. I asked God for guidance about my vocation, whether He was calling me to be a sister, wife, butcher, baker," she grinned, "or candlestick maker."

"And His answer?" asked Develyn.

"One early morning in prayer, it came to me clearly. Your misery is your ministry."

"Your misery is your ministry." Develyn repeated slowly, squinting. "What was your misery?"

Taking a deep breath, Mary Agnes looked off without seeing. After a moment, she focused on Develyn.

"It was giving up my child. After holding him close to my heart for nine months, I had to deliver my baby, not to my care, but to my cousin's." She grimaced. "It was preferable to the estranged father's choice, but my ministry has become counseling unwed

SACRED GIFT

mothers, helping them transition to the next phase of their lives, whatever that may be."

"What happened to the father?" asked Develyn, her eyes wide.

Mary Agnes's smile was wry. "After I told him abortion was out of the question, I never heard from him again."

Lifting an eyebrow, Develyn said, "Sounds familiar." Staring at her folded hands, she was thoughtful for a moment. Then she looked up. "So after God gave you His answer, what then? How did you move from the role of sinner/student to sister?"

"Why?" Again Mary Agnes shared a faint smile with Pastora. "Do you feel called to be a religious?"

Develyn flinched. "I've never heard my thoughts put into words." She took a deep breath. "I don't know. Let's just say, at this point, I'm looking at all my options, but . . . I would like to explore it." She looked to Mary Agnes for guidance. "If I did, what would be the next step?"

"Pretty much, what you're doing right now," said Mary Agnes, "talking to sisters."

"Or you might want to try a 'nun run,'" said Pastora, her eyes twinkling.

Develyn grinned. "What's a 'nun run?'"

"It's where you travel from convent to convent with other discerning women, investigating different religious communities," said Pastora.

"It's a good way to check out various orders, find a good fit," added Mary Agnes, watching her. "But could I make a suggestion?"

"Absolutely." Develyn's face lit up expectantly.

"Before you jump on the religious-life band wagon, ask yourself something. Do you know if God wants you to give up your baby?" She tilted her head as she watched Develyn's response. "You're pregnant. Could motherhood be the vocation God's calling you to?"

Develyn blinked, as if thinking it over.

"First, seek the Lord's will. Discern what He wants you to do," said Mary Agnes. "Most of us don't do a very good job of searching

241

out God's will for us . . . or accepting it once we find it." Leaning in, she lifted an eyebrow. "Your first vocation is to love God. Your second vocation is to be a good prenatal mother. Take care of your baby. Take care of yourself during this pregnancy. Go to the doctor. Take vitamins. Then soul-search. Ask God, 'do I keep or give up my baby for adoption?'"

Develyn nodded as she chewed a corner of her lip.

"At this point, I recommend you surrender and seek Him," said Mary Agnes. "You might want to find a mentor, someone to help guide you through the process. By any chance, do you have an aunt or trusted family friend you could discuss this with?"

Catching Angela's eye, Develyn grimaced. "Not really, my grandmother and I aren't very close."

"As you explore whether or not religious life's for you, you'll need someone who'll listen, be supportive. There's nothing like putting your thoughts into words to make them real. Talking it over with a confidant can help you determine if you're actually being called," Mary Agnes smiled but again raised a cautionary eyebrow, "or just searching for a way out of your current situation."

Develyn nodded. "Point taken, but I don't know anyone I could ask."

"If you're serious about talking through your spiritual journey, I'd be willing to listen."

"Like a sounding board." Though the morning was warm, Develyn lifted her head as a cool breeze fluttered through the canvas lanai covering.

Mary Agnes chuckled. "I was thinking more along the lines of spiritual director, someone who could help you pray about the direction in which God is moving you."

"If you're contemplating religious life," said Pastora, "a mentor like Mary Agnes would be an invaluable guide. She can help you consider where you are and where you're going." She turned toward Mary Agnes. "That's a generous offer." Then she turned back to Develyn. "What do you think?"

RUBBINGS

"To sleep, perchance to dream—Ay, there's the rub,
For in that sleep of death what dreams may come . . ."

— A Midsummer Night's Dream, William Shakespeare

As Angela drove out of the caliche parking lot, Develyn turned toward her.

"Do you mind if we stop at a cemetery for a rubbing?"

"Sure, you mean the one we passed the last time?"

Develyn took a deep breath. "No." Her brow furrowing, she winced. "It's near here, though. Just get me to Wimberley. I can find my way from there."

An hour later, they pulled into a country cemetery and began looking for a suitable headstone. Shaded by ancient live oaks, the grounds were relatively cool, even on an August afternoon.

As they passed several plots enclosed by low, limestone walls, Angela asked, "What are these for?"

"They keep out animals," said Develyn.

Angela nodded. Then she saw a headstone of a Confederate Army infantryman.

"Here's an interesting one. Want to take a rubbing of this one?"

Develyn turned up her nose. "Not really."

Minutes later, Angela pointed to another. "Here's the headstone of a Texas Ranger from 1889. Want this one?"

Develyn shrugged and then shook her head. "Nope."

Angela turned toward her. "Is there some reason why you wanted to come to this particular cemetery?"

"It's where my mother's buried."

Raising her eyebrow, Angela nodded. "Had a feeling it might be something like that."

"Her grave's around here somewhere." Develyn looked from tombstone to tombstone, checking. "It's been years since I visited this place. I just forget exactly where it is."

"Is her name Ginny Barona?"

"Virginia Barona."

"I'm seeing dozens of Dawsons here," said Angela, checking the names, "but no Baronas."

"It's my grandmother's family's plot, so there are generations of headstones marked Dawson. She's buried here somewhere, though. Keep looking."

Finally, Angela called, "It's over here."

The corners of Develyn's mouth slipped down as she saw her mother's tiny, rectangular marker, containing only the dates and name. Horizontal instead of upright, it lay flat on the ground. No epitaph, flowers, or shrubs softened the scene. Develyn looked from it to all the ornate headstones in the vicinity and sighed.

"How did you ever find it?"

"Easy," Angela returned a wry smile. "Your mother showed me."

Develyn's eyes grew big. "You mean, she's here."

Angela nodded, motioning to keep quiet. Her ear cocked, she strained to listen.

"What . . . ?" Develyn slumped against a nearby tree. "What's she saying?"

Angela tried to summarize. "She says you've been given some good advice, better than what she'd been given."

Develyn nodded slowly. "Anything else?"

"Ginny said to be kinder to your grandmother, to go easy on her, that . . ." Angela chuckled.

"What are you laughing about?" A deep 'V' formed between Develyn's eyes.

Angela shook her head. "I'm not laughing. It's just ironic. Ginny told me your grandmother's had her own cross to bear, echoing something that Pastora just said." Angela dropped her smile. "Apparently, no one's immune from mistakes. She says to confide in Ellen, that *this time* she'll understand."

Develyn looked up. "What do you mean, 'this time?'"

Again Angela cocked her head. "Your mother says she understands now why Ellen was so hard on her. She was only trying to keep her from making the same mistake she had."

"What?" Develyn's eyes opened wide.

Angela nodded. "Apparently, there's a family trend. Although your grandmother's situation was a false pregnancy, you're the third generation to get pregnant out of wedlock."

Develyn inhaled deeply as she looked at her mother's headstone. "Who'd have guessed?" After a moment she looked up. "Anything else?"

Angela scratched her ear thoughtfully before answering. "She said something else we've heard recently. 'Let your misery be your ministry.'"

"Wow." Develyn was silent a few minutes. Then she reached into her oversized bag and pulled out a poster tube and a box of Conté crayons. Placing a thin sheet of tracing paper over Ginny's headstone, she said softly, "I want a picture of my mother."

Angela knelt down to hold the paper in place while she made the rubbing. When she finished, Develyn carefully rolled up the paper, slipped it into the tube, and tucked it in her bag. Then she pulled something else out of her 'bag of tricks,' as she liked to call it. Develyn took out the fossilized heart and carefully placed it on her mother's headstone.

"There've been enough hardhearted women in our family," she whispered. "Let the cycle end here." Brushing her fingers with a kiss, Develyn touched the fossil. "This is for you, Mom."

When they returned to the dorm, Develyn took down her favorite rubbing from the wall. Using its matting and frame, she replaced the previous rubbing with the one of her mother's headstone and hung it over her bed.

"Family portrait." She gave Angela a wry grin as the phone rang. "Got it." Then speaking into the phone, "Hello?"

Angela could hear a whine coming through the phone.

"Want me to leave?" she whispered.

Develyn shook her head as she muted the phone. "Travis wants to say he's sorry in person."

Angela cocked an eyebrow. "You're not going to meet him, are you?"

Stepping toward the window, Develyn pulled back the curtains and pointed. "He's waiting downstairs." Then she unmuted and spoke into the phone. "Okay, but, seriously, five minutes, and that's it. I've got a couple of calls to make."

Angela stepped in front of her. "I don't think this is such a good idea."

"I'll be fine. Quit worrying so much." Chuckling as she closed the door behind her, she called, "If I'm not back in five minutes, call in the Texas Rangers."

Portents

"You changed your hair color," said Travis, his eyes running up
and down her body.

She shrugged as she crossed her arms. "Yeah, the dye's not good
for the baby." Watching him wince, she smiled inwardly.

"I thought you were going to take care of that." His eyes narrowed.

Sneering, she unfolded her arms and leaned into his space.
"What's it to you?" Her tone warned him to back off.

He put up his hands. "Just saying."

"Hey, Dev," said a girl approaching them. "When do you want to
work on that art project?"

"Oh," Develyn said, "maybe get together Wednesday?"

"It's due Tuesday." The girl heaved a sigh. "What about
this afternoon?"

"Well, uhm, I guess—"

"She's busy. Do you mind?" Travis stepped between them.
"She's having a conversation with me. Now get lost."

"Well! How rude!" Blinking, the girl opened her mouth and then
promptly shut it, turned, and began striding away.

"I'll call you later, okay, Betty?" Develyn called after her. "Betty?"
Then she turned toward Travis. "That was uncalled for. Besides,
your five minutes are up. *You* get lost."

Again, he put up his hands. "Sorry, sorry." He shook his head and sighed. "All I wanted to do was apologize to you."

"Then do it," Develyn glared at him, "and leave."

He looked at the people staring at them and cringed. "I can't do it here. There are too many," he began shouting, "*nosy people watching, listening!*" He lowered his voice. "Just get in the car. At least we'll have a little privacy." When she did not budge, he rolled his eyes. "Please."

Sighing, she looked at him, thought it over, and looked at him again. She pressed her lips together, debating.

"Five minutes." She held up her index finger, warning him. "That's it."

"Okay. Okay!"

He started toward the driver's door as she stood motionless in front of the passenger door, waiting. When she rolled her eyes, he said, "What?" Then he walked back and made a ceremony of opening the door for her. He closed it politely, walked back to the driver's side, and got in.

Then Travis threw the car into gear and floored the gas pedal. As the car fishtailed out from the curb with an ear-piercing screech, Develyn grabbed the dashboard and braced herself.

"What the hell are you doing?"

Travis swung around the corner as a cloud of bluish-white smoke hung over the street in front of the dorms. Pedestrians scrambled.

"Taking you for the ride of your life!" shouted Travis. "Yiiieeee-hah!"

"No, you're not! Now, stop it! Let me out!" screamed Develyn. "Travis, I mean it! Let me out! Now!"

"Don't worry, baby. I'm a terrific driver. The best."

Develyn glanced at him from the corner of her eye. He was smiling gleefully. His eyes were bright, too bright. She recognized the signs, but too late. His self-confidence had an alcoholic boost.

As if on cue, he reached under the seat and pulled out a bottle of Jack Daniels.

"Want a swig?"

"No! Now stop this car, Travis!" She faced him and shouted. "I'm not kidding!"

He hit the brakes hard, and she slammed against the dash, screaming.

"What, baby?" He leered at her as she pulled herself from under the dash and struggled to sit up. "I'm just doing what you said." His eyes on her, he peeled out, paying no attention to traffic.

"Travis, let me out of this car!"

He took a long swig before he turned toward her. "Shut up." Then he took another long swig as he accelerated.

She tried another tactic. "Where're you going?"

He sneered at her as he took another long swallow and wiped his mouth with the back of his hand.

"I got an appointment with death, baby, and I'm taking you along for the ride."

Suddenly, Angela cocked her head, listening internally. *Ginny?* Nodding in answer, Angela speed-dialed Develyn's cell phone.

"Put your seat belt on. Now!"

Develyn scrambled for the cell phone on her belt. "What?" she shouted over Travis's ranting.

Angela shouted into her cell. "Put your seat belt on! *Now!*" Then she heard a screech and scream, and the line went dead.

"Develyn? Dev?" When there was no answer, Angela again listened to Ginny with her inner ear. Nodding, she called Judith. "Mom? Call Develyn's grandmother. Tell her to meet me at the San Antonio Community Hospital."

"What's wrong?"

"Develyn's been in a car accident."

Judith gasped. "Are you all right?"

"I'm fine. I wasn't in it."

"Thank God!" Judith took a deep breath. "I'll call Ellen as soon as we hang up. Ceren's here with me." Her tone softened. "Angela, we'll meet you at the hospital in forty minutes. It'll be all right."

TRANSITIONS

*"What we are reluctant to touch
often seems the very fabric of our salvation."*

— DON DELILLO

Angela rushed to the hospital's emergency entrance, arriving just as an ambulance pulled in, its siren still blaring. She caught up with the attendants as they wheeled in the cart.

Develyn's face was covered in blood. Angela's jaw dropped as she gulped air.

"Got a Jane Doe for the ER," said the attendant, wheeling her into admitting.

"I can give you her information," said Angela, stepping up to the counter. "Her name's Develyn, actually Debra Evelyn—"

"And your relationship to her?"

"A friend . . . her roommate."

"Did you see the accident?"

Angela shook her head. "No, I . . . I was on the phone with her," she took a deep breath, "and heard it happen." After giving the admitting attendant all the information she could, she took a seat in the waiting room.

Judith and Ceren arrived first.

"How is she?" asked Judith.

Angela shook her head. "Haven't heard anything yet." She looked toward the door to the wards. "Hoping for some news soon." She gave them a grateful smile. "Thanks for coming."

"We wanted to be with you and Develyn," said Ceren.

Soon after, Ellen and Tim joined them.

"Any word?" Ellen's eyes were red and swollen.

"Not yet," said Angela, taking her hand.

Judith stood toward the back of the group, eyes glued to Angela and Ellen, avoiding Tim's stare.

"Thank you for calling," said Tim, his eyes piercing.

Judith managed a stiff smile, nodded, and moved toward Ellen to hug her.

"Glad you could get here so soon. Just so very sorry about the circumstances."

"Déjà vu," said Ellen. "Getting a call out of the blue to rush to the emergency room." She shivered. "It's like a rerun of a horror movie."

"Who's here for Debra?" asked a white-smocked doctor.

"Debra?" Ellen looked puzzled. "Oh, you mean Develyn. I'm her grandmother."

"I'm Dr. Madipadga." He gave her a curt smile. "Good news. They're both doing fine."

"Both?" Shaking her head, Ellen squinted. "I don't understand."

"Both mother and child are stable."

"You mean, she's pregnant?" Ellen blanched. Her face drained, devoid of emotion, she turned to Tim. "Like mother, like daughter. The leaf didn't fall far from the tree, did it? It's like reliving the nightmare with Ginny." She took a deep breath, squaring her shoulders. Then she turned back to the doctor. "You're sure my granddaughter's all right?"

"She's had a temporary loss of conscious, a mild concussion, and her speech is a little slurred. We'll do an MRI to be sure, but her vital signs are good."

Ellen gasped, her hand cupping her mouth.

"I wouldn't worry. She's out of immediate danger, and the prognosis for full recovery is positive." He raised his eyebrow. "Good thing she was wearing her seatbelt. It saved her life . . . and her baby's."

Angela caught her breath and said a silent prayer.

"Why do you say that?" asked Ellen.

"Her head hit the windshield."

"So you mean she wasn't wearing a seatbelt." Tim blinked as if trying to understand.

"She was wearing it." Dr. Madipadga gave a wry smile. "In fact, they had to cut her out of it. When the airbag malfunctioned, the seatbelt was all that prevented her from being thrown through the windshield."

Ellen groaned and put her folded hands to her face. "Can I see her now?"

He nodded. "But no more than three at a time. She's got to remain quiet until we can get an MRI and find out if there's any internal damage."

Ellen caught Tim's eye, silently inviting him to go with her. Then she looked at Angela.

"Come in with us." She gave a half-smile. "I know how close you two are."

Develyn lay on the bed, as white as the bandages on her scalp. Her face was a mass of contusions. Both eyes were black. One pupil was dilated, the other normal sized, and she looked dazed, as if she could not focus. When she looked up, she covered her eyes, moaned, and motioned toward the lights. Though her speech was slurred, she said, "Down, down."

"The lights are too bright?" Ellen dimmed the switch. "Is that better?"

Develyn tried to nod, but she winced and, cringing, gingerly touched her chest. As she moved, Angela saw the angry bruises across her shoulder. Her gown covered her chest, but the bruised welts seemed to extend beneath it. *How far? Could the seatbelt have harmed the baby?*

"Are you in pain?" asked Ellen. "Tim, can you find the doctor? Develyn needs something for the pain."

"No, you two stay here," said Angela, lightly resting her fingers on Ellen's shoulder. "I'll get him." She slipped out, closing the door behind her. After she relayed the message to the attendant, she pulled Ceren aside.

"How's Develyn?"

Angela lifted her eyebrows and took a deep breath. "She's pretty banged up."

Ceren shook off a chill. "How fast things can change."

"You don't know the half of it." Angela snorted.

Ceren's eyes widened. "How can you smile at a time like this?"

"The irony. You heard the doctor mention Dev's pregnant."

Ceren nodded slowly, beginning to understand. "So he let the cat out of the bag?"

"Closer to a herd of cats." Angela snickered. "In fact, that's what I want to talk to you about." She took a deep breath. "Esteban's here."

"What!" Her loud tone drew several stares, and she lowered her voice. "Esteban's *where?*"

"He's with Develyn, and he wants to ask you something."

"What's he doing here? What's he want?" Eyes wide, Ceren held her head back as she appraised Angela.

"Excuse me," said Tim, squeezing out the door. "Angela, Dev's calling for you."

"I'll wait out here," said Ceren.

"No, that's all right," said Tim. "You go on in with Angela." His eyes scanned the waiting room until they lit on Judith sitting near the vending machine. "Besides, I could use a cup of coffee."

Angela cracked the door and peeked in.

"Come in," said Ellen, looking drawn, wearing a wan smile. "Develyn told me you called her moments before the crash."

Angela's eyes caught Develyn's, questioning.

"S'all right," said Develyn, her speech slurred. "She knows."

Ellen nodded. "She's told me about your gift . . . about Ginny."

In answer to Ceren's questioning expression, Angela said, "Develyn's mother." Then she turned toward Ellen and Develyn. "Ginny simply used me to warn you."

"The doctor said the seatbelt saved her life." A strand of dark hair peeked out from Develyn's bandages. Ellen gently brushed it away from her granddaughter's eyes. "Both their lives." Then she looked at Angela. "But how did you know which hospital?"

Angela smiled crookedly.

"Ginny again?" Ellen sighed as a fond smile crept over her face. Then her eyes grew round. "Is she here now?"

Angela shook her head. *But someone else is.* Then she glanced at Ceren.

Tim took a bill from his wallet and fed the coffee vending machine.

"Do you take cream or sugar?"

Here it comes. Judith curled her lip and mumbled, "Neither. Black."

He handed her the coffee as he brewed his own. Then he sat beside her, positioning his chair so they could face each other diagonally. "I appreciated your phone call . . . both of them."

She raised her eyebrow but said nothing.

He sighed. "This is awkward."

She snorted in agreement. She pressed her lips together, debating whether to be civil. Then she took a sip of coffee as she looked toward Develyn's door.

"How does she look?"

He shook his head. "Not good."

"But the doctor said she's going to be all right."

"She's coherent, was asking for Angela." He rubbed his forehead. Then the corners of his mouth lifted in a wan smile as he tried to catch her eye. "Those two girls seem to have a bond."

She shifted uneasily, not liking the direction the conversation was taking.

He pulled his chair closer and spoke in a low voice. "Look, we only have a few minutes together. I don't want to waste it, so let me get right to the point." He closed his eyes and took a deep breath, as if summoning courage. "I'm truly sorry for what I did to you. I was stupid and young . . . and I honestly didn't know you were pregnant."

Judith set down her coffee. "Like it would have made a difference." Her stony eyes stared him down.

His eyebrows gathering together, he gave her a pained expression. Then, slumping, he shook his head.

"In all honesty, I'm not sure. Maybe it would have given me the courage to stand up to Ellen's and my parents. Maybe not."

Her face tight, she crossed her arms. "But we'll never know now, will we?"

He bit his lip and tried again. "In your phone message, you said you'd forgiven me. I had to see if you really did . . . do."

"I've tried." She squeezed shut her eyes. When she opened them again, she thought the lines around his eyes seemed deeper, more pronounced. "Over the years, I've tried so many times, but the anger always trumps my best intentions. This is just the most recent instance." Her fingers let go her arms. Shaking her head, she pulled her hands into fists. "I don't know if I can ever let go my resentment. After all these years, it's ingrained."

Then Judith saw her.

Suddenly, standing beside Tim, studying him, was a middle-aged woman with chubby cheeks, sparkling eyes, salt-and-pepper hair, and a wide smile. She seemed to glow from within. So bright, she seemed to light up the dark corridor. Judith felt the blood drain from her cheeks. *Helen?*

"He looks like me, don't you think?" she asked, turning toward Judith.

Judith heard the words with her mind, not her ears. She tried to move her lips, but they felt numb. Mentally, she asked, "Can Tim see you or hear you?"

The smile broadened as Helen shook her head. "No."

Judith squinted against the dazzling light. "Then why can I?"

"You need me. He doesn't."

"What?" Judith said.

"You're haunted by your past, stuck in a resentment so habitual it's chronic. You can't move forward until you can truly let go."

Narrowing her eyes against Helen's bright glare, Judith shook her head. "I can't forget what he did to me . . . what he drove me to do . . . to you."

"No one made you do anything." Helen's tone was kind, not critical. "You're the one who had the abortion, yet you blame him. Like an adrenaline rush, your resentment's become a kind of addiction, a crutch. You're so used to leaning on it that you don't want to let it go. Why? Are you afraid you'll be empty without this bitterness that permeates you? Does it feed you, fill you?"

"Of course not!"

Cocking her head, Helen fixed sympathetic eyes on Judith. "You'll have a bleak future if you can't forgive. Stop regretting what's past. You've got to let it go, move on. Forgive Tim, and forgive yourself."

"How?"

"Ask God to help. Fill your life with new experiences. Then focus on those. Don't dwell on the past."

"New faces, new places won't make up for what I lost." Judith raised her eyebrow. "You, most of all."

"The past is gone. Don't fill your mind with remorse and old grudges that rob you of the present. Only forgiveness will free you from this cycle of resentment. Only by letting go can you create a future for you."

Judith felt the tears sting her eyes. "How can you forgive him . . . forgive me after what I did?"

Helen's glow seemed even brighter. "Angela already told you how I feel. Everything was forgiven years ago, decades ago." She glanced at Tim and then back. "I feel only love for both of you. How couldn't I? I'm a part of you . . . Mom."

Judith felt her eyes filling with tears.

Tim scooted his chair closer and leaned into her until his knees almost touched hers. His smile was sad.

"What is it?"

Judith glanced at Helen, but she was gone. She looked at Tim and realized he was unaware of her visit.

"Nothing." She caught her breath. *How long was she here? Or was she? Did I imagine her?*

"So . . . do you?" he asked in a quiet voice.

"Do I what?" Automatically on the defense, Judith projected her schoolmarm scowl.

He swallowed. "Forgive me?"

Judith thought of her . . . *their* daughter Helen's words. She thought of Angela. *How generously she forgave her birth father.* She put her hand to her forehead. *Why is it so hard for me to forgive?*

Lowering her hand, she spoke slowly. "This doesn't mean I want to be friends . . . or that I can forget what happened." She closed her eyes to gather her thoughts. *In the voicemail I left, I forgave him for Helen.* When she opened her eyes again, she stared directly into his. "And it's not my call whether or not you deserve it, but . . ."

"What?"

"I forgive you . . . for *me,* so I can let go, get on with my life."

Ellen stood up and stretched. "I need to powder my nose." She looked at Angela. "Will . . . ?"

"Don't worry." Angela gave her a reassuring smile. "Ceren and I will stay right here until you get back."

With a nod, Ellen glanced at the dozing Develyn and closed the door behind her.

"Is she asleep?" Ceren stepped closer to the bed to peek.

"Either that or unconscious." Angela knitted her brows. "I don't know what's taking so long to get her an MRI." Then she smiled. "But now that Ellen's left, I can tell you about Esteban."

Ceren looked uneasy. "Why would he appear here?"

"Basically, Esteban wants you and Justin to adopt Develyn's baby."

"What?" Ceren's creamy complexion paled. She raised her eyebrows in disbelief. "I'm forty-five, much too old to adopt."

"Mom was sixty-six when she adopted me." Angela shifted her gaze from her birth mother to the little boy eavesdropping beside her, trying to tug her skirt, get her attention. "By the way, there's someone here who seems very anxious to talk to you."

"Esteban." Ceren pronounced his name like a sigh.

Angela listened to him and then relayed his words. "He said focusing on a baby would be good for you and Justin, that it would release your grip on him, allow him to move on."

"I thought we had let go." Ceren spoke softly, just above a whisper. "Justin and I finally talked about the miscarriage, brought it out in the open." She gave Angela a fleeting smile. "Thanks to the last time you and Esteban had a 'talk' with me, Justin and I've renewed our feelings for one another, forgiven each other."

Angela nodded. "I'm glad, but Esteban says your regrets still bind him to you, still call him here."

"Why?" Ceren pressed her fingers to her temples. "Justin and I have tried our best to let our son move on."

"He knows." Angela concentrated on the thoughts Esteban sent. "He said you also have regrets about another baby, a girl." As she spoke, Angela realized who he was talking about and felt the heat rise in her cheeks.

Ceren's eyes met hers. "You."

Angela swallowed before she relayed Esteban's words. "He said you love your two boys, but you've always regretted not having a daughter."

Again Ceren's eyes caught hers. "Develyn's baby is a girl?"

Angela nodded. "Esteban said adopting this girl would bring you full circle. You gave up a daughter. Now you'll gain a daughter. Adopting this baby would release you from your past and release Esteban from your psyche."

Ceren inhaled deeply. "It would let his spirit rest."

Suddenly, a breeze blew through the room. The papers on Develyn's chart fluttered. Angela brushed back her hair from her eyes and blinked.

There stood Travis, bending over Develyn's bed, shouting. "Get up! You're coming with me!"

Develyn stirred and groaned.

"Travis, leave her alone."

"Stay out of this!" Red-eyed and angry, he turned toward her. "You've interfered enough already."

Angela gasped. His eyes looked like hollow slits as his pupils reflected an eerie red color, like photos with redeye.

He glared at her and then, turning, he reached for Develyn's arm. "I said, *get up!*" His arm passed through her body like light shining through glass. He jumped back. "What the . . . ?" Again and again, he tried to touch her, but his hand made no contact. It simply passed through the air.

But at each attempt, Develyn squirmed and moaned. Somehow, she sensed it.

"Travis, get out of here," said Angela.

Ceren's eyes darted left and right. "Who's Travis? Who are you talking to?"

"Develyn's boy . . . ex-boyfriend."

In a flash, as if fast-forwarded, Travis rushed toward Angela. The hem of Ceren's skirt rustled as he flew by. He stopped abruptly, millimeters from Angela's face, then loomed over her. As if trying to intimidate her, he fixed his red eyes on her.

"What do you mean 'ex?'"

"Don't you get it, Travis?" Toe-to-toe with him, Angela peered up into his face. "You're dead."

He sneered. "And I told you to stay out of this."

He whooshed back to Develyn, put his hands on the bed, and tried to shake it. "Get up, damn it! I told you I was taking you for the ride of your life, and I meant it."

Each time he tried to shake the bed, he appeared to increase his strength until Angela saw the mattress begin to spring up and down. Develyn writhed and whimpered more with each of his moves. She began panting. Her mouth took on a pale blue tinge.

Ceren yelped at the sight. "What's happening?"

Angela looked at the monitor over Develyn's bed. The top green line that read "Heart Rate" shot up. The next blue line dipped. The white and bottom blue lines skyrocketed. The line on the ICP monitor soared. As their lights started flashing, an alarm sounded.

"Get the doctor," said Angela. "I don't know what Travis is doing, but it's obviously affecting her."

Ceren rushed out, Esteban dogging her heels. Without warning, Ginny appeared between Travis and her daughter. Angela froze in her chair.

"Stop it!" Guarding the bed, Ginny positioned herself as a buffer. "Leave my daughter alone!"

"Get out of my way!" His arm connected with Ginny's shoulder, and he threw her aside.

Angela watched silently, powerless. *They're on the same plane. If Develyn's mother can't help her, what can I do? Her mother . . . .* Suddenly, Pastora's early teachings came to mind, and she began praying out loud.

"Hail Mary, full of grace. The Lord is with thee. Blessed art thou amongst women, and blessed is the fruit of thy womb, Jesus. Holy Mary, Mother of God, pray for us sinners, now and at the hour of our death. Amen. Hail Mary, full of grace . . ."

Travis's red eyes glared at her. Then he turned back toward Develyn. "Come with me, Dev. I want you with me always. You know I want you, baby. Come with me!"

Angela kept up her prayer. "The Lord is with thee. Blessed art thou amongst women, and blessed is the fruit of thy womb, Jesus.

Holy Mary, Mother of God, pray for us sinners, now and at the hour of our death. Amen. Hail Mary, full of grace . . ."

"Dev, I told you I was taking you for the ride of your life. Come on. The ride's not over yet! I want you with me . . . now . . . always." He turned toward Angela. "Shut up!"

Angela kept on. "The Lord is with thee. Blessed art thou amongst women, and blessed is the fruit of thy womb, Jesus. Holy Mary, Mother of God, pray for us sinners, now and at the hour of our death. Amen. Hail Mary, full of grace . . ."

Putting his hands to his ears, Travis suddenly began shrieking. Ginny moved to her daughter's bedside and laid her hands across her womb, as if using them as a shield, as a blessing.

"The Lord is with thee. Blessed art thou amongst women, and blessed is the fruit of thy womb, Jesus. Holy Mary, Mother of God, pray for us sinners, now and at the hour of our death. Amen. Hail Mary, full of grace . . ."

Angela opened her eyes wide as she watched Travis gradually lift off the ground, but she continued praying.

"The Lord is with thee. Blessed art thou amongst women, and blessed is the fruit of thy womb, Jesus. Holy Mary, Mother of God, pray for us sinners, now and at the hour of our death. Amen. Hail Mary, full of grace . . ."

Once his feet left the ground, he began drifting gradually, like smoke. For a split second, his spirit seemed to enter Develyn's body.

Angela watched her face momentarily take on an agonized, masculine appearance. Frightened, she began praying louder.

Something appeared to be yanking Travis's spirit out of Develyn's prone body. Then his spirit jerked back, as if wanting to remain in her, hide in her. Finally, the greater force wrenched it from her. Shrieking and flailing its arms and legs, his spirit struggled against the invisible force. Apparently powerless against it, his spirit began rising. Just before it approached the corner ceiling of the room, it reached out to Develyn. "Help me!"

Then it was gone.

Drained, Angela slumped against the wall.

When the doctor rushed in with Ceren, he glanced at the monitors and checked Develyn's pupils. "Wheel her into radiology."

Two hours later, Dr. Madipadga met them in the waiting room. Angela waved to Ceren, talking on her cell, and she joined them.

Ellen reached for Tim's hand. "How is she, Doctor?"

"Her ICP was twenty-five millimeters, so high we were considering a craniotomy."

"A what?" Ellen's eyes widened.

"We considered drilling a hole in her skull to release the cranial pressure, but luckily we were able to raise her blood pressure and dilate the blood vessels enough in her brain to reduce the swelling."

Ellen gasped. "Will she be all right?" At the doctor's nod, she asked, "Were there any other injuries?"

"She has a bruised liver and a fractured rib, which caused a small pneumothorax—"

"A what?" asked Ellen, her eyebrows a deep 'V.'

"A partially collapsed lung. Anti-inflammatories and a week of bed rest, and the leak will seal over on its own. The good news," he smiled, "is that there shouldn't be any permanent damage."

Ellen closed her eyes, seeming in silent prayer. "She's not in any pain, is she?"

"She'll be sore from the bruising, but other than the small fracture, nothing's broken. Nothing's ruptured. However, I won't mince words. She came very close to meeting her maker today. She's one very lucky lady." He shook his head. "God must have big plans for her."

"When can we see her?" asked Ellen, rising from her chair.

"Any time," said the doctor, looking from one to the other, "but she's been asking for Angela and Ceren."

Her brow furrowed, Ellen's spine slouched, and she slumped back onto the chair.

Angela gave Ellen a warm smile. "Why don't you go in first?"

"Would you mind?" Ellen's eyes lit up. "I just need to tell her something . . . something I should've said a long time ago." She started toward Develyn's room and then looked back. Her tone shy, she spoke to Tim. "Are you coming with me?"

His eyes crinkled as they met hers. With a nod and a gentle smile, he joined her.

Judith's eyes followed them until they shut the door behind them, locking out the rest of the world.

Then the doctor turned to Angela. "As I recall, you're also a friend of the driver's—"

"He didn't make it, did he?"

He shook his head. "We did everything we could to save him, but when he was thrown from the vehicle, he sustained multiple fractures, broken ribs, and a ruptured spleen."

Angela frowned as she glanced at Ceren. "What a waste."

Ceren's eyes wide, she asked, "What about Develyn's baby?"

"We'll follow up with prenatal monitoring, but from all indications, the baby's doing just fine." He smiled and with a slight bow said, "Now, if you'll excuse me, ladies, I need to attend to my other patients."

Judith turned to Ceren. "Who've you been talking to on the phone for two hours?"

Ceren shared a mischievous grin with Angela. "Justin." She winked. "Suddenly, we have a *lot* to talk about."

A few minutes later, Ellen and Tim emerged from Develyn's room.

"Do you want to come in with us?" Angela asked Judith.

She shook her head. "No, you two go ahead."

"I'll wait with you," said Ellen. "Tim, why don't you bring the car around? I'll join you in a few minutes." When they were alone, she turned to Judith. "I knew I liked you the instant we met at the retreat, but I didn't know we had so much in common."

Judith blinked. "I'm not following."

Ellen took her hand. "I heard your voice mail for Tim."

Judith opened her mouth, but no words came out.

"I put two and two together—your story at the retreat and then the message you left on the answering machine. Tell me if I'm off base here, and I'll pretend this conversation never took place."

Judith shook her head. "Ellen, that was over decades ago. There's nothing—"

"I know that." Ellen smiled gently. "In fact, what I really want to do is thank you."

"*Thank me?*" Judith scoffed. "For what?"

"I'd told you when we met that our marriage was stable but loveless." Ellen grunted. "I knew there'd been someone else. I knew Tim had never forgiven me for, as he called it," she sighed, "trapping him, and he'd never forgiven himself for letting go the love of his life . . . until now."

"What do you mean, 'until now?'" Judith studied her. "Nothing's happened."

Ellen watched her with smiling eyes. "Your forgiving Tim took a great burden off him, one that had caused many . . . if not most of our marital problems. When you forgave him, it freed him. He was able to forgive himself. Now he has no cause to resent me, and for that, I'm grateful."

As soon as Develyn saw Angela and Ceren, her eyes lit up behind the swelling and bruises.

"Were you here earlier, or did I dream it?" Her speech was still slurred but improved.

Angela smiled. "We were here."

Shaking her head, she winced. "I had nightmares. I saw, *was surrounded by* horrible, hideous creatures shaking the bed. Skulls that spoke tried to trick me, lure me into going somewhere with them. For a moment, I felt," she turned bloodshot eyes toward Angela, squinting, as if recalling painful memories. "I felt like something was in me, *inside* me, something evil trying to kill me." Her shoulders drooping, she added in a whisper, "My baby along with me."

Angela took a deep breath. "Nothing but synapses firing off in your brain. The doctor said the ICP monitor—"

"The what?"

Angela pointed to it, reading its label. "Intercranial Pressure, he said yours was so high they were considering drilling a hole in your head to release it."

"Wow, then that was my third close call." She looked up, confused, unfocused. "Was Travis here? I seem to remember—"

"What you had was just a bad dream." Angela crossed her fingers behind her back. *You don't need to know the details.*

"Maybe so, I can't seem to separate the dreams from the waking moments." Develyn frowned, as if struggling to concentrate. "What about Travis? Is he badly hurt?"

Shaking her head slowly, Angela said, "He—"

"Travis didn't make it, did he?" Her voice monotone, her question was a statement. She looked off in the distance, accepting the truth with no show of emotion.

"I'm sorry."

Develyn looked up at them, her eyes dark. "He tried to kill us, you know." She sighed. "He'd been drinking, but I'd never seen him act that way before. I wonder what got into him."

So do I. Recalling his actions and his eerie, red eyes, Angela shuddered.

Suddenly Develyn's eyes brightened. "Was there a little boy with you when you visited earlier?"

Angela caught Ceren's eye before answering. "Why do you ask?"

"Was that part a dream?" She paused, seeming to choose her words. "I'm not sure, anymore, but in it, a little boy tried to talk Ceren into adopting my baby."

"Is that an idea you might be interested in pursuing?" Ceren watched her response closely.

Develyn's black-and-blue eyes flickered and then gleamed. "Very much." She stretched out her hand. "Would that interest you?"

"Definitely." Sharing a conspiratorial smile, Ceren clasped her hand. When Develyn winced, Ceren immediately let go. "Sorry, are you all right?"

"I'm fine. Just bruised." Develyn smiled crookedly. "Can we discuss the logistics later?"

"Absolutely." Ceren and Angela turned to leave.

"But before you go, can I ask a favor?"

"Sure."

"Would you invite Pastora and Mary Agnes to visit me?"

"Of course." Her interest piqued, Angela asked, "Why?"

"I had another dream." She turned to them, her eyes shining. "This one must have been a dream. In it, my mother told me what a miracle it is that I'm alive." Develyn's eyes danced. "Then she showed me what I was born . . . and saved a second, *no, third time* . . . to do."

CALL TO ORDER

*"If God gives you something you can do,
why in God's name wouldn't you do it?"*

— STEPHEN KING

Three days later, Angela brought Pastora and Mary Agnes to visit. Pastora smiled her hopeful, childlike grin as she took Develyn's hands in hers and pressed a rosary in them.

"This is my favorite, the one I used at the Rosario Chapel in Mexico." Pastora gave her hands a friendly squeeze. "I'd like you to have it."

"Thank you." Develyn kissed Pastora's cheek and then examined the beads. "Onyx?"

"Yes, it was the local stone in Puebla."

"It looks like moonstone, it's so translucent." Develyn suspended it from her hand, letting it rotate as the morning light reflected through it. "I don't recall the last time I held a rosary."

"As Bishop Sheen said, the rosary's the best therapy because it combines the physical, the vocal, and the spiritual."

Develyn smiled as she fondled the beads. "Prayer's something I can do *here*," she gestured to the hospital room, "and now."

"Prayer's something you can do anywhere, anytime." Again, Pastora smiled her little girl grin.

"And I'd like you to have this blessed medal of St. Raphael, the archangel of healing and journeys," said Mary Agnes, carefully placing a necklace over Develyn's head. "He'll help guide you to better health, as well as to your calling."

"Thank you." Develyn kissed Mary Agnes's cheek. "I need help in both areas." One by one, she looked at the three women gathered around her. "And that's why I asked Angela to invite you here." She took a deep breath and then winced.

"Are you all right?"

Develyn waved off their concern with her hand. "I'm fine. Just have to remember to breathe shallowly." She smiled.

"You've had quite an experience," said Mary Agnes.

"More than you know." Develyn's lip lifted in a half-smile. She glanced at Angela, catching her eye, and then turned back to the two sisters. "Thanks to my friend, I'm here to talk about it. After the accident, I had a dream. In it, my mother showed me what God's saved me twice to do."

"Twice?" Mary Agnes squinted. "I don't follow."

"When I was born, I survived a botched abortion, and now I've survived a car accident. If I didn't get His message the first time, I get it now. God's got a plan for me."

"You've had time to contemplate here."

Develyn smiled. "No distractions."

"It's good to listen to God's silence." Mary Agnes nodded. "It's there you'll find His message, His mission for you."

Develyn lifted her head. "I finally know what it is, and I accept it. Ceren—"

Pastora's ears perked. "Did you say Ceren?"

A smile animated Develyn's features. Her eyes twinkled. Her face seemed to radiate. "Ceren and Justin have decided to adopt my baby."

"An open adoption?" Pastora beamed. At Develyn's nod, she glanced at Angela. "We know first-hand how well that works."

"Then you'd remain a part of your child's life?" Mary Agnes watched her response.

"As Ceren's been to Angela, I'd be an auntie to my child. I've had plenty of time to think about it lying here." Develyn gestured to the room. "God's shown me His plan. He's called me, and I'm eager to start His journey." She reached for Mary Agnes's hand. "After the baby's born, I'd like to become a postulant. If you're still willing, I'd appreciate it if you'd mentor me."

SOUNDS OF SILENCE

"There's a lot of difference between listening and hearing."

— G.K. CHESTERTON

That Friday night, Angela joined Kio for a star party on the planetarium's observation deck.

"Using these powerful telescopes," said the visiting astrophysicist, "we can see objects so far away, their light's taken nearly the entire age of the universe to reach us. If not space voyagers, we're space voyeurs. In a vicarious way, we're witnessing the creation of the first stars. Now, using clusters of galaxies as giant telescopes to bend light and magnify distant images, we're pushing past even those boundaries."

Following the lecture, they peered through the telescopes and watched as the speaker pointed out the constellations with a laser.

"It brings those tiny pinpricks of light to life," whispered Angela, holding onto Kio's arm.

Afterwards, they found a bench on campus where they could look up at the stars.

"It makes you think, doesn't it?" Kio asked.

She nodded. "And makes you feel small, insignificant." She caught his eye. "I mean, we're tiny creatures on a speck of rotating dust out in the middle of this universe. With telescopes, we can see billions of light years away, yet we have trouble seeing what's right in front of us."

"You're thinking of Travis, aren't you?" His tone was hushed.

"Him and how he's impacted Dev and their baby . . . and Ceren and Justin and their family." She took a deep breath, the evening air cool, almost bracing. Then she turned toward him. "You were his roommate. How has his death affected you?"

"It hasn't really sunk in yet." He gave her a wry smile. "Travis's parents cleaned out his things. The dorm seems empty without him." He grimaced. "Yet it somehow seems he'll walk through the door any minute. It's hard to believe he's gone."

She nodded but kept silent, reluctant to share her thoughts about a soul that has passed.

"Is Dev back yet?"

"No. They released her from the hospital, but she's spending the rest of the week at her grandparents, resting . . . contemplating."

"Becoming a nun," Kio shook his head. "That's quite a change from the Develyn I met."

"That's for sure," Angela said, "but when you're called, you're called. The problem's hearing God's voice."

"I think you have to be attuned to hear God's voice."

"To use computer jargon, are you talking about more bandwidth?"

He shrugged. "Something like that."

Grinning, she turned toward him. "You mean, as in adding more cell phone towers in your service area for better reception?"

"Not exactly." He smiled. "Have you ever heard about the Green Bank Telescope?"

"Sounds familiar, but I don't know anything about it."

"The GBT's one of the world's largest radio telescopes. It's huge, as tall as the Allegheny Mountains near it."

"What's it do?"

"It operates in the radio frequency area of the electromagnetic spectrum, where they can detect radio sources." He grinned at her blank expression. "Basically, it listens."

Her head tilted, she asked, "To what?"

"Quasars, pulsars, in fact, discovering cosmic, microwave, background radiation that was the beginning of the Big Bang theory."

She squinted, trying to follow his line of thinking. "Okay, so what's this got to do with Develyn being called by God?"

"There's so much noise out there." He gestured with his hands. "There're so many frequencies, channels, stations, so much *racket*, it's hard to hear the sounds of space. The GBT's like a giant ear, listening through all the different frequencies of the universe for the voice of God." He lifted one eyebrow. "You have to listen for the silence first before you can hear God. Somehow, Dev was able to do it."

"Funny." Angela said as she looked from Kio to the stars. That's almost what Mary Agnes said. 'You have to listen to God's silence.'"

ENLIGHTENMENT

*"Look at how a single candle
can both defy and define the darkness."*

— ANNE FRANK

The alarm went off at five thirty. Angela groaned but pulled on her robe and padded next door to Develyn's room.

"It's time."

Develyn's light snoring continued.

"C'mon, get up. We're meeting Kio in half an hour."

Develyn groaned and rolled over.

"Dev," said Angela, shaking her arm. "You said you wanted to see this. If you're not up and dressed in the next ten minutes, you're going to miss it."

"The idea sounded a lot better last night." She pulled the covers over her eyes. "I can't, seriously. The spirit's willing, but this baby's sapping my energy. Next time, next year on October fourth."

Ten minutes before sunrise, Angela pulled into the nearly empty parking lot at San Antonio's southernmost mission, San Francisco de la Espada. A lone car flashed its headlights, and Angela pulled alongside it.

Kio rolled down his window. "Morning, sunshine."

Angela grinned. "Was hoping that was you." She looked at the full moon floating above the façade of the old stone church. "That's optimistic, a good omen if I ever saw one."

"Unfortunately, there's cloud cover." Kio shrugged in the moonlight.

Angela noted his disappointed body language. "Sorry, hope it clears for St. Francis's solar illumination." She grinned, hoping to cheer him. "Maybe he'll intercede. After all, this mission was named for him."

Another car pulled alongside them. When the driver rolled down his window, they recognized him as the docent from Concepción. "Pray for the clouds to break."

Getting out of their cars, they nodded and began walking toward the white limestone structure. Its front façade rose above the adjacent walls, with three built-in bells high above the main door.

"If I remember correctly, you said this was built in 1731." Angela looked at the docent.

"Actually, this is the state's oldest Spanish Colonial mission. Founded in 1690 as San Francisco de los Tejas in East Texas, it was relocated here in 1731 and renamed Mission San Francisco de la Espada."

Cocking her head, she studied the structure in the fading moonlight.

"It reminds me of a church in the Hill Country."

He nodded. "Several churches are architecturally designed after this mission, including St. Stephen's Episcopal Church of Wimberley."

As the gloom faded, mist began rising off the San Antonio River, creating an eerie scene. Angela felt they were walking through a cloud.

"I can't see more than a foot or two ahead of me. Hope the sun can pierce this fog."

"In all the years I've tried to view this illumination, I've only seen it once," said the docent.

Angela shared a look with Kio. "Those aren't good odds."

"This particular illumination is illusive, but the friars built solar illumination into the Missions Concepción and Espada."

"Why was that?" asked Kio.

"The sun was especially important to the Native Americans that the missionaries met here. It was part of their world view, religion, and lifestyle. To help the natives' transition into Catholicism, the Franciscans began using the sun as a metaphor for Christ, a symbolic part of Catholic worship. Architecture began imitating life. Several missions were built to 'capture' the sun's rays on significant religious and seasonal days."

"Church holidays, such as Assumption," said Angela.

"And seasonal celebrations, such as winter solstice," said the docent, turning toward her. "Be sure not to miss that."

"Welcome." The pastor opened the ornate, mesquite door for them. "Are you familiar with the Franciscan culture related to the mission?"

Angela shook her head. "Very little."

"Then let me share its background." The pastor smiled. "Franciscans over the world traditionally gather on the Feast of St. Francis. Friars in the San Antonio area would probably have met here, at the church named for him, San Francisco de la Espada. The night before, they would have held the Transitus, the traditional Latin service indicating Francis's transition through death to the new world above. Then the next morning at sunrise, they'd have celebrated the Mass of St. Francis."

"Was there any Biblical basis for the mission's solar illumination?"

The pastor nodded. "The traditional reading for the Mass of St. Francis is from the *Book of Sirach*. Most likely, that's what inspired the solar illuminations with its allusion to 'a star shining above the clouds.' That passage would have been read just as the sun was rising in the sky and illuminating the statue of St. Francis." He pointed to the statue above the altar.

Angela's eyes followed. "So that's what the sun illuminates."

Pointing overhead, the pastor stepped back to better see the window above the door.

"The sun enters through that window," he pointed, "and shines on that wall. Then its beam glides down until it illuminates St. Francis's statue."

More people began arriving and taking their seats in the pews. At seven thirty, a reader began reciting the Canticle of the Sun. Just as he read the words, "Be praised, my Lord, through all your creatures, especially through my lord Brother Sun, who brings the day," two things happened.

The sun broke through the clouds, casting its beam through the window, lighting the wall above the statue of St. Francis. Although most eyes focused on that, Angela noticed a kitten walk through the partially open door, jump onto the holy water font, and begin drinking.

Grinning, she nudged Kio and pointed it out. With a quick smile, he nodded.

"Not holy cow, but holy cat." Then he turned his eyes back to the illumination progressing down the wall. A moment later, Angela felt something jump on her lap. Before she could react, she heard purring and saw the kitten making itself comfortable on her lap. Silently, she began stroking its soft, gray coat.

As the reader finished the Canticle with the words, "Praise and bless my Lord, and give thanks, and serve him with great humility," the sunbeam illuminated the statue of St. Francis, and the Mass began.

All during Mass, the kitten stayed by Angela, either purring in her lap or sitting on the pew, cleaning itself, when she knelt in prayer.

Afterwards, Kio turned to her and scratched the kitten's head. "Looks like you've made a friend."

"I wonder if anyone owns . . ." she did a quick medical examination, "him."

"I doubt it." Kio shook his head. "A lot of people drop off unwanted animals outside the city limits."

Groaning, she held the kitten tighter. "He's such an affectionate little thing. Let me check." On the way out, as they shook hands with the pastor, Angela asked, "Do you know who might own this kitten?"

"No one. Everyone." He shook his head. "There are so many abandoned and feral cats in this area. It's a shame. Are you going to keep him?"

She hunched her shoulders. "I hadn't planned on adopting a cat today."

"God doesn't always choose opportune moments to share His will."

Angela chuckled. "That's close to what Mary Agnes said." Then she thought of Develyn and Ceren. With a determined nod, she made up her mind. "Yes, I'm going to adopt him."

"Since this is the Feast of St. Francis, this is his namesake mission, and St. Francis is the patron saint of animals, let's bless this kitty." The priest dipped his fingers into the holy water.

"Heavenly Father, our human ties with friends of other species is a wonderful gift. We ask You to grant this special animal companion your Fatherly care. Give us, his human friends, new understanding of our responsibilities to these creatures of Yours. May your abundant blessings rest upon . . ." He looked at Angela.

She thought quickly and then grinned. "Francis. Frank for short."

"Frank," he repeated. "May we speak to this creature of Yours with kindness and affection, respecting his life and purpose in our communal creation. In the name of the Father, of the Son, and of the Holy Spirit." He sprinkled Frank with holy water from his fingertips and then, grinning, scratched the kitten under the chin. "You're one lucky kitty."

On December twelfth, the Feast of Guadalupe, Angela, Kio, Judith, Pastora, Ceren, Justin, Mary Agnes, and Develyn gathered at Concepción Mission. They watched as the illumination struck the left corner of the wall at the intersection of the cruciform church, crossing in front of the painting of Our Lady of Guadalupe.

"She's wearing a crown," whispered Mary Agnes afterwards.

"It's an unusual painting." Develyn nodded. Six months pregnant, she knelt in front of it in prayer, asking for Mary's intercession as she had done in August.

When she finished, Justin helped her to her feet.

"Thanks." Develyn smiled. "Could I ask you and Ceren another favor?"

"Of course." Ceren looked from her to Justin and back. "What is it?"

She pointed to the painting. "On August twenty-ninth, in this very spot, during the previous illumination, I prayed for guidance. I'd just discovered I was pregnant. With three hundred dollar bills in my hand, I debated what to do. Travis wanted me to get an abortion. I was lost, scared, unsure which way to turn."

"I remember," Pastora murmured.

"God's worked through a series of events, through each of you," she looked in the face of each and then turned to her roommate, "especially through Angela, to guide me back here. Do you recall what the docent said about the analemma that night?"

Angela made a face. "Vaguely."

Grinning, Develyn used her hands to demonstrate. "He said the crossing or 'waist' of the analemma figure eight occurs twice: August twenty-ninth and April thirteenth. On those two days, the sun tracks across the tabernacle on the main altar. August twenty-ninth is sixty-nine days after summer solstice, and April thirteenth is sixty-nine days before summer solstice. The docent named it the Last Judgment illumination." She winced. "Trust me, when I prayed here August twenty-ninth, I felt it was my 'Last Judgment.'"

Ceren asked softly, "What would you like us to do?"

"Do." Develyn gave her a crooked smile. "My 'due' date's April sixth. Would it be possible to have the baby baptized here, at Concepción Mission, on April thirteenth during the second Last Judgment illumination? Instead of a Last Judgment, it would be a final blessing. It would complete the top half of the analemma's figure eight." She looked down, trying to hide her quivering chin.

"I'm hoping it will also give me closure."

Ceren grabbed her hand. "Girl talk," she called over her shoulder as she led Develyn to the original baptistery. Then she added in a whisper, "Where we can speak in private."

When they were out of earshot, Ceren turned and saw Develyn's eyes were brimming with tears. She put her arms around her shoulders. Hugging her to her chest, she felt the baby between them.

"If anyone understands how you feel, it's me." Ceren spoke softly, remembering her own pain in giving up Angela. She let go Develyn's shoulders to look at her. "You're doing the right thing for your baby, for yourself . . . even for me."

"What do you mean, for you?"

"Giving up Angela was the hardest thing I ever had to do."

"I can imagine," said Develyn, "but look how she turned out."

Ceren nodded, smiling. "That's exactly what I mean. Justin and I want this baby . . . your baby. Our baby. The boys are nearly grown, and though this baby won't make up for Esteban's miscarriage, she'll fill the gap he left in our lives."

Develyn blinked, trying to smile.

"She'll be the daughter I've always wanted—the daughter I've waited for all my life." She looked into Develyn's eyes, her lashes still damp. "You mentioned how having the baptism here on April thirteenth would give you closure. Raising a daughter will bring me full circle. I gave away a daughter in adoption, and now I'm adopting a daughter."

Tears starting again, Develyn hugged Ceren. Swallowing, she whispered, "Thank you."

Ceren shook her head. "No, thank you for this blessing." She drew a deep breath. "Finally, life is flowing again. After the miscarriage, our marriage stagnated. I felt blocked, obstructed, but now this baby is proof."

"Proof of what?"

Ceren narrowed her eyes, trying to find words to describe her thoughts. "Proof that life goes on after death, both here on earth," she thought of Esteban, "and above in heaven."

Pastora pulled in a few favors, but they were able to have the baptism in Concepción on April thirteenth. Develyn sat in the front row of the mission, near the painting of Our Lady of Guadalupe. Wearing a postulant's black jumper over a white blouse, she chatted quietly with Pastora and Mary Agnes as they waited for the baptism to begin. Ellen and Tim sat behind them, dividing their attention between their granddaughter and great-granddaughter.

Ceren and Justin sat in front of the altar, while Angela and Judith sat directly behind them. Watching Ceren and Justin fuss over the week-old baby, Judith chuckled.

"They're like newlyweds with their first child."

Angela turned her gaze from Develyn to the tiny baby, dressed in an ornate baptismal gown made of white satin, organdy, and ribbon. So small, the baby was nearly lost amidst its frothy fabric, her long gown flowing over Justin's arm.

"Was that really my baptismal gown?"

"It's the one the convent nuns made for you in Puebla." Judith nodded as a smile tugged at the corner of her lip. "I thought Ceren would like to borrow it for her daughter's christening."

Angela nodded. "It adds special significance. I'm sure she appreciates it."

"Maybe, one day, your baby will wear it."

Angela felt the heat rise in her cheeks. She cleared her throat. "I don't foresee any babies in the near future."

Raising her eyebrow, Judith glanced at Kio sitting behind them with Ceren's sons.

"Maybe in a few years."

Angela followed her eyes and hunched her shoulders. "We're just friends. That's all." *Isn't it?* She purposely looked away, not ready to pursue that line of thought.

Instead, she turned her gaze to the baby, focusing on her blue eyes. They were so wide, Angela wondered if she could see what was going on, if she had any idea of the ceremony. Then she glimpsed Develyn. Though dry, her eyes were glued to the baby's. Her yearning was obvious.

Angela compared Develyn's current image to her goth girl look. *Was that less than a year ago?*

"What are you thinking?" asked Judith, watching her.

Angela sighed. "Develyn's still wearing black, but everything else has changed. She's a postulant, on her way to becoming a Sister. Ceren and Justin have a new daughter." She looked at the baby and then glanced at Kio. "People have come into our lives." She thought of Travis. "And people have gone." She looked at her mother and smiled. "How about you? Do you feel things have changed?"

"You mean, aside from your moving out and living on campus?" Judith gave her an affectionate smile. Then her eyes focused past Angela, resting on Ellen and Tim. A beat later, her focus returned to Angela. "Yes, I've changed. My life has changed, and in no small part it's because of you."

"Really? How so?"

"Because you introduced me to Helen, I found the courage to attend a postabortion retreat. Finally I was able to forgive Tim-hmhmm . . ." she cleared her throat, "myself and the baby's father. Yes, a lot's changed."

As Justin held the baby, Ceren adjusted their daughter's white headband among her curling wisps of dark hair. Then she looked up into his face.

"Do you realize we're completing two circles here . . . actually three?"

Justin shook his head. "I'm not following."

"When did we have our first date?"

He squinted as he wracked his brain. "Is this a trick question?"

Ceren gave him a wry smile. "Angela's baptism was our first 'date,' remember? Judith and Sam set it up so you'd have to drive me back to Puebla."

"Oh, yeah, now that you mention it."

"We've made a full circle since we met."

He shrugged. "I guess you could say that."

"Plus, at Angela's baptism, I gave up a daughter. Today, at this baptism, we're gaining a daughter."

He nodded. "That's true."

"And the godparents we chose couldn't be more suitable. Angela, the daughter I gave away in adoption, will be her godmother, and Justin Junior, our adopted son, will be her godfather. That way, all three will have been adopted: godparents and godchild."

He smiled as he leaned over to kiss her. "That's just one of the reasons I love you. The woof and warp of life," he said, repeating one of their first conversations. "You're so good at tying up loose ends."

Ceren grinned as she glanced at Angela. "Actually, she is."

Angela took a small packet from her purse, stepped out into the aisle, and crossed in front of the pews. She stopped in front of Develyn and smiled, waiting until she had her attention.

"This is for you," she said, handing it to her.

Develyn weighed the daintily wrapped gift in her hand. "Though small, it's heavy. What is it?"

"Open it and see." Angela gave her a mysterious smile.

Develyn undid the ribbon and tissue paper to find a heart-shaped stone. She raised her eyebrow, silently asking a question.

"This is to make up for the fossilized heart you left on your mother's headstone. The day you met Mary Agnes, as we climbed the stone path to the open-air chapel, I prayed you'd find what it was you needed. At that moment, I literally stumbled across this rock. I hope this stumbling block becomes your stepping stone because it's a sign if I ever saw one."

"A sign?"

Angela nodded. "Since this turned up during a prayer for you, I'm taking it as a sign from God that you're doing exactly what you need to do. You're on the right path. Just have heart. Keep on going."

Develyn's chin quivered. "You've saved it all these months."

Angela grabbed her hand and leaned over to whisper. "Just waited for the right occasion."

Develyn swallowed hard and took a deep breath. Then she looked up at Angela, a mischievous glint in her eye.

"So you're calling me hardhearted."

Chuckling, Angela shook her head. "Anything but. Something tells me you've ended the cycle of hardhearted women in your family." Again she leaned over to whisper. "You don't fool me. You're an old softie, but I promise I won't let on."

The two shared a grin. Then Angela winked, squeezed Develyn's hand, and returned to her seat.

One of the docents began playing a recorder, its reedy sound a haunting blend of a clarinet and flute. Then the deacon stepped into the cruciform church's transept.

"Friends," he began, "today's a special day for two reasons. The illumination, which has already begun." He gestured toward the beam of light silently making its way toward the main altar. "And, more importantly, the baptism of this baby." He smiled at the small congregation of relatives and friends. "Would the parents and godparents please come forward to present this child for baptism?"

Ceren turned to cue Angela and her adopted son, Justin Jr. With nods, they stood and joined her, Justin, and the baby as they approached the altar.

"My dear sisters and brothers," said the deacon, "as we welcome this child into the Church, let us recall she's a gift from God, the source of all life."

Angela glanced at Develyn and saw her nodding in agreement.

"Not only is this a rite of admission, it's also an adoption." He looked at each parent and godparent. "Just as Ceren and Justin legally adopted this little girl, today God divinely adopts His daughter." He turned to Ceren and Justin. "What name do you give your child?"

Ceren glanced at Develyn and her grandparents before answering. In a clear voice, she said, "Virginia. Ginny for short."

Angela watched Develyn cup her hand over her mouth, trying to hide the sob that escaped. Tears started down her face, as Ellen leaned forward to hug her. Through wet lashes, Develyn glanced at Angela, her eyebrow raised questioningly.

In answer, Angela nodded. *Yes, I knew.* She smiled.

Then the illumination's bright sunlight caught her eye as it beamed through the west wall's round window. While the light tracked across the sanctuary toward the tabernacle, Angela watched the original Ginny glide toward her namesake grandchild. She stooped and caressed her tiny cheek. In response, the baby gurgled and kicked.

Angela glanced at Pastora, and their eyes met. Smiling as she brought out her rosary and began praying, Pastora nodded. *She sees her, too.*

The deacon asked, "What do you ask of God's Church for Ginny?"

"Baptism," Ceren and Justin replied.

Looking at the older Ginny, Angela quickly added, "Eternal life."

Instantly, Develyn's mother lost her troubled frown. Ginny turned toward her with eyes that looked soft, luminous. Angela watched her lined, haggard face relax into a peaceful smile. Instead of sunken cheeks, her now rosy cheeks shone with a youthful glow.

Angela blinked at the transformation.

With a relieved sigh, the older Ginny began to rise with the light as the illumination climbed above the main altar. The brilliant sunlight continued to ascend, highlighting the painting of the Immaculate Conception.

Angela studied the artwork. The illumination lit it with a radiance that seemed to bring it to life, as if heaven itself were opening before them. Then Angela noticed.

Ginny's gone.

S͢G

READING GROUP GUIDE
FOR SACRED GIFT

Why is the title, *Sacred Gift*, significant? Why do/don't you like it? What would you have named *Sacred Gift?* Is the title a clue to the theme(s)?

Did you enjoy *Sacred Gift?* Why/why not?

What do you think *Sacred Gift* is essentially about? What is the main idea/theme of *Sacred Gift?*

What other themes or subplots did *Sacred Gift* explore? Were they effectively explored? Were they plausible? Were the plot/subplots animated by using clichés or were they lifelike?

Were any symbols used to reinforce the main ideas?

Did the main plot pull you in, engage you immediately, or did it take a chapter or two for you to 'get into it'?

Was *Sacred Gift* a 'page-turner,' where you couldn't put it down, or did you take your time as you read it?

What emotions did *Sacred Gift* elicit as you read it? Did you feel engrossed, distracted, entertained, disturbed, or a combination of emotions?

What did you think of the structure and style of the writing? Was it one continuous story or was it a series of vignettes within a story's framework?

What about the timeline? Was it chronological, or did flashbacks move from the present to the past and back again? Did that choice of timeline help/hinder the storyline?

Was there a single point of view, or did it shift between several characters? Why would Bartell have chosen this structure?

Did the plot's complications surprise you? Or could you predict the twists/turns?

What scene was the most pivotal for *Sacred Gift?* How do you think *Sacred Gift* would have changed had that scene not taken place?

What scene resounded most with you personally—either positively or negatively? Why?

Did any passage(s) seem insightful, even powerful?

Did you find the dialog humorous—did it make you laugh? Was the dialog thought-provoking or poignant—did it make you cry? Was there a particular passage that stated *Sacred Gift's* theme?

Did any of the characters' dialog 'speak' to you or provide any insight?

Did the quotes at the beginning of the chapters 'set the tone' for the subsequent action? Which ones? How so?

Have you ever experienced anything that was comparable to what occurred in *Sacred Gift?* How did you respond to it? How were you changed by it? Did you grow from the experience? Since it didn't kill you, how did it make you stronger?

What caught you off-guard? What shocked, surprised, or startled you about *Sacred Gift?*

Did you notice any cultural, traditional, gender, sexual, ethnic, or socioeconomic factors at play in *Sacred Gift?* If you did, how did it/they affect the characters?

How realistic were the characterizations?

Did any of the characters remind you of yourself or someone you know? How so?

Did the characters' actions seem plausible? Why/why not?

What motivated the characters' actions in *Sacred Gift?* What did the sub-characters want from the main character, and what did the main character want with them?

What were the dynamics between the characters? How did that affect their interactions?

How did the way the characters envisioned themselves differ from the way others saw them? How did you see the various characters?

How did the 'roles' of the various characters influence their interactions as sister, coworker, wife, mother, daughter, lover, and professional?

Who was your favorite character? Why? Would you want to meet any of the characters? Which one(s)?

If you had a least favorite character you loved to hate, who was it and why?

Was there a scene(s) or moment(s) where you disagreed with the choice(s) of any of the characters? What would you have done differently?

If one of the characters made a decision with moral connotations, would you have made the same choice? Why/why not?

Were the characters' actions justified? Did you admire or disapprove of their actions? Why?

Ceren and Judith both had moments where they struggled with their faith. When was the last time your faith faltered? What helped you get through that time?

What previous influence(s) in the characters' lives triggered their actions/reactions in *Sacred Gift*?

Did *Sacred Gift* end the way you had anticipated? Was the ending appropriate? Was it satisfying? If so, why? If not, why and what would you change?

Did the ending tie up any loose threads? If so, how?

Did the characters develop or mature by the end of the book? If so, how? If not, what would have helped them grow? Did you relate to any one (or more) of the characters?

Have you changed/reconsidered any views or broadened your perspective after reading *Sacred Gift*?

What do you think will happen next to the main characters? If you had a crystal ball, would you foresee a sequel to *Sacred Gift*?

Have you read any books that share similarities with this one? How does *Sacred Gift* hold up to them?

What did you take away from *Sacred Gift*? Have you learned anything new or been exposed to different ideas about people or a certain part of the world?

Did your opinion of *Sacred Gift* change as you read it? How? If you could ask Bartell a question, what would you ask?

Would you recommend *Sacred Gift* to a friend?

Chocolate and Chilies
Mexican Recipes

"God gave the angels wings, and He gave humans chocolate."

— ANONYMOUS

Mushroom and Squash Blossom Quesadillas

Ingredients

1 tbsp. butter
¼ cup onion, diced
¼ lb. mushrooms, sliced
¼ lb. squash blossoms, washed and stems removed
¼ tsp. salt, or to taste
¼ tsp. pepper, or to taste
4 corn tortillas
½ cup Oaxaca cheese

Ingredients for Garnishes

Avocado, salsa, and sour cream

Directions

In a skillet, melt the butter and sauté the onion.
    Add the mushrooms, stirring constantly for 5 minutes.

Add the squash blossoms and season to taste. Stir until the blossoms are limp, about 2 to 3 minutes. Do not overcook.

One at a time, warm the tortillas on a griddle over low heat for 30 seconds on each side. Divide the mushroom and squash blossom mixture, spooning one-fourth of the mixture onto each tortilla. Top with 2 tablespoons cheese.

Fold the tortilla in half, and heat each side on a griddle for 2 minutes, or until cheese melts. Serve warm. Serves 4.

QUELITES SALAD

The name quelites is a catch-all term applied to a variety of wild greens in Mexico, but true quelites are lamb's quarters, a European green, used as a pot herb. Pigweed, better known as amaranth, or bledo in Spanish, is a native Mexican green often referred to as quelites. Similar in texture to spinach, quelites have a unique flavor.

INGREDIENTS FOR SALAD

¼ cup olive oil
3 garlic cloves, minced
6 green onions, thinly sliced
½ jalapeño or serrano chili, seeded and minced (optional)
Salt and pepper to taste
1 bunch amaranth greens, well rinsed and patted dry

INGREDIENTS FOR DRESSING

The fruit of the prickly pear cactus is called the tuna. A rich burgundy red color, it has a subtle flavor that pairs well with balsamic vinegar. If tuna jelly is not available, substitute pin-cherry jelly, or, in a pinch, grape jelly.

2 tbsp. tuna jelly
3 tbsp. balsamic vinegar
1 tablespoon amaranth or toasted sesame seeds

DIRECTIONS

In a large skillet, warm all but 1 tablespoon of the oil over low heat. Add the garlic and stir 1 minute or until a golden brown. Add the green onions, chili, salt, and pepper and stir 1 minute.

Add the amaranth leaves. Using tongs, turn to coat the amaranth evenly with the onion-garlic mixture. Stir constantly 1-2 minutes or until just wilted. Remove from heat.

Combine the remaining tablespoon oil, jelly, and vinegar. Toss with the amaranth leaves. Adjust the vinegar and seasonings, adding more if needed. Garnish with amaranth or sesame seeds and serve immediately. Serves 4.

About the Author

 Born to rolling-stone parents who moved annually, Karen Hulene Bartell found her earliest companions as fictional friends in books. Paperbacks became her portable pals. Ghost stories kept her up at night... reading feverishly. The paranormal was her passion. Wanderlust inherent, she enjoyed traveling, although loathed changing schools. Novels offered an imaginative escape.

An only child, she began writing her first novel at the age of nine, learning the joys of creating her own happy endings—usually including large families.

Professor emeritus from the University of Texas, Bartell and her husband live in the Texas Hill Country with five rescued cats.

Connect with Karen Online

KarenHuleneBartell.com

Twitter: @KarenHuleneBart

Facebook: @KarenHuleneBartell

THE MISSION OF DIVINE MERCY, a monastic and contemplative Community in New Braunfels, Texas, is creating a retreat center and sanctuary to spread the message and ministry of God's mercy—year round. As of this writing, its chapel is open air, and its dining hall is a lanai spread beneath live oaks of the Texas Hill Country.

MORE INFORMATION AT:
www.MissionOfDivineMercy.com

Made in the USA
Charleston, SC
27 April 2015